Written by my friend:

RACHEL MATHEW

The Great

Exposure

HALLARD
PRESS

Library of Congress Control Number: 2023905627

Publisher's Cataloging-in-Publication data
Names: Mathew, Rachel, author.
Title: The great exposure / Rachel Mathew.
Description: The Villages, FL: Hallard Press, LLC, 2023.
Identifiers: LCCN: 2023905627 | ISBN: 978-1-951188-75-7 (print) | 978-1-951188-76-4 (ebook)
Subjects: LCSH Third parties (United States politics)--Fiction. | United States. Congress--Fiction. | United States. Congress.--Officials and employees--Fiction. | Political fiction. | Christian fiction. | Love stories. | BISAC FICTION / Christian / General | FICTION / Political | FICTION / Thrillers / Political | FICTION / Women
Classification: LCC PS2613.A84 G74 2023 | DDC 813.6--dc23

ISBN: 978-1-951188-75-7 (Paperback)
ISBN: 978-1-951188-76-4 (Ebook)

To the LORD Jesus Christ
Who is worthy of it all.
Nothing of value exists,
but that has come about because He is.

CONTENTS

The light in the darkness did shine
and the darkness could not perceive it.
John 1:5

THE GREAT EXPOSURE

Six years before, scandal after scandal had been revealed to the American public and the two main political parties had been decimated. Career politicians left office in droves. The minor parties saw their chance to ascend and suddenly were desperate for candidates. Anyone remotely qualified to hold public office had been courted.

PROLOGUE

A working breakfast had just been served in the president's inner dining room adjacent to the Oval Office. The participants were engaged in a highly charged argument about how to manage the coming midterm election. No one had touched the food. The president was trying to be heard, yelling "Order! Come to order! Take your seat, general!" He started to rise but fell back into his seat, too weak to stand all the way up. An aide stepped quickly to his side and offered his arm for support, but the president pushed it away. Frustrated, he slapped the tabletop with his palm and yelled a strangled, "Shut the hell up!" Spit flew, and drool ran down his chin.

The Chairman of the Joint Chiefs, whom he had addressed, was red-faced and shaking with fury. He ignored the president's shouts and kept his eyes riveted on a shadow president who was leading the meeting. "I will not!" he continued, as if the president had not spoken. "We risked everything for this pathetic attempt at world domination, and we were promised we would be off the hook in four years. I will not, I repeat, I will not follow one more diabolical command that those monkeys on our backs are shoveling out! Each one of us has a noose around our necks already. This would kick the stool right out from under us!" He took a breath and glanced at his cell phone. It was dark. "What the hell?"

Everyone jumped at the crack of doors slamming open in the adjacent Oval Office. The shadow president jumped to his feet. The hand of the Chairman of the Joint Chiefs moved involuntarily to his belt where he had hidden a tiny pistol. He had smuggled it into the White House that morning and was prepared to use it if he had to. He had had a nightmare the previous night and felt a premonition that he might need it. He knew that he could be court-martialed for having it, but that consequence was minor compared with what would happen if the misdeeds of everyone in the room were exposed. He figured that having the firearm would increase his possibility of escape. Secret service officers swarmed the room. "This is not the time for a drill, morons!" the Chairman of the Joint Chiefs shouted, "Stand down!"

Ignoring him, the detail advanced without missing a beat. "This is not a drill. I repeat, this is not a drill," one of the officers said. The shadow president calmly walked out of the room right past the secret service. They were used to him coming and going at will. None of them had ever had the nerve to oppose him. They knew that he would have his own plans for this moment securely in place. He had hoped that it would never come but had lived in dread for the past two years knowing that it could. He would be out of the country within an hour.

The president looked up in confusion as the two largest officers approached him, one on each side, and lifted him in a two-man carry. "Get your hands off of me!" the president shouted. "What is it? Are they storming the building? Where's the first lady?"

He was excised quickly from the room. His protests echoed loudly all the way down the hallway. The others grabbed their laptops and ran out without any urging. Each quickly grasped that this was some kind of credible immediate threat. The press secretary and the president's personal physician were jostled to the back of the pack. When the way cleared, they jogged to catch up. The room was then empty except for the Chairman of the Joint Chiefs. He was still trying to turn his phone back on but kept glancing up at two members of his own security team.

"Sir, all communications have been down for two minutes," one of them said calmly. "It is our duty to escort you to the safe room."

"Screw your duty! I'm not going down with this sinking ship. Back off!" He reached inside his jacket and dug under his belt for his pistol. He pulled it out and trained it on them. They stopped cold, shocked. The general shot a round into the wall between them, and they hit the floor, scrambling furiously back into the Oval Office. Satisfied that he had bought some time, the general turned and exited through the service door. He had not been caught entirely off guard; he had known for several weeks that the administration was a house of cards ready to tumble. He had even prepared his escape plan before agreeing to be a part of the debacle, rehearsing his getaway regularly for the past few months. Now, he wondered whether enough time remained to get to the airport and take off before they noticed that he was missing. He was rattled by the communication blackout. He had no idea what had happened, but he wasn't going to wait around to find out.

There was pandemonium down in the bunker. The president kept demanding to know what was going on. The Secretary of State calmly told him, "Communications are shut down completely, Sir. The secret servicemen waited two minutes, as is protocol, and then followed routine orders to get us all to safety."

"I didn't order this!" the president shouted.

The Chairman of the Joint Chiefs usually got things under control when necessary, and it had become increasingly necessary lately, but he was not there to take control. The president had never been the one in command, but only recently had he fully realized this fact. Nonetheless, he tried. His attempts to gain control were futile, laughable, really. In the absence of the Chairman of the Joint Chiefs, no one was sure what to do. Only the secret servicemen knew their role in a situation like this. They stood their ground and remained silent. They had no answers to give anyway and refused to speculate. The president's Chief of Staff usually stepped up when the Chairman of the Joint Chiefs was not around, but he had not been at the luncheon, nor was he present now. Unknown to the rest of them, he was being held on suicide watch in the brig at Andrews Air Force Base. Having left the White House in an unmarked car, he had driven himself to the base an hour earlier after suffering another debilitating panic attack. He could not stand the tension and guilt for one more day. He turned himself in and was in protective custody.

The Attorney General had a cool head, but he couldn't get phone service either. He kept shouting, "Does anyone have phone service?" None of the computers were on, and none would boot. The huge video monitors that covered the walls were blank. The president kept yelling, "Turn the damn things on! That's an order."

"We're trying, Sir. The power seems to be out."

"The power's not out. We have lights, don't we? Use the generators. Why aren't they running? Where's my wife? I want my wife!" he whined.

The secret service counted heads and came up short. Only the president, his physician, his press secretary, Attorney General, Secretary of Defense, and Secretary of State were present. Normally, they would have had full access to the locations of the rest of the members of the Cabinet through their communication devices, but now they had no idea where the others were or whether they were safe. All communications had been completely cut off. Everyone in the room, with the exception of the president, knew that, if they could not establish communications soon, they would have to leave the White House. It could not be protected without communication and coordination with the armed forces.

At this moment, the monitors lit up.

"Thank God!"

"Finally!"

"Now we can get some answers!"

"Oh my God! What the hell?"

A video played on every screen. Jaws dropped as they saw footage of themselves. It was a recording of a secret meeting that they had held under the strictest security. They had no idea where the video had come from. Their eyes turned slowly from the screen to each other with pupils narrowing as the tension built. Each wondered which of the others had somehow brought a hidden camera into their meetings. Scrolling slowly across the bottom of the screen were these words, "Proverbs 5:21-23: *For a man's ways are before the eyes of the LORD, and the LORD examines all his paths. The iniquities of a wicked man entrap him; the cords of his sin entangle him. He dies for lack of discipline, led astray by his own great folly."*

The beeping of cell phones rebooting next grabbed the attention of everyone in the room. Their hearts lifted only to crash again when they saw the same video playing on their personal devices. What they saw horrified them. It was real, raw, unedited footage of a series of meetings in which they themselves had authorized murders, torture, breaking and entering, and other crimes. What was worse, as the video continued they saw paid operatives talking to middlemen and the middlemen reporting to their superiors. They saw the superiors standing soberly before their handlers nodding in agreement to the verbal orders given in top secret meetings that had, somehow, been recorded. They heard the words. The names of each person appeared on a banner underneath the video feed as they appeared. No one in the safe room said a thing. The only sounds audible in the room over the soundtrack of the video were the sharp intake of jagged breaths of shock, gagging, and moaning as each step in these crimes was more completely revealed. Now, the faces on the screens were their own. They saw themselves nodding, raising their hands in unanimous votes, and then leaving to pass along the orders to those under their command. They saw their secret conversations and deals made with foreign leaders laid bare. They saw enough evidence to put every one of them behind bars for life. They saw enough to put most of them on death row for treason. The worst was yet to come.

They saw the ledgers of offshore bank accounts, their secret code names in black and white. They saw the dates for deposits of enormous amounts of money. They saw the bodies of innocent people whom they had agreed must die. They saw satanic rituals that they had participated in. They saw depraved sexual orgies and sexual assaults involving multiple victims. Some of them saw their own naked bodies in these acts. They saw women and children kept in cages like slaves for other depraved persons like themselves. They saw money leaving their hands to buy these slaves. The president was retching. The Secretary of Defense was hyperventilating. A gunshot rang out. The president passed out onto the floor and lay there in his own vomit. Everyone hit the deck. Some scrambled under the conference table. The Secret Service quickly assessed the situation. One of them crossed to a body sprawled out on the floor. It was the Secretary of State, who had shot himself through the head. There was a mad scramble to control the weapon he had used. The Secret Service quickly gained possession. "How the hell did he get a firearm in here?" they asked. "We have to get you all out of here. We are evacuating now!"

Fifteen minutes later, the president's motorcade was speeding to a safe haven in the mountains. They had to be driven because Marine One and Air Force One were grounded, unable to navigate without the assistance of computers. The trip took over three excruciating hours though they raced at high speed non-stop with lights and sirens. Their destination was White Sulphur Springs, West Virginia. It was a tense drive, with everyone in the motorcade constantly scanning for danger, especially from the air. The drivers were anxious. They had never transported the president with so little security, much less with no communications. No one knew who the enemy was, how the exposure of their crimes had been accomplished, or what kind of attack might come next. Traffic was heavy, with civilians filling the highway, weaving back and forth, and even pulling between the vehicles in the motorcade. The president's driver was cursing a blue streak, punctuating his profanity with, "My apologies, Sir," though the president could not hear him behind the glass partition. The driver obviously had not seen the video. Otherwise, he would have run for his life rather than remaining with such a high-profile target in his care and he certainly would never have apologized to him.

The president would not have noticed the driver's language even if he had been able to hear it. He was struggling. What he had seen would not only end his presidency but probably lead to his execution for treason. The best that he could hope for would be life in prison.

His personal physician was at his side, lamenting the lack of medical equipment in the limo. "I need you to relax, Sir," he cautioned. "I can't give you any more sedation, or your blood pressure will tank. Breathe in slowly through your nose and out through your mouth."

He demonstrated what he meant, but the president would not follow his lead. His jaw was clamped tightly. The doctor turned to the first lady, who had always been able to calm him down. Everyone relied heavily on her and called her when he became upset. "Ma'am, can you try to—" he started to say but ceased speaking when he saw the symptoms of shock in her enlarged pupils, her rigid and still posture, the empty gaze, and ashen skin.

"I had just started to relax," she mumbled. "I thought we'd gotten away with it."

The doctor gently guided her into a prone position and elevated her feet on one of the pillows that the president kept for his lower back, taking off his jacket to provide her with a covering. He drew a series of deep, cleansing breaths. It took everything in him to keep going. He was on autopilot. He had seen his transgressions on the video as well. They were not as heinous as those of the others but damning enough, especially his treasonous claim that the impaired president had a clean bill of health. He was desperately concerned about his wife and family and couldn't wait to get away and look after his own affairs. He kept barking orders into his watch phone, forgetting that it wasn't working. He could barely control himself as the phone kept streaming video of compromise after compromise that he had made. He squirmed as he saw the 7-figure payoffs that were transferred into his bank account. He began to feel genuine remorse. As the tears flowed down his cheeks, he bent over, put his face in his hands, and prayed, "Father, forgive me. I don't deserve it, I know. Have mercy on me, I pray, for the sake of my children and grandchildren. It's my fault, not theirs." He was still praying when a Marine shook his shoulder and asked, "Doctor, where do you want us to move the president and first lady? Shall we take them to the infirmary?" The doctor hadn't even noticed that the caravan had stopped.

PART ONE

CHAPTER 1

AIDA DELIVERED TO HER DOOR

A blast of frigid air shocked Aida awake the moment her driver, Tony Romano, opened the car door. She did not want to move. She shook her head, still overwhelmed by all that had happened to bring her to this night. The years since The Great Exposure had been full of incredible change and rebuilding. Part of that process was the rise of a handful of new political parties. She still found it hard to believe that she was now officially a member of Congress. Gratefully taking the hand that Tony offered, Aida let him help her out of the limo.

Tony spoke softly, "Congresswoman, may I help you to your door?"

"No!" She answered too quickly and with more energy than she thought she had left. She raised an apologetic hand. "Forgive me, Tony, I spoke too quickly and forcefully. That's very sweet of you, but I can make it," she said with a smile.

"No apology necessary, ma'am," he replied and tipped the bill of his chauffeur's hat with one hand.

"Thank you, Tony. You must be beat, too."

Tony bowed his head slightly and said, "I'll be back bright and early Monday morning. Have a good weekend." He could see that she was unsteady on her feet and wished that she would let him help her. She was a tiny woman, about five feet tall and no more than 90 pounds. He could easily have carried her to her second-floor apartment. It had been quite a couple of days, not only for Aida and him, but for the whole country. He had never seen so many fireworks and parades and parties before, and he was grateful just to have been a part of it. He climbed back into the limo, watched until she reached her door safely, and then started the engine.

Aida gazed up at the old sandstone townhouse. It was in the middle of the six residences in her building. She lived upstairs, and her landlord lived downstairs. She felt the weight of every step she took toward the front door and realized that her feet were killing her. She regretted her stubborn independence as the edifice loomed over her. She really could use a strong arm to lean on right about now. She hadn't been to bed in more than 48 hours; indeed, she'd hardly sat down. Steeling herself for the five wide cement steps that she had to climb just to reach the front door, she wobbled on her glittery gold sling-back heels but made it to the top. Only after she had opened the front door and stepped into the entry did she hear the limo roll quietly down the street.

When he stopped at the traffic light at the end of the block, Tony instinctively turned to scan the back seat. He saw that Aida had left her warm wrap behind. He wanted to kick himself for not noticing it sooner. Leaning back to retrieve the garment, he brought it to his face, inhaling her fragrance, and smiled. "What a dame," he said aloud.

As soon as Aida closed the front door behind her, she felt the gaze of her landlord, Mr. Wafi, through the peephole of the downstairs apartment. She forced herself not to look, having grown accustomed to his spying. It was a price that she paid every day for this choice apartment. A heavy sigh rose from deep within her. Every bone was aching. She wasn't sure what she wanted more—a hot bath, some food, or just to hold baby Emmit. Tears sprang to her eyes, and now, in the privacy of the lobby, she did not bother to brush them off, though she stifled a sob.

Aida had never understood quite how she ended up with this apartment. Fraz, her campaign manager, had sent her a link to a rental advertisement, and when she saw the location—halfway between the Islamic Mosque and Cultural Center and the Capitol Building—and the low rent, she at first thought that the figure must be a typo. After taking the virtual tour and seeing that the space would be adequate for her, Karen, and the baby, she called immediately to request a showing. Surprisingly, Mr. Wafi had offered to lease it to her over the phone. Fraz still had not told her how he managed to find it but kept emphasizing how close it was to the mosque, though Aida did not attend the services regularly. All things considered, putting up with a nosy landlord was a tolerable annoyance, though she wondered if Mr. Wafi ever slept. What Fraz had neglected to tell her was that Mr. Wafi was the imam at the nearby Islamic Mosque.

Aida gathered up the tail of her silky gold ball gown before starting up the next set of steps to her apartment. It crossed her mind that the landlord would probably think that she was drunk, but she was too tired to care. Clasping the railing tightly with her right hand and the hem of her garment with the left, she began making the ascent. Her best friend and roommate, Karen, came out the door and ran down to meet her after she had climbed just a few steps.

"Congresswoman!" she whispered loudly. "You certainly partied the night away—" but her big grin transformed into a frown when she saw the expression on Aida's face. "Here, give me your shoes and lean on me. I'm so glad Tony let me know you were on the way. You must be dead on your feet!" Karen craned her neck to peer over Aida's shoulder and through the window in the door to the street. "Is your hunky driver gone already? Anyway, how were the inaugural balls?"

Aida gratefully felt Karen wrap her arm around her and support some of her weight. The tears began to fall faster now that the sight of her friend had stirred her emotions. The other woman's expression changed to one of concern.

"Are you okay?" Karen asked. "What is it?"

"All—" Aida started to speak, but another sob interrupted her.

"All what, honey?"

"Used," she took a breath, "up."

Karen threw her head back, unable to suppress a laugh. "Ha! I can't believe it! The nonstop perpetual motion machine has run out of gas!" She shook her head. "Well, come on, Representative Adams. I can't carry you, and I don't want to drag you, so dig deep and work with me here."

The pair toiled up the steps, taking them one at a time. Aida kept her eye on the goal, the landing at the top of the stairs. Karen had left the door to their apartment ajar, and, kicking it wide open, she half-carried Aida inside and down the short hall to her bedroom. Leading her to the edge of the bed, she dropped her there unceremoniously in a heap. "Have you even eaten today?" she asked.

Aida whispered dully, "Um, not really." She turned her attention to the little crib in her closet. "Is he okay?" she mouthed, nodding at the sleeping baby.

"Absolutely," Karen whispered back. "You just sit here a minute and I'll get you a protein shake, and then you can crawl into the sack."

Aida didn't answer, and Karen slipped quietly from the room. When she returned two minutes later with the promised shake, she found Aida slumped over on the bed fast asleep with the baby snuggled close beside her. Karen carefully pulled the sleeping infant out from under Aida's arm and returned him to his crib. She then turned to Aida and unfolded a soft, warm blanket over her. She heard Aida's phone buzzing from inside Aida's beaded clutch, so she took it with her as she backed out of the room, leaving the door open a crack since she wanted to be able to hear the baby if he woke in the night. Walking to the tiny kitchen, she set the purse on the counter and pulled out the phone. Nothing else was in the purse except eye drops, lip gloss, and a tissue. The phone buzzed, and Karen punched the mute button and heard herself say, "Oh, shut up and let the poor woman sleep!" She put the phone on the charger and turned off the lights, eager to get back to her own bed.

CHAPTER 2
TONY

Tony was Aida's driver and bodyguard. She hadn't thought that she would need either service, but, immediately after her nomination, she had begun to receive death threats from hate groups. Some on the far right objected because she was Muslim, while some conservative Muslims objected because they still thought a woman's place was at home. Still others objected because her skin was dark. The vitriol in their words was especially shocking to Aida because she had been relatively sheltered growing up. Her parents were born and raised in Ethiopia and had come to the U.S. on student visas in their twenties, eventually completing the legal process and becoming full citizens. The day that they stepped onto American soil, they gave up most of their Muslim observances and practices and even some of their native foods. They spoke only English and adopted American dress and speech and customs as much as they could. Though they never denied being Muslim and Aida always knew her heritage, their home was strictly secular. Aida attended private schools with students primarily of other minority groups, most of whom did not know her ethnic origin. It just wasn't an issue. She prided herself on being without prejudice.

Recently, after some especially horrific and graphic email threats, Aida reluctantly informed Telly Gavin, the chairwoman of the Egalitarian Party, about the situation. Telly immediately arranged protection for her. A retired cop named Joe showed up at her office the next day. He was short and balding, with the stereotypical pot belly of a middle-aged man who exercised too little. Joe told Aida that he was only there to drive her, but it was obvious to her that he had been told to keep an eye on her, too. He huffed and puffed just climbing behind the wheel of the car. Aida was unimpressed and started a little game that she and Karen called "avoid the cop." He didn't seem to care as long as he kept receiving his paycheck. When Telly called Joe in for his first review and found out how little time he actually spent with Aida though, she was furious and fired him on the spot. She also gave Aida a dressing down, which she and Karen did not find funny at all.

Tony was Joe's replacement. After one look at him, Aida and Karen were through playing "avoid the cop." Karen especially was interested in playing with this particular cop. Tony was medium height, about five-nine, and well-built. As far as Karen was concerned, he was a major upgrade indeed. It did not take her long to find out that he was single, never married, and had no children—not because he didn't like women and children, though, because he very much did.

Tony Romano had grown up in a tight-knit Italian Catholic family in New York City. He had five sisters, and they all remained very close. He had started graying in his twenties, and now, at forty, his hair was not only mostly gray but also receding rapidly, leaving very little on top. He liked hats, perhaps for this reason; he certainly looked younger when he had one on. When Aida saw him, he was usually wearing either a navy blue chauffer's cap, similar to that of a police officer, or, when he picked her up after hours, an old battered navy blue baseball cap. She did notice that his blue eyes twinkled when he grinned in the rearview mirror while teasing her. He was keenly interested in government, having moved to the city so that he could spend his free time exploring the museums and monuments and, whenever he could get in, sitting in the galleries in the Capitol building. He considered the security clearance that his job gave him to be the best perk of all, for his nightlife consisted of frequenting the Lincoln Center alone.

Tony kept fit by body-building. He had exactly the right body type for it. When others noticed his rapid progress he was encouraged to enter competitions. He didn't want to devote the time necessary to do so, however. More importantly, he was modest about his body and had no desire to pose shirtless. He had achieved a good balance, working out just enough to keep fit and look imposing but still having time for his other passions. Tony, then, would be quite a catch, and all of his sisters and relatives were on the lookout for potential matches for him, though he was in no hurry to settle down. He was stubborn too, flat out refusing every offer to be introduced to a woman. He had decided when he joined the police force that it would not be fair to a wife to have to live with the daily fear that he might not come home from work, and that mindset had stayed with him even now that he was no longer a policeman. With no wife or children, Tony lived very simply. He earned good money but didn't spend much of it apart from being very generous toward his sisters, nieces, and nephews. His family members could always count on him to cover emergency expenses if they got in a pinch. His only extravagances, if they could be called that, were season passes to all of the museums and libraries in Washington. He bought a new one every year, moving from one destination to another in rotation in his off-hours. When he wasn't tending to Aida, he was either in a library, museum, or gym. He didn't mind living alone or going out alone. He had retired early from the force after investing his spare income wisely and now received a partial pension to supplement his substantial investment income and his salary from the Egalitarian Party. He had moved to D.C. just as a kind of extended vacation, inspired by his fascination with politics. Right away he had contacted his congressman for tickets to tour the area around the White House and Capitol, where he became a familiar sight.

After a couple of months, though, he had grown bored with sightseeing, and it was about this time that a recruiting offer for a "driver/bodyguard" in his inbox caught his attention. Police officers current and former are constantly bombarded with such offers from private contractors, but this one was from the federal government. Tony responded, scheduled an interview, and was hired on the spot. The master's degree in political science that he had earned in his spare time while still on the force had helped to seal the deal. He received his credentials as soon as he cleared all of the background checks. Although he did not work directly for the federal government he had to go through the screening before he could be hired and given clearance to protect members of the government. His employer was actually the Egalitarian Party, and he reported to its chairman, Telly Gavin. He was amazed at how fast his life changed. Not long before, he had resolved never to work in public service again, and even now, he wasn't completely certain why he had taken the job with Aida. Maybe he just wanted to be where the action was. He was content in his job as a driver but often frustrated by Aida's stubborn disregard for her own safety.

CHAPTER 3

FRAZ

Fraz Abbas returned from the downstairs fitness room frowning at his phone as he entered his hotel room. He had left four texts for Aida and several voicemails last night before giving up and going to sleep at four a.m. He was up again a mere two hours later, as he never missed a workout. He squinted at the Florida sun streaming through the gap between the drapes. He had rented a small suite for the weekend of the inauguration. He hadn't been invited and tried to act as if he didn't care, but of course, he was deeply insulted. He had tried to dull the pain with alcohol and women. His beautiful home was only a few miles away, but he never took women there. He didn't want to let them know where he lived.

"You would think she'd have the decency to pick up the phone for the man who won this election for her," he grumbled.

A muffled, "Hmmm?" came from the bed behind him.

Fraz glanced behind him and then turned his attention back to his phone, irritated to find the blonde still there. He absent-mindedly rubbed his chin. He had always been fastidious about his appearance. He wanted a shower and it was time for his next shave. He was impatient for the girl to leave. There were naïve young college students everywhere in Gainesville, so he never lacked a bed partner. He was no longer

19

interested in this one. He turned to the bed where the young woman was lying. She was pretty and shapely, but he had no respect for her or her behavior. He slapped her on her rump.

"Hey, you!" he said. "Time to move. You'll have to take the stairs. Make sure no one sees you leave this room, either." He didn't even try to remember her name as she squinted up toward him with her hand shading her eyes.

"Good morning to you, too!" she replied.

He frowned and turned back to his phone, scanning to see if Aida had answered yet.

"Call me," she offered.

She stood up slowly. Her head was pounding and she felt like retching. She looked pitifully at Fraz, still hoping that he would let her stay. She had nothing to wear but her thin swimsuit cover-up and no remembrance of where she had left the hastily discarded bikini. She pulled on the thin gauzy tunic. Fraz felt her eyes on him, but he did not return her gaze. He smiled to himself, knowing that her swimsuit might still be floating in the hotel pool, amusing the little children he heard splashing and squealing in it below. She looked longingly over her shoulder at his face and body as she headed toward the door. Seeing that he was not looking, she glanced around quickly for some sort of souvenir and surreptitiously snatched one of his dirty socks off the floor and stuffed it in her small handbag. Now she had a reminder that, for one night at least, she had been part of the high life

Fraz was glad when he heard the door slam behind her. He wished he could just stay in Florida. The average January temperature in D.C. was thirty-five degrees. It was seventy-five and sunny in Gainesville. Fraz loved the Florida weather. It reminded him of his childhood in Egypt.

His father had encouraged and supported his move to the United States when he was only eighteen years old and paid for his college education and law school. Fraz had been required to work to earn his own spending money, however. Fraz was an exceptionally handsome and vain man, so when one of his classmates pointed out an advertisement for male models, Fraz had jumped at the chance. The agency had a studio in Gainesville where all of the photography was done and that was very convenient for him. The job paid well for little work on his part and also provided him with connections to beautiful women. He concentrated more on parties than his studies, and his grades in law school were not good. His father complained about his academic performance, but he did not expect a lot from Fraz. He had always considered Fraz the slowest of his sons. Fraz, for his part, was determined to enjoy himself thoroughly in America. He had been forced to live a very austere life in Egypt. He wanted to sample, even gorge on, everything that America had to offer. His studies came easily enough to him, so he gave them little attention. His father never caught on that his mediocre performance was due to a lack of diligence rather than of intelligence.

Fraz's father was a blunt and harsh man, so Fraz had made it his goal to be articulate and charming. In contrast to the negative examples that he had known in his formative years, his time at law school introduced him to no end of male role models to emulate. He copied the bearing and manners of his professors. He used these manners with everyone whom he considered to be of any importance. Other men laughed at him behind his back, but they could not help being jealous of his success with women. He had no friends. Women found him irresistible, at least at first, but he never gave them a chance to know him since he rarely saw the same one twice. Dates with Fraz Abbas ended poorly for young ladies. As charming and polite as he was in public, he was just the opposite in private, blunt and demanding like his father. Young women threw themselves at him, and he was indiscriminate and foolish in his associations with them. He had no respect for women who were "easy." Considering them promiscuous, he felt free to treat them as their supposed lack of morals deserved. He gave little thought to his own morals, however.

After passing the bar, Fraz specialized in corporate law. He had settled happily into his career and quickly became the most sought-after attorney at his firm. Two years passed, and then, one day, he had received a call from the head of the Egalitarian Party. It was from Telly Gavin that he first heard about that party's ambitious plan to fill some of the many empty seats in Congress that The Great Exposure had emptied. Fraz had never heard the name Aida Adams and was surprised when he realized that Telly was trying to recruit him to serve as Aida's campaign manager. She informed him that the party was running candidates who represented various minority groups and considered Aida a very promising Muslim candidate since her moderate views would be palatable to the constituents of this conservative central Florida district.

Managing a campaign, especially for a woman, was the last thing that Fraz wanted to do. He told his father about it as a joke, but was surprised when his father actually wanted him to do it. Fraz quickly found himself on the receiving end of unrelenting pressure. Even his mentors in Egypt urged him to interview for the job. They were convinced that, provided that a man such as Fraz was pulling her strings, this woman could advance their interests in the United States. A large deposit directly into his bank account by his father and the promise of further monetary incentives if he delivered results finally changed Fraz's mind. He comforted himself that the campaign would involve only a year-long commitment.

When Fraz first laid eyes on Aida, he found her boring and unattractive. She did not wear makeup or have her hair professionally styled or use any products on it. It was long and frizzy, and she usually wore a headband to hold it back out of her face. Beyond her appearance, her Ethiopian ancestry had biased Fraz against her immediately, though he took comfort in the fact that her skin was exceptionally light. She could pass for Egyptian should any of his countrymen see him with her.

Fraz did not make a good first impression on Aida either, and he knew it. She did not respond to his charm at all during their interview. She was all business. She informed Telly that she had ruled him out because he had no experience in politics. The chairwoman replied that they had chosen him for other reasons. She said he was a no-nonsense organizer with an uncanny ability to anticipate and avoid legal snares. She did not tell Aida about the large campaign contributions the party was receiving that were conditional on Fraz receiving the job. Fraz did not know it either. Telly pretended not to know that the funds came from outside of the country. She knew that ignorance was no defense if she would be caught, but her ambition and arrogance deceived her into thinking she would not be caught.

CHAPTER 4
KAREN AND EMMIT

Frost covered the small window and the weak winter sun dimly illuminated Aida's bedroom. She opened gritty eyes and tried to focus on the clock.

"It's only three a.m.," she muttered to herself. "Why do I have to pee so badly?" Rubbing her itchy eyes, she felt the thick mascara caking her eyelashes. Groaning, she realized that she had fallen asleep without washing off her makeup. She hated the cosmetics and the heels and all of the ridiculous rituals that women were expected to perform. Fraz had insisted that she wear formal attire, though, and the other party officials had agreed. The inauguration of a new president was a formal event, and those lucky enough to be invited to an inaugural ball were expected to dress appropriately. When the guest had been recently elected to office herself, the pressure to conform was even greater.

She remembered pulling off her gown and lying down to cuddle for a minute with the warm, sweet, sleeping baby boy. Where was Emmit? Aida felt a shot of adrenalin hit her system. She sat straight up and threw back the covers. Just then she heard the school bus brakes squeal and the sound of laughing children thumping down the big steps of the bus. She frowned and then hit herself in the forehead. Of course the baby was not sleeping now, she realized. She looked at the clock again. It was three p.m.! Karen must have gotten up with him so he wouldn't disturb her.

"Thank God for Karen," she breathed. "How could I ever make it without her?"

Aida groaned again and staggered to her feet. She felt hung over, but she had not been drunk; what she was experiencing was pure exhaustion. The whole past year had been a sleep-deprived fog. It seemed that the campaign, the trips, the speeches, and the meetings would never end. On the other hand, it all seemed to have happened so quickly. She still couldn't believe that the citizens of Florida's Third Congressional District had voted her into the U.S. House of Representatives. She had never held any kind of public office, but now she had been elected on the ticket of the Egalitarian Party, beating out the incumbent Republican as well as an up-and-coming former sheriff representing the Democrats in the general election.

Aida headed down the hall to the bathroom that she shared with Karen. Soon, steam was rolling out of the shower stall along with strains of "God Bless America" in Aida's lusty contralto.

Karen looked toward the bedroom as she heard the shower and singing. She was sitting on the floor in the tiny living room letting Emmit have some "tummy time" on a soft blue-and-white puffy baby quilt. Emmit held his head up and bobbed a few times before face-planting into the quilt.

"Oops! Are you okay, baby boy?"

Emmit lifted his head again just long enough to turn it to the side and then plopped it down on the floor again. His squished cheek and eye looked funny to Karen and she laughed. The baby was tiny. He had been born a full two months early. He was thriving now but very small for his age.

Karen was the same age as Aida and, though neither of them could see a resemblance between them, they were often mistaken for sisters. Karen was proud that she was a whole inch taller than Aida. Her 5-foot-1-inch frame was about 15 curvaceous pounds heavier, too. She had lively brown eyes, and her hair was a couple of shades lighter than Aida's dark brown. Aida was a first-generation, truly African American, but her coffee-and-cream complexion left people guessing at her ethnic origin.

Aida herself had been born prematurely in Washington, D.C. while her parents were visiting the city early in the third trimester of her mother's pregnancy. They had planned a last hurrah, a whirlwind weekend of theater, opera, fine dining, and couple-time before the baby came. The only grand entrance that they saw, however, was Aida's red and screaming face, and the only fine dining that they enjoyed was hospital food. Even though she grew up in Gainesville, Florida, Aida made it a point to say that she was born in Washington, D.C. whenever she had a chance.

Karen had a perpetual tan and an olive complexion in keeping with her Italian roots. Karen and Aida thought it was especially hilarious that they were mistaken for sisters because they saw themselves as opposites. Karen always seemed on the verge of laughter, and she teased the more serious Aida relentlessly. They found that being "sisters," though, worked to their advantage in many situations. "Blood relatives or not," they agreed, "we couldn't be closer!"

When it came to dress, however, the similarities ended. Karen wore what most young women did—skin-tight jeans and form-fitting tee-shirts. She had a cute little figure and was not afraid to show it. When she dressed up, she added high heels to the look. Aida, on the other hand, had hidden her figure behind loose, baggy caftans throughout the entire campaign. She also wore her head covered in various plain scarves. The inaugural ball gown had been a huge change in that respect.

The women each had one tattoo. Karen's was on her chest just below her collarbone. It said, "Semper fi!" in flowing blue cursive. She had never been in the Marine Corps, however, nor had she ever dated a Marine. She had had the tattoo done on graduation day on a dare from Aida. They had gone to the parlor together after too many celebratory drinks. Because Aida rarely drank alcohol, after just two drinks, she was beyond tipsy. She had a "Semper fi" tattoo of her own, but in a spot normally covered by clothing. The sentiment was a promise between the two women to remain friends forever, and each took it seriously. Karen soon regretted the placement of her tattoo but never the promise, and she kept it faithfully—even when doing so meant putting her entire life and career on hold to move to Washington, D.C. and be a stay-at-home mom after Aida's election to the House.

Karen was a native Floridian, or almost, being the offspring of transplanted New York Italians. The Rizzo clan had tired of the northern climate and made the move when Karen was a baby. Her parents still had the Brooklyn accents to prove it. This was one reason that Karen liked Tony so much: he sounded just like her dad. Karen had the characteristic drawl of those who had grown up in the Sunshine State and the relaxed unhurried friendliness to go with it.

Aida emerged from the bathroom wearing one of her long, loose-fitting caftans.

"That's enough for now," Karen said as she gently rolled the baby over to pick him up.

"No, no, no, let me!" Aida rushed across the kitchen to her and the baby. "Auntie Aida is here, little one! I missed you so, so, so much!"

Aida bent over and carefully scooped up the tiny boy.

"Ooh, let me smell you and feel your soft preciousness!" Aida rocked the baby back and forth in her arms, but he started fussing. "Oh no, what's wrong? Do you want mama?" Aida's face scrunched with concern. "Have I been gone so long that you forgot about me?"

"He hasn't forgotten you. You're unforgettable, remember? It's his bottle he wants." Karen had anticipated the baby's needs, and a bottle was waiting on the bottle warmer.

"Oh perfect! I get to feed you, little Emmit bug! It's coming, hold on!"

Karen handed Aida the bottle, and she looked at it as she bounced the baby gently up and down.

"I wish he could still have breast milk."

Emmit popped his fist in his mouth and started sucking hungrily. Karen heard the catch in Aida's voice. Emmit fussed louder and let out an angry squawk.

"Aida, he had it for his first two weeks and those are the most important. We've been over this. Are you going to feed that child, or shall I?" Karen demanded.

Karen noticed that Aida's shoulders had risen, and she heard her let out a deep breath to compose herself.

"Emmit, here you go. Move that little fist. That's not going to fill your belly."

Emmit let out another angry squawk before Aida successfully maneuvered the nipple of the bottle into his mouth. She moved to the rocking chair and settled in with the baby close against her breast. Aida smiled as he hungrily nursed the bottle, but Karen noted a tear sliding down her cheek. Karen thought of all of the decisions that she and Aida had made together regarding Emmit. She was the more pragmatic of the two, and, once the decision had been made, she didn't dwell on it. Aida, on the other hand, tended to rethink things whenever she was forced to choose between two relatively equal choices.

"We ran out of all the frozen breast milk, but we still have plenty of halawa left," she offered.

"I love that stuff!" Aida exclaimed.

"You can have it, thank you very much. I don't care how much it's supposed to help new mothers! I guess it did help with all the milk that was pumped and stored in the freezer."

"Now I know what I will have for lunch: a nice halawa sandwich!"

"Yuck!" Karen replied.

She had tried the stuff once—a solid yellow gritty loaf full of sugar and with no nutrition to speak of—and that had been more than enough.

"I bet Emmit will like it when he's old enough."

"I'm sure he will at 24 grams of sugar per serving."

"Oh, look how big you are getting!" Aida declared. "You'd never know you were that tiny red naked bird who made his surprise appearance so early in the morning last October twenty-first. That was your birthday, little boy!"

"Right; tell me about it after you've fed him every two hours day and night!"

"I did feed him every two hours day and night, Karen."

"Oh, sure, for exactly two weeks. It was such a blur, I almost forgot."

"I will feed you day and night every two hours this weekend, though," she said to the baby. "Yes I will! I don't have to go to work for two whole days." Emmit gazed up into Aida's eyes and patted her chest with his little hand. Aida was in heaven. Another tear slid down her cheek, this one of joy.

Aida looked up at Karen, who stood there smiling at them. "Hey, Karen, it's January twenty-first. Emmit's three months old today!" She turned her attention back to the baby. "Little boy, you're three months old. How do you like the world so far?"

Emmit turned his head away from the bottle and blew some raspberries with his tongue. Milk spilled and started running down his chin. Aida laughed and dabbed at it with the corner of the baby's shirt. Then she picked him up and held him over her shoulder for a burp.

"Remember how terrified we were to feed him at first?" Aida recalled.

Karen nodded solemnly. Aida had been terrified, but Karen had been calm and cool, as if she'd done it all her life. As it happened, Karen had tended more than her share of babies while working at a daycare center part-time during college.

Aida kept chattering. "Karen, remind me what the doctor said at the three-month checkup."

"She was very pleased. Of course, Emmit's below the curve for weight and length, but he's growing steadily, and that's what we need to focus on."

"How much did he weigh?"

"Six pounds and one ounce."

"Six pounds, Emmit? Good boy!" Aida kept patting the baby's back and rubbing her lips across his velvety hair. "You smell a little sour, precious. I predict a bath in your future."

"Six pounds *and one ounce*," Karen added. "Don't forget the one ounce."

"Oh no, I won't forget it. I'm so proud of you for being such a good eater!" Emmit replied with a huge belch. Both women laughed.

"Impressive!"

Aida slid the baby down in her arms again and looked deeply into his eyes. They were a smoky blue. Aida had been told that all babies' eyes were that color at first. She smoothed the baby's hair with her fingertip and watched as his eyelids grew heavy and he began to lose focus. Aida kept feasting her eyes on the little one. She couldn't get enough of him. He had lots of jet-black hair so thick that it almost seemed to overwhelm the tiny infant.

"I had no idea it would be so hard to be away from him," Aida mused. "Karen, I'm sorry I slept so long. I never sleep like that."

"No, you don't. You must have been exhausted, because you hardly ever sleep more than a few hours. I bet you'd been up for at least three days."

"There you go, exaggerating again."

"You deserved a good sleep-in, and I wasn't going to wake you up no matter how many times that phone rang."

"What? Where is my phone? I can't believe I haven't had any calls yet—maybe the battery died. I didn't even think to put it on the charger last night."

"You mean this morning? You didn't lie down until 4:30, you know. I took your phone and put it on the charger."

"Oh, thanks, Karen, but it's not ringing."

"I might have put it on mute," Karen confessed.

"What! Oh no, I'd better check it."

Aida jumped up and hurried to her phone, still holding the baby. Picking it up, she saw twenty missed calls and a hundred new emails. Most of the calls were from Fraz. She groaned.

"Are you mad?" Karen asked.

"What? Mad at you? Never! You're my hero. I couldn't make it if it weren't for you. If I didn't have you looking out for me, I don't know where I'd be now. And you have Emmit all the time! The one who's probably mad is Fraz. That man has no patience. I can't wait until I see the end of him."

She put the phone back down. Karen couldn't believe it. "She must have really, really missed that baby," she whispered to herself.

"Karen, this is absolutely your weekend," Aida said. "If you want to sleep, sleep. If you want to go out with some of your other friends, go. Go shopping, have a spa day, whatever. I'll take care of this little one. I convinced you to move here with me away from your family to be my support system. I can never thank you enough."

"Congresswoman, would you please give it a rest about me moving here? It's awesome to be in D.C. As for caring for the baby all weekend, well, you should rest."

"Would you stop calling me 'Congresswoman'? And I got enough sleep already, so go, make some plans. Get dressed up and go out without baby burp on your shirt."

"Yes, Congresswoman," Karen replied with a grin.

"Hey, Squiggy! What I wouldn't do to you if I didn't have this baby in my arms!" Squiggy was a nickname that she had given Karen on the day that they had moved into this apartment. They were making a list of household items they would need when Karen noticed the window was dirty and said that Aida should add a "squiggy" to the list. "Do you mean 'squeegee'?" Aida had asked and then teased her mercilessly, using the new nickname when she needed a comeback. Karen, predictably, got all worked up and then shut up, which was just want Aida wanted.

Aida looked down at the baby.

"Look, he's falling asleep again. Wake up, Emmit!" she whispered. "Auntie Aida wants to play!"

Another burp erupted from the baby. Milk ran from the corner of his mouth and into a crease in his neck. He gave a little shudder and his head lolled back.

"Sorry, Auntie, that's a sure sign. He's down for the count now." She waved toward the phone and said, "If you want to check your messages, you should have about an hour-and-a-half until his next meal."

"I better get busy, then," Aida sighed. She stood up and reluctantly started back to the bedroom. Then she stopped and turned around. "I don't have to, and I'm not going to!" she eased back into the rocker. "I'm just going to sit here and enjoy this baby and anyone who doesn't like it can just kiss my—Squiggy!"

"I heard that!"

"And you deserved it!"

Aida chuckled. She loved getting Karen's goat. "What if my mom has been calling, though?" she asked. She made her way back to the bedroom while scrolling through her phone.

Karen shook her head. She was already in her room. She did not understand the strange relationship between Aida and her mother, Gloria. Apparently, Aida's mother had never been very attentive to her. She had divorced Aida's father and moved to Israel with her lover right after Aida went off to college. Since then, she seemed to have forgotten that she had a daughter. Perhaps it was because she did not want her new husband to be reminded that he was only three years older than Aida.

Karen sat on the edge of her bed to call her friend Dana. The apartment had two tiny bedrooms. Karen's hardly had room for her bed, and it had no closet. Karen didn't mind, though, because her wardrobe was limited to the jeans and tee-shirts and sweatshirts that she kept folded neatly in the double row of stacked cubes that held all of her belongings.

Aida wanted Emmit in her room, and she had given up half of her closet to prove it. She considered the dry cleaner's her closet for her work clothes, and the rest of her wardrobe was in the other half of the closet in more of the stacked cubes, which she and Karen had selected together at IKEA. Emmit's crib was really a Pack-n-Play, and it fit perfectly in the other half of the closet. Aida wasn't home enough for this arrangement to be a problem, and it worked well for Karen since she slept better with some distance from the baby's little noises.

Karen confirmed her plans with Dana. Surprised but happy, Dana told Karen that she wanted her to come over as soon as possible so that they could start their girl-time. Karen headed to the shower to get ready. She had already rescheduled with Dana three times before. Aida had promised her a Saturday off several times during the campaign when she thought that she would be home but each time had been unable to make it. Aida wouldn't let her arrange for any other babysitter, insisting on caring for Emmit herself when Karen wanted to go out. She had been home at random times and never on the weekends.

Karen had friends who would gladly watch the baby, but Aida wouldn't hear of it. She kept begging, "Just let him get a little older and let him bond better with us before we introduce someone else. Can you honestly say that there is anyone else you would fully trust with him who wouldn't get nosy about his father?"

They were both overprotective of the infant. After his rough start, it was natural that they were especially careful. He had been in the NICU for a full month before they brought him home. Karen wished for the millionth time that her mother was still alive or that Aida's mother was not thousands of miles away in Israel.

CHAPTER 5
FIRST DAY ON THE HILL

During her time off between the election and the inauguration, Aida made several decisions. The first was to start wearing typical American clothing again. She had started with the gold evening gown and was very pleased with the reaction that she received in terms of news coverage. She made the front page of the *Washington Post*, and talking heads were speculating on what the change signified. She followed up that success with a bright red jacket and a black pencil skirt for her first official day on the job.

Her second decision was to wear her hair uncovered and pulled back from her face into a smooth bun at the nape of her neck. With the right hair care products, it was actually easier than keeping a head covering in place.

The third decision was that she was done with Fraz Abbas. That resolution would prove to be the hardest to keep.

Tony gazed after Aida as she power-walked with her shoulders back and chin held high as she walked toward the Capitol building. He whistled softly through his teeth as he followed the blaze of her jacket across the wide pavement on that first foggy Monday morning. She looked ready to take on the world. "What a dame!" he repeated for at least the hundredth time since he had met her.

Aida moved quickly through security. She had a photographic memory and was confident in finding her way around the vast complex of buildings. She headed to her office by a route that was not the most direct but allowed her to make a pit stop at Dunkin Donuts. There, she bought the first of what would be countless cups of the house blend with double cream. A beautiful young lady with dark hair and darker eyes waited on her with a cheery smile that put Aida in an even better mood. Aida pegged her as a grad student, overqualified for her job but happy to be in D.C. She resembled some of the Middle Eastern immigrants with whom Aida had worked, but her demeanor was very different. Her smile lit up her whole face, and she seemed delighted to serve Aida, nodding as she took the order. Her eyes were wide and bright, and her gleaming white teeth had a gap in the middle that added to her charm.

Soon Aida was in the elevator sipping the hot beverage as she headed to the fifth floor of the Longworth Building, where her office was located. When the door opened she eagerly stepped out and hurried around the corner, juggling her drink and briefcase and handbag. Her secretary, Roger, was standing in the hallway at the open doorway to her office. He gasped when he saw her struggling with her drink and briefcase.

"Congresswoman, I'll take that! You don't need to trouble yourself!" His blue eyes were clouded with concern. He looked quickly around for Tracy, the young intern. Aida recognized Roger immediately. He looked even better than he had on the video calls. He was about five-eleven and slim, with close-cropped blonde hair parted and combed up and to one side.

"Tracy, Tracy!" He repeated, snapping his fingers and glancing around.

Tracy was staring intently at her monitor and typing rapidly, but she jumped up like she'd heard a gunshot when Roger called her name, crossing the small room to hover near him.

Aida was amused but also a little concerned. She made a mental note to let the handsome young man know her policy about respect for those both above and below on the pay scale.

Tracy did not seem to mind Roger's somewhat rude means of

summoning her. Another good-looking young person, she was the picture of sophistication. Aida felt another pang of mild concern. Fraz had hired most of her staff, and it occurred to her that he may have chosen them on the basis of looks, which could cause big problems. She had talked to members of her staff on the phone many times before today but had not yet met this intern. Tracy was also tall and slim. She wore a black suit and heels. Her black hair gleamed and was smoothed back into a long ponytail that reached almost to her waist in the back. Not a hair was out of place. Her lips were painted bright red. Aida remembered facing down feelings of inferiority when encountering prosecutors who looked like this in the courtroom.

"Congresswoman, what is that beverage, please? Is Dunkin your favorite?" Roger looked expectantly at Aida as he beckoned the intern closer. "Pay attention, Tracy," he instructed. "The congresswoman likes —" He paused and looked at Aida with raised eyebrows.

Aida threw back her head and laughed. "Roger, is this about my getting my own coffee? Don't be silly! I feel badly. I should have brought some for you! Where are my manners? What do you like, Roger? Tracy, how about you?"

A bewildered look came over Roger's face. "I—I—I'm sure it will be fine, I mean—" he stuttered, then cleared his throat and stood up a little straighter. "Congresswoman, welcome to your first day at the House!"

He motioned toward the doorway and nodded to Tracy, who rushed back to her computer with a cute little half-smile on her shiny red lips. She moved her hand over the mouse and clicked, filling the small room with the strains of the Triumphal March from Verdi's *Aida*. Aida gasped and threw her hand across her mouth.

"My favorite!" she squeaked. "How did you know?" Tears came to her eyes.

The sounds of the blaring trumpets penetrated the corridor, and soon, curious faces leaned into the room.

"We have our sources, Congresswoman," Roger teased, "and they shall forever remain anonymous!"

When the song was over, everyone clapped, and Aida treated them to a deep, graceful curtsy.

"Bravo!" They cried as if she had performed the whole opera herself.

"Thank you, Roger! And thank you all for doing such a great job of getting this office set up for me. It's perfect!" Aida beamed as her eyes traveled to each of the people looking happily back at her. She took in the jumble of desks and chairs that were practically on top of each other. She knew that this was the fate of a freshman House member. There would be no privacy, but nothing could damper her excitement on this memorable day.

Her grin grew even bigger as Roger announced, "Ladies and gentlemen, let's get to work!" Then he turned to Aida and motioned toward the farthest corner of the crowded room with his eyes. "Ma'am, if I may have a word in private?"

"Of course," she answered, asking as she followed him, "What is it, a sensitive problem already?" Her merry eyes made it clear that she thought he was being overly dramatic.

"Congresswoman, I have several urgent messages for you from Mr. Abbas," Roger said as he hurried forward. "Of course, I put him off per your request, but, just a few minutes ago, I also had a call from Ms. Gavin. She insisted I ask you to call her as soon as possible. I um, well, it's none of my business, but I got the distinct feeling that her call related to Mr. Abbas."

Aida could hear the concern in his voice. "Don't be afraid to trust your instincts or to give me news, whether it's good or bad," she instructed. She flashed her best smile. "Don't worry; I won't shoot the messenger!"

Aida was very pleased with Roger. She liked everything about him. He was the former chief administrative assistant for the outgoing Secretary of State. She wondered how Fraz had secured him, but not enough to force her to have a conversation with her campaign manager about it. She was sure that she would get along famously with Roger. She reflected on what a contrast he was to Fraz. Both men were young, good-looking, and whip-smart, but they had completely different personalities. Roger had a certain humility that made him a breath of fresh air in D.C., and Aida prayed that he wouldn't change. Fraz, by contrast, could not change enough in a lifetime to suit her.

In her usual ultra-efficient fashion, Aida had filled her staff positions before the votes had even been tallied. She had made the task of securing her staff part of Fraz's job description when she hired him. He had been incredulous when she insisted that he find and secure promises from future staff members before she had any reason to believe that she would even be elected. He had protested fiercely that to do so was a colossal waste of time. When she asked him about his progress four months into the campaign, they had had one of their major fights, ending in threats by him to quit and promises by her to fire him, after which she had inhaled the bitter words still on the tip of her tongue and hung up on him. Fraz showed up at her office the next day with a bunch of flowers and a lukewarm apology. She found the flowers and apology confusing because he had never shown a hint of humility before.

Telly called Aida as soon as she learned of the rift and insisted that Fraz remain on board. Her reason for doing so was that a huge donation to the Egalitarian Party was contingent on Fraz's remaining at his post. It was also contingent on the Egalitarians seeking support for rebuilding Palestine. These conditions were bad enough, but the foundation, called the Enterprise for International Justice (E.I.J.) was incorporated outside of the U.S.A.

When Telly was first contacted by the E.I.J. she went online and read all that she could about the organization. It sounded like a charitable organization dedicated to helping third world nations rebuild. Later, Telly talked at length to a member of their board. He confirmed everything Telly had read. When she read the mission statement of the organization she found it very compatible with the goals of the Egalitarian Party. The board member insisted that E.I.J.'s participation be kept strictly confidential. Telly finally agreed to take the money, but she was painfully aware that her party would be ruined if the source of the donation was ever discovered. The situation was enough to give Telly an ulcer. In the end, Telly agreed with the terms that E.I.J. offered.

Aida and Fraz had no knowledge of this aspect of Fraz's employment. Aida felt trapped and angry because she was forced to keep Fraz on her staff. Fraz felt furious because he often disagreed with Aida, yet could not quit.

In the end, Aida's foresight had been correct regarding early staff selection. Aida now had Roger and several reliable staffers, some of whom had worked for various Republicans or Democrats who had lost their seats after The Great Exposure. Many, in fact, had fled the country and were in hiding; others were in prison; and not a few had committed suicide. Many were still awaking trial. It would take years before all of them concluded. With many positions in Congress and in the government in general still vacant, large numbers of stellar former senior staff members had been left without jobs. Aida insisted that Fraz hire the applicants with the most experience for her team since she was painfully aware of her own inexperience, and she hoped that he had done so. He had come through, whether by accident or design, with a team of career public servants more knowledgeable than a junior member could have dreamed of.

Roger relaxed slightly as Aida took out her phone and sat at her desk. She wanted to put her staff at ease by example, but being called on the carpet by the Egalitarian Party Chairwoman, and about Fraz, no less, keyed her up immediately. She turned her chair around to face the wall and give herself a modicum of privacy. She made a mental note to ask Roger to find a big landscape for the blank wall that she now faced. They would just have to squeeze the funds out of the meager budget that she had received for furnishing the office. She would add cubicle dividers for her desk to that request as well. Otherwise, she would be spending a significant chunk of her time gazing at that beige wall. She took a deep, cleansing breath and hit "call."

Before Aida's call went through, though, her phone buzzed with a video call from none other than Telly. When she accepted the call, it was on speaker phone.

"Aida, what party did you run for?" The party leader did not look, or sound, happy. Her voice was loud and sharp.

"Good morning, Telly, I was just—"

Telly cut her off, raising her voice. "Aida, I asked you a question!"

Aida heard a quick intake of breath from Roger. The rest of the office staff went dead silent. Recovering quickly, Roger spoke quietly to the others.

"Let's get back to work, please."

Telly was surprised by her own tone as well. She had been alarmed by a call from Fraz and called Aida in a near panic. He asked if Aida was in the hospital because he hadn't been able to get a hold of her for three days. Telly knew he was fishing for information and that could only mean one thing. Aida had decided to shut him out. Telly's stomach lurched again, not at the thought of losing Fraz as a staff member, but out of fear of losing the income from the mysterious financial backers who gave her a kickback for keeping him on staff. She would need that money for the next election cycle. Not only that, she feared that if she offended the donor, whoever it was, that she risked being exposed for taking foreign funds.

Aida quickly turned down the volume on her phone, drew a quick breath, squared her shoulders, and then replied calmly,

"I ran for the Egalitarian Party, ma'am," Her voice was clear and strong, just as she had learned to speak on the debate stage. She managed to hide her irritation at this demeaning line of questioning.

"Well, here's your chance to start being the peacemaker you just convinced Florida voters you are," she said. "How do you think you're going to run a full staff, much less contend with Republicans and Democrats, if you can't even work out differences with your own campaign manager?"

Aida stared wide eyed at the screen. She noticed an aide who tiptoed up to Telly with a stack of papers. "Campaign manager?" she repeated. "Telly, Fraz's job is done now.

Telly waved the aide away and went on as if she hadn't heard Aida. "You're going to have to keep your staff in line but still happy to serve you. That's exactly why I agreed with your strategy of recruiting them early, while they and their families were sweating about their future livelihoods." Her agitation remained evident. "I had a conversation with your campaign manager this morning, and he told me that he has been unable to reach you since the election. He was calling me to see if you were still alive!" Telly glared at Aida through the phone. Aida opened her mouth to reply, but Telly cut her off again. "Aida, I don't have time to spoon-feed you information on how to negotiate relationships in D.C."

Aida could see the aid tiptoe slowly back toward the party leader, who continued to let Aida have it, and drop the papers that needed signing in front of her boss. Telly looked down and absentmindedly started signing the documents where they were highlighted while she went on about politicians being snide and crafty snakes-in-the-grass with whom Aida would have to come to amicable agreements if she wanted to get anything done.

"Aida, you are representing a party of peacemakers who know how to get along with people of differing views. You'd better get busy working with Fraz Abbas, because he is good at what he does, and there's no time to find a replacement."

Aida thought that Telly would have a point if the campaign were still going. Her resentment toward Fraz was deep and painful. She was certain that, if Telly only knew what Fraz had done, she wouldn't be so insistent about him remaining on her staff.

As if she could read Aida's thoughts, Telly added, "I know that the campaign is over, but we hope to run you for more than one term, and we need him now as a legal advisor just so you don't make any mistakes that make a second term impossible."

At this, Aida's stomach hit the floor. She hadn't thought that far ahead.

"Aida, men can really do a number on us. We don't have to take it lying down, though."

Aida rolled her eyes at that apt choice of words. Luckily, Telly had been looking at the papers she was signing and did not see Aida's rolling eyes or flaming red cheeks.

"Remember what they do, but go on as if you don't. The time will come when you can use whatever he's done to your advantage." Telly straightened up and reached for the off button on the camera. "I want you to call him back and make up."

"Okay, but—"

"I have retained him as legal counsel, and I want you to work closer with him. Offer him a job on your congressional staff as a public policy adviser. The man has a good read of the public."

Aida gasped. "Telly! I can't possibly—" but the other woman ended the call and the screen went blank. "Argh!" Aida growled deep in her throat. She turned around and saw Roger standing silently before her.

He cleared his throat and quickly looked down.

Dressed down on her first day, Aida felt her happy mood evaporate. She turned away from Roger's puzzled face and said to him, "Would you please call Mr. Abbas for me and invite him up on the Hill sometime next week? I'd like to meet him in one of the conference rooms downstairs if you can squeeze it into my schedule, please."

"Yes, ma'am," Roger replied. "I'll see to it right away. Now, I'm afraid, you are running a tiny bit late for a party meeting—"

"Oh no! Where is it, Roger?" she asked as she jumped up and buttoned the jacket of her suit.

"Down one floor, conference room five."

"Thank you so much," she replied over her shoulder as she hurried out the door.

CHAPTER 6
METRO MENACE

Aida sighed contentedly as she stepped outside. The crisp air and weak sunshine were invigorating. She had forgotten to call Tony with a pick-up time, so she decided to hop on the Metro for the short ride home. She had thoroughly enjoyed her first day in the House, apart from Telly's call. She was actually shocked at how much she liked her new job. She had studied and memorized the names of every incumbent representative before winning her seat. Now she also knew the names of all the receptionists, legislative aides, caseworkers, press secretaries, and office managers whom she had met. She was one of those rare people with a photographic memory. She had also learned the name of Farah, the lovely, dark-haired server at Dunkin, with whom she was developing a rapport, and she smiled as she remembered their easy banter.

She shifted her briefcase to her other hand. It was packed heavy with material for her to go through at home. She was not going to have any nightlife. In fact, Aida was a unique type of people-person. Though she loved others and was endlessly polite and engaging with them, she only related to them in the context of work. If she was not at work, she was by herself or with Karen and Emmit.

There were no open seats on the train, so Aida stood. She felt her stomach rumble and realized that she had not eaten all day. She loved feeling lean and light. She was quite fit, though she rarely actually worked out. She had always been active and had an athletic build. She walked any time the distance was less than a mile to her destination and, when she could, took the stairs. She was up and down out of her seat constantly and walked as fast as most people jogged. As the train rounded a corner, Aida easily kept her balance, taking advantage of what she thought of as the free exercise that the Metro was offering, a workout that didn't take any extra time. She planted her feet wide and bent her knees, moving in response to the motion of the train.

Aida became so lost in her thoughts that she failed to notice a young, dark-haired man taking photos of her with his phone. She did not notice that he exited the train right behind her and followed her, either. The young man blended in with the dozens of others at the Jeffries Lane stop in his blue jeans and black leather jacket. He also wore a beanie that covered his hair except for a few dark curls in the back. He was of average height, thin, and had a dark complexion and dark, hooded eyes that gave him a sleepy look. He was good at his craft and had already gotten to know Aida's neighborhood like the back of his hand. He took a couple of shortcuts that allowed him to arrive at her building a few minutes before she did.

Others were watching for Aida, of course. Karen and Emmit were at the window upstairs and had seen the young man arrive, though he didn't see them. Karen expected to hear the doorbell, but instead she saw him leave a few seconds later and stroll leisurely to the other side of the street. From there, he watched Aida come around the corner. She was talking on her phone and oblivious to her surroundings.

"Stupid fool," he muttered to himself. He leaned against a tree and lit a cigarette.

Aida raised her voice to be heard on the phone, and the young man was able to make out what she was saying—to her driver, he surmised.

"Tony, I'm home already! I took the Metro. Why? Because I like the Metro. Okay, okay, I get it. Okay, I'm sorry, I wasn't thinking. Please take the rest of the evening off. I'm not going anywhere. Okay, okay, I'll see you in the morning."

He lingered a moment before he left. He liked the thrill of hiding in plain view. Then he noticed an eyeball peeking through the downstairs window blinds. "Looks like Mr. Wafi's on the job, too," he murmured. The holy man would have to be kept in mind if things heated up, the young man reflected. It wouldn't do to take out an imam. He watched as Aida leaned toward the window and waved.

"Good evening, Imam!" she called. The eye quickly disappeared. Aida checked the mailbox before she went inside. It was empty.

Pulling open the left side of his jacket, the young man made sure that the envelopes that he had retrieved from the mailbox were safe. Patting the right side, he made sure that his Glock was secure. Then, he leisurely turned to make his way back toward the Metro. As soon as he rounded the corner and was out of sight of Aida's building, he stopped at a trash can. Sorting through the mail, he threw Karen's into the trash and kept the envelopes addressed to Aida for hand-delivery to his boss.

Aida jogged up the steps to her apartment and immediately went to find the baby. "Hello, family!" she called.

Emmit was on the floor in the living room having some tummy time. He lit up when he saw her and stretched out his little arms. She scooped him up and started smothering his cheeks with kisses.

"Oh, you precious angel! You make me feel so good inside!" What a nice welcome home!" "Mmm mum mum, you are so sweet! Are you my little boy? Yes, you are! You are the sweetest child in the world! You are sweeter than anything, do you know that?"

"Aida, was there any mail today?" Karen asked.

"None at all. Oh, you are so funny!" Karen laughed at the baby's goofy grin and suddenly noticed a sliver of white.

"Aida, that's three days and no mail."

"Is that what I think it is?!!" Aida looked at Karen with wide eyes. "Karen, did you see this? Come here and look! Emmit's getting his first toofer! Oh, you big boy!"

Karen had seen the tooth; in fact, she'd been bitten by it, too, but she wanted to let Aida have the joy of discovering it, so she played along.

"Oh, how cool! It'll be time for steak before long!" After giving Aida a minute to enjoy the baby undisturbed, Karen continued. "Aida, I'm concerned about the mail," she started, and when Aida looked up, added, "and about something more."

Aida looked over when she heard the tone of Karen's voice. "What is it?"

"Emmit and I were watching out the window for you and saw some punk kid wearing a beanie come right up to the building. I expected to hear the bell or the door open, but there was nothing. Then he left again. I think he took our mail! We haven't had mail for three days now. He crossed the street and stood there as if he was waiting for someone. When you came around the corner, he watched you all the way to the door, and then he turned and headed back down the street the way he came.

"It's no biggie. Let's just change our mail delivery to a P.O. box."

"Aida, you have to be kidding! You've got to tell Tony and Telly!"

"Why? I already got dressed down by Tony for taking the Metro. I agreed to let him drive me back and forth to work every day. That's who I was talking to when that creep, whoever he was, was stalking me. I don't want to be put on full lockdown. Remember what it was like during Covid?"

"Aida, this isn't just about you. What about Emmit and me?" Karen's voice was shaking. "We've got to tell Tony and Telly, and even Mr. Wafi downstairs."

Aida fell silent, and, when Karen looked at her, she saw in her eyes a stubbornness that she knew all too well. This was not the first disagreement that they had had about safety. In desperation, Karen pulled down the neck of her sweatshirt to expose her tattoo, "Semper fi." The fact that this was the first time that Karen had used that trump card made clear to Aida that Karen was serious. Karen stared with steely resolve at Aida. Emmit picked up the tension in the air and started crying.

Aida handed the crying child to Karen and started down the hall. "Fine! Just fine! I can't believe you used the tattoo for something this small!"

"Aida, you know what some people are capable of! Don't you remember The Great Exposure?" Aida's bedroom door slammed.

It did not take long for Aida to see Karen's point, though, and she informed Telly and Tony about the stalker the same evening. As a result, Aida's security detail increased, and unmarked cars started cruising in and out of the cul-de-sac on a regular basis. The added protection helped Karen deal with the situation. Soon, she and Aida were joking about the stalker, whom they took to calling Beanie Man.

CHAPTER 7
THE CONFERENCE WITH FRAZ

The week flew by, and soon it was time for the conference with Fraz. Aida kept him waiting for five full minutes before she calmly walked into the conference room. She scanned it quickly, finding it much smaller than she would have liked. Fraz was looking out the window with his back to the door. Aida imagined that he was already angry to have been kept waiting, and his stiff posture seemed to confirm her surmise.

The tiny room had a small, low table with matching upholstered chairs on opposite sides. Tracy had left a tray on the table with a pitcher of ice water and two glasses. Fraz turned slowly when he heard Aida enter. Aida could not help being affected when they made eye contact. He was every Muslim woman's vision of a perfect man as far as appearance went. Aida's father was not nearly as handsome, but the two men looked enough alike that Fraz's appearance stirred up feelings of deep affection in Aida. Fraz also stirred within her something less welcome. She was in the middle of her cycle, and unwelcome sexual urges had been plaguing her all day. Catching herself, she silently cursed her hormones.

Fraz was impeccably dressed in a custom-tailored navy blue suit paired with a starched white shirt, gold cuff links, and a simple pale blue silk tie. The suit fit his tall, lean build perfectly. His personal grooming reflected the same careful attention. His thick, shiny black hair looked as if had just been trimmed, short on the sides and slicked back on top. His intentional two days' growth of black beard was likewise crisp along the edges. It was his eyes, however, that especially knocked Aida off-balance. Whenever they met, he looked right into her eyes and held her gaze for a few seconds before either of them said a word. His eyes were a deep brown that almost looked black. The light brown tone of his face was a shade or two deeper around his eyes, giving them a smoky effect. His eyelashes were thick and long and black.

Aida was aware that her practiced look of authority was fading from her face, but she was helpless to stop it. When his intense scrutiny turned slowly into a big, welcoming grin, she felt her own features match it.

"Aida! Thank you so much for making time to see me. I know you must be very, very busy!" He stepped toward her and stretched out his hand. He was turning the charm on full-strength now and he looked truly humble. Aida knew what he was doing but could not bring herself to reply with the vitriol that she had felt just moments ago. She stepped toward him and held out her hand.

"Hello," she said, faltering as he took her small hand in his and then slowly laid his other hand gently on top, completely engulfing it. She was not sure, but she thought she saw a flicker of triumph in his eyes as he realized that he had moved her again. The look was gone so fast that she did not quite trust having seen it, especially as he still had her hand in his. He increased the pressure just slightly and leaned in a little further. She almost thought he was about to raise her hand to his lips and kiss it. She managed to compose herself enough to withdraw her hand and straighten herself as she said, "Of course, please forgive me for neglecting you. As we parted on bad terms, I assumed our business with each other was concluded."

Fraz's lips formed into a slight pout, and he looked contritely at the floor. When he looked up again, there were actually tears in his eyes. "Aida, forgive me for trying to change you. Look at you." He held onto her upper arms, took a step back, and looked her over from head to toe. "You have stepped into a new look, a confident one. You are going to be wonderful in your new position." He turned to pick up a newspaper from the table. "You even made the front page of the *Washington Post*." He stepped a little closer and held it up for her to see. "I saved a copy for you from last week. Have you seen it?" Aida gasped before she could catch herself. There was a photo of her on the Metro in her bright red blazer, one hand above her head holding a bar and the other grasping her briefcase. Her skirt was higher on her thigh than she would have liked. The headline read, "Aida Adams Stands Out on First Day on Hill."

"Oh!" she gasped. "I had no idea my clothes would make such a stir."

Fraz's eyes flashed, but Aida was distracted by the article and did not notice. Fraz breathed in deeply through his nose, trying to discreetly calm himself. Her carelessness with her public image angered him. Nevertheless, he decided that this was the moment to make his apology since she avoided eye contact when she was flustered and he didn't think that he could stand to meet her gaze at the moment. He shook his head slightly to prepare himself and then turned his gaze to Aida. "I know I can be hard to deal with." He tried to maintain a gentle tone. "I have such strong opinions, and, when I see trends and what the people respond to, I get on a mission to help you please them." He lifted his chin, "Every vote counts, you know!"

He was uncomfortably close, in her space, but she did not want to give the impression of being intimidated and held her ground.

Gulping, she gestured toward the chairs. "Shall we get started?"

Fraz bowed slightly. He waited for her to sit and then did so himself, scooting his chair a little closer to hers. He picked up the pitcher of water from the tray, filled a glass, and looking at her over it, raised his eyebrows in an unspoken question. Aida's mouth was dry, and before she could think, she nodded and reached out her hand. His fingers brushed hers as she took the cool glass. She wished that she could splash some of the water on her face. She was sure that she was blushing. She realized suddenly that she did not want him to know that her mouth was dry, so she set the glass down within reach and looked calmly at him. Having the table between them gave her a bit of relief, and she rallied as she began her prepared speech.

"Fraz, I want to thank you for your work on the campaign. You were very helpful, and I'd be happy to give you a strong reference if you want to continue working in politics."

She was in control now. Aida knew how to deliver a speech. Public speaking was her forté, as was debate. She had been thrown by his presence, but she was determined to recover. His casual demeanor became somewhat apprehensive. He opened his mouth to speak, but she raised her hand to stop him.

Fraz closed his mouth, and she could see his jaw clenching. This confirmed her hope that he was unaware that Telly had ordered Aida to keep him on. She was determined to maintain the upper hand even though she would have to keep him on her staff. It wouldn't hurt him to squirm for a few minutes as she challenged his pride. That was exactly her goal—and not just for today, either, but for every day that he was in her employ.

Aida continued, "Fraz, you are as aware as I am that we don't see eye to eye on most things. I know that I have been a source of—" Aida checked her internal thesaurus quickly. There was no way she was going to use the word frustration, so she began again. "I have opposed some of your plans for the campaign and the image you hoped I would project. Your vision of the first Muslim Egalitarian in the House was, let's face it, an airbrushed female version of yourself."

Fraz had to jump in. He thought that he was about to lose his job and could not let that happen. "Aida, I know it might seem that way, but, honestly, I only meant to offer options. You have good instincts. When you chose otherwise than I suggested, well, I just wanted to see how strong your commitment to a course of action was. We're both strong personalities, and I apologize again if my lawyerly ways discouraged you or seemed disrespectful. I have great respect for you, and I am proud that we were a part of such a worthy cause as this—"

"Fraz, you interrupted me again. Perhaps we should just, you know," she made a motion to stand up.

"Aida, ma'am, please continue." He gave her a pleading look, slid back in his chair, and, trying to look patient, folded his hands in his lap.

His pleading look did not move Aida. She knew that he was putting it on. She was tired of this discussion and keeping him in the hot seat was not as fun as she had fantasized.

"Fraz, my intention was to make this appointment an exit interview for you. We said our goodbyes over the phone, and I am convinced you were as happy as me to part ways. However, Telly has suggested to me that you might be a perfect fit to be my surrogate at the home office."

Fraz stiffened in his chair and his eyes shot back up to her face.

"I prefer to let Jackie keep running the show, but, if you really want to stay on the team, I can offer you a part-time job in Gainesville helping her when things are extra busy. If you wish, you can still work at the firm as well. Of course, we will still keep you on retainer to give us legal counsel. I'll have Roger send you a formal job offer by email. Please respond within three days if you're interested." She smiled and glanced his way. "Okay? Good. Thanks so much for coming today; I really appreciate it."

Aida then stood quickly and exited the room before Fraz had a chance to reply. He jumped up and hurried around the table as quickly as he could but refused to call out to her until he caught up to her. However, when he stepped through the doorway and looked up and down the hallway, she was already striding quickly around the corner and out of sight before he could open his mouth.

CHAPTER 8
FRAZ REACTS

Fraz walked down the hall to the elevator. His chiseled jaw pulsed with the violence of his clenched teeth. He breathed deeply through his nose as he struggled to keep his composure. He punched the elevator button several times before he caught himself and stopped. He glanced around quickly and then relaxed somewhat when he saw that the hall was empty. Aida had disappeared in the opposite direction and apparently, was not coming back.

"She must be as eager to get away from me as I am from her," he muttered to himself as he stepped into the elevator.

He longed to pound on the walls and yell, but the sight of the surveillance camera on the ceiling convinced him to restrain himself. By the time the doors opened, he had regained control over his expression. Three young female staffers were waiting to get in as he got out, and they gave him a quick glance, and then a double-take caused all three to light up. He barely noticed their overly welcoming smiles. He breezed past them without a second glance though one of them had movie-star looks. He could not wait to get outside and into his car. It was a brisk winter day, and the frigid air helped to calm his fury. He noticed the sensation of sweat under his armpits, and that caused his smoldering anger to flare back up. He would have to go home and shower and change every item of clothing. It was a good half-mile to the parking deck, and he wished that he could run and work off some of his rage, but of course, he could not.

When he reached the parking deck, he took the side door into the stairwell and jogged quickly up to the sixth floor where he had parked. He pressed the key fob in his pocket, and his sleek red Ferrari 812 chirped. He rarely took this supercar out of storage; a $350,000 vehicle was too much to risk in D.C. traffic. He had only driven it that day because he had planned to invite Aida to lunch and hoped to impress her, so her brush-off infuriated him all the more. He climbed into the driver's seat and slammed the door. When he engaged the ignition, the V-12 engine roared to life. The guttural roar echoed off the concrete walls and pillars of the parking deck. He had forgotten having cued up "Every Story is a Love Story" from the Broadway *Aida* by Elton John and Tim Rice on the sound system. It started with the engine.

> *Every story, new or ancient,*
> *Bagatelle or work of art;*
> *All are tales of human failing.*
> *All are tales of love at heart.*
> *This is the story*
> *Of a love that flourished*
> *In a time of hate.*

Hearing those lyrics now, Fraz felt as if his head would explode. He fumbled to mute the sound before he heard any more. He selected his heavy metal playlist and turned the volume up to an ear-piercing scream.

He threw the Ferrari into reverse, turned around, and headed out with tires squealing. He underestimated the thrust as he shot across the tight rows of vehicles. He was driving a vehicle capable of reaching 60 miles per hour in a mere 2.8 seconds and had to brake hard as he roared toward the exit, barely in control of the beast. The quick-responding braking system took him to a full stop in only 142 feet; the beast obeyed its master. He pounded the steering wheel with his fists until a golf cart came floating around the corner with a courtesy driver and a heavy-set, well-dressed elderly man in the passenger seat. The realization that he could easily have plowed into them was enough of a shock for Fraz to regain his composure. He felt like a stick of dynamite with a lit fuse. He hit the off button on the audio as the courtesy cart rolled up next to him and the driver called "Is there a problem, sir?"

Fraz rolled down the window and forced a grim smile, "Oh no, just checking for an important message before I get on the road. Thanks for asking."

The driver gave Fraz a salute. His passenger didn't even look over. It was obvious from the way he was scanning the parking deck that he was searching for his car.

"There it is!" he shouted, causing both the driver and Fraz to jump.

The rage rushed back into Fraz, but, luckily, the courtesy driver had floored the cart in his surprise at his passenger's outburst and was silently rolling away in the direction of the man's car. Fraz doubled his fists and raised them to strike the steering wheel again, but then froze.

"She's not worth it," he muttered as he pulled out onto the boulevard. He started plotting how to get his revenge once his assignment with Aida ended.

Back in his hotel room, after enduring a long, cold shower and dressing in fresh clothes, he contemplated his next move. He was confident that he still could get under Aida's skin in person—he had seen her reaction to his presence and how she had to focus on her memorized speech in order to keep cool. She was just another stupid, wanton woman, in his opinion—but he would be handicapped trying to manipulate her from a distance. He had contempt for all women, but none so much as Aida Adams. Normally, he would not give a woman like Aida a second glance. Now, he had to try to handle her from afar, yet come up with reasons to takes trips to D.C. so he could see her in person. His direct report regarding Aida was Mr. Wafi, the imam who was Aida's landlord. Fraz hoped to handle this with him because he would rather deal with him than his father. He had not checked in since the inauguration and was overdue to do so. Fraz was determined to work something out with the imam before his father, Omar Abbas, became involved. When he had himself under control again he sat down to call the imam.

CHAPTER 9
BEATRICE

Time went by in a blur as Aida settled into her new job. She and the other junior representatives took every opportunity to meet their colleagues and were alternately amused and offended at the self-importance of the senior members. Few veteran politicians were left in the aftermath of The Great Exposure. These few were deep into jockeying for power. They were desperate to build support for their party's agendas and had little time for the junior legislators, so the new office-holders had it rough. Nationwide, voters had elected ten Egalitarians, but the Republicans and Democrats in Congress had no real need of their input, at least at first. They would need their help soon, when they were ready to pass some serious legislation. Only then would they be given a meaningful role to play. Even the few veteran representatives left in office that were from Florida ignored Aida's messages.

A month passed. Aida organized a luncheon with the other junior representatives from the Egalitarian Party in the House cafeteria. The gathering quickly deteriorated into a gripe session. Murray Saunders from New York was the worst. "When the hell are we going to be done with these endless briefings?" he complained.

Aida soon had her fill of the complaining. She tried to change the subject. "Murray, attending briefings is boring," Aida interjected, "but do you—"

He carried on as if she had not spoken. "I told Telly to her face that I've about had my fill."

"And how many party meetings is a man supposed to be able to take," Jack Benson, a newbie from California asked, "without dying of boredom?"

Aida cut in, turning quickly to him. "Jack, how have you been?"

"I don't even know, Aida. I'll let you know when I climb out from under the piles of endless forms on my desk and can concentrate on getting floor procedures straight."

Aida rolled her eyes but bit back the stinging words on the tip of her tongue. Instead, she said in her head (and in a thick New York accent that she had learned from Tony), "Ahhh, quitcha bellyachin'!"

Murray wiped his greasy lips on his napkin and broke in. "I propose that we commit to one another that, unless we have a speaking engagement or a visiting delegation from our home state," he sucked his teeth for a moment and continued, "or, even better, if we manage to get a lunch date with a more senior member of the House, that we will start a firm tradition to keep meeting here," he waved expansively around the hall, "for lunch at this greasy spoon every Monday!"

He raised a glass of water high toward them each, one at a time. "All in favor, say, aye!"

Aida reluctantly raised her glass with a weak "Aye." It was their first vote on Capitol Hill. Turning her head away from the group to roll her eyes again, she saw the senior congresswoman from West Virginia, Beatrice Gainer, bustling toward the table.

As she approached, slightly breathless from the exertion, she said politely, "Forgive me for intruding. You all look like you're in the middle of some important policy decisions."

The sound of several chairs being pushed back from the table was followed by hands reaching out to be shaken and a jumble of comments.

"Not at all, Congresswoman!"

"Please join us!"

"Congresswoman Gainer, I'm so pleased—"

"Have you eaten?"

"Oh, my, no, no," she replied to the last query. "Thank you so much. You're all too kind. I just wanted to say howdy-do to you all," she smiled, "Welcome to the House, and please, please, call me Bea!"

Representative Beatrice Gainer was about five feet five inches and a trim hundred-and-twenty-five pounds. She was serving her third term in the House as a Republican representing West Virginia's Third District. She had already been in office a full term before the Great Exposure. Aida took in her smiling hazel eyes and rather heavy dark eyebrows. Beatrice had an outdated, no-nonsense brown bob that was obviously molded into submission with lots of gel and hair spray every morning. When she shook her head enthusiastically, her hair didn't even move. She was wearing a royal blue polyester pantsuit that looked like it had come from a vintage thrift shop. Her bright, multi-colored floral blouse had a little gap between the buttons down the front of her ample bust, and Aida had to force herself to keep her eyes on the congresswoman's face. Beatrice was smiling broadly, and her voice had a happy lilt to it that made it seem as if a chuckle was about to erupt.

Aida had heard that Beatrice was a friend to everyone but that few took her seriously because she acted more like a doting grandmother than a politician. Telly, however, had told her to be careful of Congress-woman Gainer because "Bea," as she liked to be called, was known to be a very skilled and articulate communicator. She had a reputation for expressing her point of view in a manner so down-to-earth and conge-nial that opponents had been known to nod their heads in agreement as she spoke, oblivious to the fact that she had just changed their minds. Telly called it "The Gainer Greasing."

"Let me see," she murmured, turning first to Aida. "Unless I'm mistaken, you are Aida Adams from Florida's District Three, aren't you?" She smiled at Aida, and her sparkling and honest eyes gave Aida a happy feeling in her stomach. The feeling surprised her, not because it was unpleasant, but because she suddenly realized that it was the return of a feeling that had been absent for quite a time.

"Yes, ma'am, I'm District Three in Florida, and you are District Three in West Virginia!"

"That's right! We have something in common. Three is a good number, I always say."

After they exchanged a firm handshake, Bea turned to the others and greeted each in the same confident manner. Bea straightened up and said, "Speaking of three, I'm so thankful that you all are here to help us pass term limits—even though they will boot me out of here after this term. It limits us to three terms, you know. I just wanted to let you know that there is immense pressure on the Speaker to get the ball rolling, and it should be happening soon. We all promised to support term limits in our campaigns, and I can assure you that no one who opposes it will see another term—not after The Great Exposure! Even those who think they're all that and a bag of chips are learning that the voters are in charge now!"

Aida and her associates sat with silly grins on their faces, nodding along with Bea.

Jack spoke up enthusiastically, "Yes, ma'am, we are with you all the way!"

Murray turned to Aida and behind his hand muttered, "I think we've just been greased."

Aida ignored his comment. She hadn't been greased; she'd been graced—that is, she felt grateful not only to have connected with a senior representative but to have met someone whom she found worthy of her respect. In particular, she was impressed that Bea was willing to vote for a bill that would end her own time in the House. The next day, when Aida arrived at her office, she found a handwritten note from Representative Gainer inviting her to lunch the following Monday.

CHAPTER 10
LUNCH WITH BEATRICE

The week sped past, and Aida soon found herself sitting across the table from Beatrice Gainer in the quietest corner that they could find in the House cafeteria. Beatrice was the only person in Washington she had met so far with whom she longed to spend time, not just for political connections, but to get to know her and just enjoy her company. Aida started to realize how much she longed for a female mentor. Her own mother lived so far away, and her grandmother had been gone for several years. Aida had rarely seen her mother since her senior year of high school, when her parents had divorced and her mother had moved to Israel with her new husband. They spoke on the phone once a month, but it was always one-sided: her mother talked nonstop about herself, her husband, and their social life. She always started the conversation with a quick, "Aida, how are you?" but did not wait to hear the answer before jumping into a thorough rundown about her life.

"Aida, how are you?" Beatrice asked.

Aida looked up expectantly but said nothing.

Beatrice leaned forward a little more and spoke a little louder. "How are you and your family adjusting to Washington?"

Beatrice leaned back and waited for Aida to answer, but she was so caught up in thoughts about her mother that she expected Beatrice to continue without waiting for her to say anything. When she realized that Beatrice was waiting for her reply, she quickly gave the standard answer.

"Fine, thank you. It's just such an honor and privilege to be here in Washington. How are you?"

Beatrice ignored the question.

"I remember what it's like arriving from civilian life in this city. I felt like a hound dog pup that had been picked up by the nape of its neck and dropped into shark-infested waters. I called my mama every night and cried and bawled like one, too. I crept into the House chambers that first day like a weaned puppy in a strange place wondering where its mama and littermates were, cold and confused with new owners shouting and arguing in a language I didn't understand. I would have quit the first week if Mama hadn't kept telling me, 'Child, you are ready for this! You wanted to go to D.C. and make a difference. That's all I heard from you for years. Now you've got your chance, and you had better stick it out. I don't want to see you coming home with your tail between your legs. Don't you remember your farewell party? The whole town of Philippi is rooting for you! You have a calling. Put your big girl panties on and git 'er done.'"

Aida did not have any experience with dogs; much less a hound dog, but Beatrice's vivid description painted a clear picture in her mind, and the two ladies enjoyed a hearty laugh together. Tears suddenly sprang to Aida's eyes as she realized how the cute but pitiful picture was accurate for her experience in the House so far, too. She blinked rapidly to keep the tears back.

"I didn't know until much later that Mama would hang up the phone and just bawl and squall on Daddy's shoulder after we talked," Beatrice continued. "He said that she wore the carpet out just pacing and praying every morning for me. Thank God for family!"

Now tears sprang to Beatrice's eyes, but she did not fight them as Aida did. She picked up her napkin and wiped her face. Then she gave a heavy sigh and leaned in closer to Aida.

"Now, darlin', tell me. How are you adjusting to life in Washington?"

Her motherly concern touched Aida, but she did not know how to respond to it. She certainly was not ready to confide in anyone, but she desperately wished that she could. Now, it was Aida's turn to sigh. She was afraid to trust anyone, even this apparently sweet lady who looked like she had enough love in her to nurture the world. "I have studied wordsmiths and speechwriting extensively. What you just said was perfect, just perfect. This city-raised lawyer relates more to what you just said than you might think!"

Beatrice studied Aida's face and nodded thoughtfully. Aida went quiet, unwilling to say more. Beatrice made a quick decision. This girl needed a friend. She had no time in her schedule to take another junior representative under her wing, but she decided that she would make time for Aida.

After more small talk, Beatrice asked Aida about her work with immigrants. She noticed right away that Aida's eyes lit up as she talked about it.

"I heard about the good work you did in Florida. I saw the show about Melting Pot Justice on *We Are America*."

"You did? I can't believe it!" Aida blushed and moved to hide her face behind her napkin. "I'm sure that you saw that awful photo, too!"

"Oh yes I did! It was priceless! I never miss that show. I absolutely love it. It is so real and inspires everyday people to step up and make a difference—but, Aida, why are you blushing?"

"Oh, Bea, I'll never forget the day I first heard that I had been selected for that show. It was so embarrassing!"

"Oh, I've got to hear this! Tell me. Dish, girl, dish!"

"It seems so long ago, yet it has only been two years. It was right after the presidential election, but before the inauguration." Aida got a distant look in her eyes as she thought back to that day. "So much has changed."

"Oh yes, life happens fast," Bea chimed in. "So, where were you when you found out about being chosen?"

"I was in the hallway of the Orange County Courthouse in Orlando with an Iranian family. I was representing them."

Aida had been very pleased with herself as she left the courtroom. The middle-aged Iranian couple she represented had been awarded a favorable and just settlement. The whole family was crowded around her in the lobby, crying, hugging, and laughing. Her clients, Mohammed and Era Ibrahim, had three grown sons who were there with their wives and children. They were all talking at once in Farsi. Aida nodded and laughed with them though she only understood a few words. She saw a camera crew and news anchor approach. The reporter stretched out her microphone ahead of herself as she shouted,

"Counselor! Ms. Adams!"

Mr. Ibrahim saw them coming first and shushed his family immediately. He had no love for the media, though the press had undergone many positive changes since the Great Exposure. Aida knew his feelings and was determined to shut down this ambush. "Mr. Ibrahim, take your family immediately to the car," she told him. "Don't speak to anyone or make eye contact. I will take care of this and join you later at your home for the party."

Her eyes bore intensely into his with a gleam that told him she was looking forward to the confrontation. He obeyed immediately. Turning to his wife and offspring, he stretched out his arms and herded them quickly down the hallway toward the exit to the stairs. They responded to the sober intensity in his eyes and moved quickly down the steps to the parking garage. His sons hurried their wives and children along, scooping up the little ones into their strong arms. The patriarch peered through the crack in the door for a brief moment to confirm that they weren't being followed before turning to jog down the steps himself. All of this drama proved unnecessary, however, when Aida discovered the reason that she had been pursued. "Ms. Adams, I'm Lucinda Moran of the Reeltime Network," the reporter introduced herself. "What is your reaction to finding yourself chosen as one of the shining stars highlighted on *We Are America*?"

Aida knew all about *We Are America*. She watched the show every day and rejoiced in the many ways in which more and more Americans were stepping up to rebuild the nation. The camera zoomed in on her face, and she blinked a few times as she struggled to shift gears from the confrontation that she had expected. Her jaw was still set firmly, and her eyes had not lost their fire; her arms were at her sides, but her fists were tightly clenched. As she registered what the reporter was saying, however, her jaw dropped and her face froze in a brief moment of confusion, as when she had once picked up and sipped a glass of ginger ale thinking it was water.

The photographer was thrilled to discover that Aida hadn't heard the news that she had been selected to be on the show. He took several still shots. To Aida's chagrin, these were the images that accompanied every headline following the announcement. They were not flattering, to say the least. Karen had howled when she saw them and teased Aida mercilessly. Later, when Aida ran for office, her opponents used them in negative ads with the catchphrase "She doesn't have a clue!"

Aida had not been happy with this first step into the public spotlight, but she did appreciate the fringe benefits. Donations to her nonprofit, Melting Pot Justice, started pouring in, and many eager volunteers showed up to the next orientation. Her workload had always been heavy, but, after she became known, it skyrocketed. More and more immigrants found Melting Pot Justice. She had to train and supervise additional volunteers and hire staff to keep up with the phones call, email, and requests for interviews that followed. She was now a model for private-sector charities seeking to protect Americans against adversaries with deeper pockets. Other advocates for justice contacted her and begged her to help them get started. Later, when Aida arrived in Washington, she had naively assumed that she would be called on by the congressional leadership to help with immigration policy, but, so far, this had not happened.

"Hello! Aida, are you still with me?" Beatrice laughed and waved her hand across Aida's field of vision.

Aida blinked and looked back at her.

"Oh, Congresswoman, I'm so sorry! I just got caught up in the memories. Please forgive me."

"How about this? I'll forgive you if you put whatever you were reliving into words so I can get in on it, too!" Beatrice chuckled deep in her throat, her hazel eyes sparkling.

Aida was embarrassed at how rudely she had behaved. She quickly told the story. The women knew that they only had a few more minutes together before Beatrice would have to leave for a committee meeting in preparation for the coming actions on term limits. Aida wanted to ask her so many questions, but they were out of time.

As if reading her mind, Bea looked at her watch and said, "Aida, I know that you probably have a lot of questions for me. Do you have a quick one before I have to get going?" She had finished her salad and was reapplying lipstick in preparation to leave.

Aida had not touched her food. Her coffee sat untouched as well. She looked at Beatrice gratefully, thinking how generous it was of this busy woman to spend time with her. And she was not even in the same party. Aida's thoughts turned to Beanie Man, to Fraz, and to Karen and Emmit. So many things were troubling her. She could figure out the nuts and bolts of the political world by herself, but what she longed for was some personal advice. This motherly woman had put her at ease. She looked hopefully into Beatrice's warm eyes but hesitated. Actually, she reminded her of her grandmother. Her mother had always been distant and busy with various social activities. She had often left Aida in her grandmother's care. She shook her head at Beatrice.

"Thank you, but no, nothing urgent."

"Are you sure?"

"It'll keep. We need something to talk about next time!"

"Yes!" Beatrice agreed, "Next time. Aida, I want to see more of you. What do you say? Shall we make this a regular thing?"

"Oh, yes ma'am! I'd love to!" Aida immediately felt hopeful.

"It's a deal then, a truly bipartisan decision. But stop calling me 'ma'am,' young lady. It makes me feel old!"

"Deal!" Aida repeated. "But please, stop calling me 'young lady'!" A huge smile broke out across Aida's face and expanded into a big toothy grin. It was a physical sensation that she had not felt in a long time.

"Deal!" Beatrice agreed. "Now let me get out of here so you can eat a bite. I kept you so busy you haven't touched a thing. You have to eat when you can around here. Please don't get in a habit of skipping meals!"

"Yes, mmm—"

The other woman's eyebrows shot up, and she gave Aida a stern look.

"—mmmBea!" Aida laughed and Beatrice echoed it.

"Good girl!"

Another wave of that wonderful feeling that she had when she was with her grandmother washed over Aida. She remembered her grandmother telling her, "You're a good girl, Aida. There's nothing wrong with you! You just need a dose of Grammy! Come here and let me give you a hug."

Aida smiled as she picked up her sandwich. While she ate, she mused about her entry into politics. It had all started with the *We Are America* opportunity, she reflected with a wry smile—maybe the jury was still out on whether getting into politics had been a blessing or a curse. The server quietly served her another hot cup of coffee. She savored it as she thought back to the impact of her brief, ten-minute interview on *We Are America*.

CHAPTER 11
RECRUITMENT

Aida continued reminiscing. It was only a week after her interview with *We Are America* that one of the volunteers interrupted her during a conference with a troubled student from Ethiopia. Her heart had warmed just looking at the young man who reminded her so much of her beloved friends at the international school she had attended when she was his age. She was about to ask him a question when her favorite volunteer, Lizzy, a tall, dark-skinned African American beauty, burst into her office in a state of obvious excitement.

"Ma'am, ma'am, I'm so sorry to interrupt," she stammered as she approached Aida. "And excuse me, sir," she said, turning to acknowledge the young man as well. Aida had trained all of her staff and volunteers to treat their clients with the utmost respect. "I'm so sorry."

"What has gotten you into such a tizzy, Lizzy?" Aida queried. Her impatience was obvious in her tone despite her attempt at humor.

"You have a phone call, Ma'am, from someone very important."

"Is it an emergency?"

"No, but it's someone very important and I left her on hold."

Aida frowned, now truly annoyed. "Is it my mother?"

"No ma'am."

"Then take a message. Whoever it is, they are not more important than Tadele, who is sitting right in front of me." She gave Lizzy a hard look. "Please, take a message."

Lizzy looked shocked but backed away quickly, half-bowing as she whispered, "Again, I'm so sorry to interrupt both of you. I just got—" Her words trailed off as she turned and fled the room. Lizzy had been there long enough to know that she had nothing to fear except a lecture. Aida was a forgiving boss. She did know that Aida would expect her to remember this lesson, though.

By the time Aida finished with Tadele, Lizzy had regained her former excitement and was more exuberant than ever when she finally got a chance to tell Aida, "It was Telly Gavin!"

Aida stared at her expressionlessly.

"Telly Gavin! You know, the head of the Egalitarian Party?!"

So began Aida's political journey.

PART TWO

CHAPTER 12
BEA ASKS A FAVOR

Aida's heart did a happy dance when, two months later, Roger reminded her of her lunch date. She arrived early and sat near the door of the House cafeteria so that she wouldn't miss Bea, who soon joined her. A tired-looking, middle-aged server with dark hair in a messy bun came and stood in front of their table with a coffee pot. Aida glanced up at her and then waved her away. Looking at Beatrice, she said, "I've had too much coffee already."

Beatrice glanced up at the server and took note of her nametag.

"Linda! I don't think I know you. I'm Bea. How are you doing?" The server perked up at the mention of her name.

"I'm fine. Thanks for asking. Would you like some coffee, ma'am?"

"No thanks, darlin', but, oooh, I love your earrings!"

"Thanks, my little boy gave them to me for Christmas."

"How sweet! That makes them extra special, doesn't it?"

Aida was a little annoyed. They did not have much time, and she wanted to take full advantage of it. She said to the server. "I'm ready to order." She nodded to her companion, "Bea, are you?" Beatrice smiled back. Aida continued quickly, "I'll have the chef salad with ranch on the side and just ice water to drink."

"Make that two, please, Linda," Bea added. "I appreciate it."

"Coming right up," the server responded as she turned and walked toward the kitchen. Aida noticed that she had a little more energy in her step and made a mental note of what a difference a little bit of positive attention could make. She felt a little pang of guilt for her abruptness. She was amazed at the kindness and patience that Bea constantly showed. It was such a contrast with the fake charm of the other legislators. It took Aida a moment to adjust to it.

"Well, Aida, you have survived two months in this pressure cooker. How are you adjusting to Washington?"

"Oh, Ms. Gainer," she started.

"Remember, Aida, to call me Bea. We're friends, aren't we?"

"Oh, I hope so!" Aida replied. "It would be wonderful to have a friend in the House."

"Well you do, so now that we've got that straight, I'm sorry for interrupting you. You were saying?"

"Sorry, what were we talking about?"

"About how you like your current job."

"Right! I feel like I'm in grade school again."

"Uh-huh," Bea nodded. "I remember."

"There is so much to learn. I'm afraid my term will be up before I know what I'm doing. So far, I haven't voted for one resolution, much less a bill. And I haven't been able to get a word in at any of the committee meetings. It's so different from my previous job, where I was in the thick of things constantly and really felt that I was making a difference for my clients." She stopped herself abruptly. "Oh, Bea, I'm sorry I'm complaining. Just what I hate others to do!"

"Darlin', you're just answering my question," Bea replied. Her warm hazel eyes held Aida's, and the younger woman felt comforted. It was a relief to confide in someone.

"Well, if you really want to know, frankly, I find this job boring!"

Bea threw back her head and laughed.

Aida covered her mouth with her hand. "Did I say that out loud?"

"Oh yes, you did!" Bea continued to chuckle. "And you told the truth. You are a rare one, Aida! I may have just met my first honest politician."

Aida chuckled nervously, still not entirely at ease with her new friend. She was still in awe of this career politician.

"Aida, I want to ask a favor of you today. I have a close personal friend who requests to remain nameless. I will honor that request just as I will honor any request you give me."

Aida's heart skipped a beat. Maybe, just maybe, Bea could help Aida with her troubling secrets. She had never trusted anyone, not even her own mother or father, with the problems that she was facing. Only Karen knew. Aida was so grateful for Karen. "Praise be to Allah," Aida said without even realizing she was speaking.

Bea looked at her and paused briefly. Aida blushed but gave no explanation.

"This friend is a brilliant young Ethiopian woman living here on a visa that is about to expire," Bea went on.

"I can probably help with that," Aida interjected. "I used to help students all the time. She is still in school, isn't she?"

"She is graduating next fall with a Ph.D. in computer science. She doesn't qualify for a visa extension, and she is not trying to get one. What she's seeking is asylum in the United States."

"Why? I mean, on what grounds?"

"Because she has departed from her family's faith and become a Christian."

Aida's dark eyes flashed as she abruptly set down her cup.

"Aida, I know that you might find her choice troubling, but this friend has every right to her beliefs, and to change them, doesn't she?"

"Who is it?" Aida demanded.

Beatrice sighed and went silent. The server returned and quietly placed a salad before Bea with one hand and then seamlessly gave Aida hers with the other.

Bea looked up at her and smiled. "Thank you, Linda." She continued. "Aida, I will keep my word to my friend to protect her anonymity. To do otherwise could put her very life in danger. Her father and brothers are very strictly observant Muslims. She said that she was beaten throughout her childhood for minor infractions of Islamic law, laws that her father and brothers did not even keep themselves. She gave me examples of two other family members who simply asked a question about Jewish beliefs and were beaten so badly that they were hospitalized. One of them is permanently disabled."

Aida's nostrils flared and her jaw tensed. She spoke again, using her diplomatic politician's voice.

"I'm sorry, Beatrice. It is not my business to interfere in the domestic lives of foreigners."

"Aida, although you and your family are Muslim, you grew up in the United States. Do you have any firsthand knowledge of what it's like for Muslim women in other countries?"

"Of course I do, Bea, but this is the United States of America. Her life is not in danger here!" Aida immediately regretted the sharp edge she heard in her own voice and wondered to herself why she was so defensive.

"Yes, Aida," Beatrice patiently responded. "She is much safer here, but she is still in danger. Have you ever defended a Muslim woman who tried to escape trial by Sharia law?"

Aida took a sip of her ice water and composed herself. "No," she answered honestly.

"Aida, this woman has many relatives in Dearborn, Michigan. They are all devout Muslims. She is convinced that, if they find out that she has converted, they will bind themselves to an oath to kill her for the honor of the family. Their plan for her is for her to return to Ethiopia and marry someone her father has made an arrangement with, someone she has never met."

"Then that is what she should do!" Aida could not believe what she heard herself saying. Where was this venom coming from? "Am I not a Muslim? Didn't my parents grow up in Ethiopia?" Aida pushed back her chair as if ready to leave the table. "It is an honorable culture! I'm tired of every American thinking they know what is best for us!"

The abrupt movement and squeak of the chair legs against flooring caused heads to turn at the adjacent tables.

Bea remained as cool as ever, but she did not back down from her point.

"Your father is a Muslim and a wonderful man, Aida, I know that. He is also an anomaly when it comes to believing in the equality of women. Did you ever wonder why your parents never took up residence in a Muslim community? How many Muslim constituents do you have in District Three?"

Aida stood and threw her napkin on her plate. "I must go and prepare for my next meeting. Excuse me, please." She reached for the check. Her cheeks were flaming red. She had lost her composure. She regretted it already and knew that she would regret it even more later. She did not want to risk staying and saying anything else.

"I'll pay this on my way out."

"Thank you, Aida," Bea said, still smiling.

Aida turned abruptly and walked quickly to the register. She handed the cashier some cash and turned immediately to head out the door. She did not see her only true friend in the House looking sadly after her.

Bea watched Aida's retreating back. After Aida was out of sight, Bea took a deep breath. She had lost her appetite. She pushed her salad around on her plate as she watched and then pecked at a bite of it.

She told herself that she needed to eat and commanded her stomach to cooperate. She smoothed the napkin in her lap and straightened her back, determined not to waste the meal. She bowed her head. "Thank You, Lord, for my daily bread, and for my Muslim friends. I ask You to help all of them find their way."

CHAPTER 13
AIDA AGREES TO LISTEN

The weeks fell into a routine. Aida started every day on the Hill with a stop at Dunkin Donuts to get coffee for herself and her staff. She always looked for the pretty server who had been her favorite since impressing her on her first day on the Hill. Aida knew that, as soon as she located and made eye contact with the young woman, her daily order would be filled quickly and perfectly without a word. Since that first day, Aida had insisted on bringing her staff members their favorite drinks. Roger was very uncomfortable with this arrangement, but the rest of the staff was delighted. It became a complicated order, and Aida had delivered it the first time written out on a note. She needed to do so only once, though, since this server seemed to have a photographic memory.

Aida had learned the server's name from her name tag, and, on this day, she used it. "Farah, how are you today?"

The young woman hesitated before answering, conscious that this was the first time Aida had called her by name. Looking up, she saw Aida's genuine smile. Aida was glad that she had followed Bea's lead and used her server's name when she saw Farah's face light up. Farah, for her part, interpreted Aida's increased attention to her as evidence that

Congresswoman Gainer must have kept her promise to ask Congresswoman Adams to help her.

Aida had turned her attention to her phone and did not say more, though, so Farah hurriedly filled the order. Aida received it and turned away without a word, balancing the cardboard tray of hot cups of coffee in one hand and scanning the phone held in the other. She was calling her father to ask whether he thought the situation for Bea's friend could be as dire as she had described it. She was unaware that this friend was the young lady who had just served her. To Aida's surprise, her father confirmed what Bea had said was sadly possible.

The weeks passed, and soon the monthly reminder for her lunch with Beatrice popped up on Aida's schedule again. Her stomach lurched. She had never dreaded seeing Beatrice before, but this time she knew that she was going to have to eat crow. Still, she was eager to make up with her only friend besides Karen.

At the end of the morning legislative session, Aida looked around for Beatrice. It was Good Friday, and the House had adjourned until Monday. The long weekend would be a welcome break. Aida didn't see her friend and, since she was too short to see over the heads of her colleagues, sent her a text.

Beatrice heard the notification as she was walking into the ladies' room around the corner from the House chamber. She laughed as she read Aida's attempt at a veiled apology.

Friday 12:00 Aida Adams

Ummm, this is your sometimes not-so-egalitarian friend wondering if we are still on for lunch if I promise to listen more and talk less.

Bea immediately replied *yes.*

Aida breathed a sigh of relief. Ignoring the gaggle of reporters dogging her steps, she walked briskly forward with her eyes fixed ahead. The hallway was crowded. She saw a pair of broad shoulders and cut deftly through the crowd to follow closely behind six-foot-seven-inch Representative Vance Packer, a decorated military veteran. He was not only huge in size; he was also a huge hero. He played a pivotal role in The Great Exposure. He laid his reputation and even his life on the line when he gathered evidence against the traitors. As they proceeded down the corridor, he cut off a reporter who narrowly missed tripping. He stopped for no one, and Aida was happy to use him as a shield to make her way outside quickly. No one could see her behind him, and she was past the reporters before they realized that she was there.

"There are advantages and disadvantages to being small," she said to her shield as she patted his back lightly. She then stepped around him and grinned.

Representative Packer craned his neck around to see who had touched him. "No touching allowed!" he barked and then, realizing who it was, softened his voice. "Aida, how are you?"

"I'm fine," she replied happily. "How are you on this beautiful spring day?" Not waiting for his answer she gave him a salute. "Thanks for the cover, sir!"

"Any time! My pleasure. Let's get through this holiday, and then we can come back and do some serious work for a change."

"Term limits!" she shouted to his retreating form. "Woo hoo!"

He gave her a return salute and a lopsided grin before striding confidently on. He had never lost his soldier's gait and posture.

When Aida arrived at the House cafeteria, the hostess greeted her with a cheery "Good afternoon!" and led her toward the table where Beatrice was sitting. She watched Aida approach and gave her a big smile and a wave when their eyes met.

Aida's tense shoulders dropped just a notch, and she wasted no time in launching into her overdue apology. "Beatrice, I want to apologize for over-reacting last time—"

Beatrice jumped in, "Aida, please, no apology is necessary!"

"Yes, it is. I'm determined to be egalitarian, and yet I find myself constantly being slapped in the face by my own biases. Your friend has every right to her beliefs and to whichever faith she chooses without any judgment from me, and you do as well. I am willing, wanting, and waiting to see what you have to share about your other Muslim, or former Muslim, friend."

Beatrice burst out in a ready laugh. Catching her breath, she said, "Wow, how articulate you are, even letting the alliteration flow in your apology. I predict that you will soon be called the poet of the House!" Then she looked earnestly into Aida's eyes. "I am also willing and waiting and wanting to tell you anything you want to know about my friend, who happens to have been born a Muslim, but I refuse to categorize my friends by religion." Both ladies laughed, and Beatrice leaned forward to add, "I know, however, that you stole that quote from Eliza Doolittle's father!"

"What are you talking about?" Aida replied. "Who is Eliza Doolittle?"

"Aren't you familiar with *My Fair Lady*?"

"No. What is it, a book?"

"No, it's a famous musical that became a classic film with Audrey Hepburn and Rex Harrison. Sorry, I keep forgetting how young you are. It was released in 1964."

"That's an important time period for many of my constituents. Should I see it?"

"No, I think it would just make you mad, and we have enough stress in our lives as congresswomen, don't we? I recommend comedies only. *My Fair Lady* is about a very arrogant and superior man who tries to mold a poor flower girl into a lady to trick people and show off his skills as a linguist by teaching her to speak properly. He uses her and then is horrified to find that he's fallen in love with her."

"Yuck! I suppose she feels so honored and falls at his feet? I hate those predictable scripts!"

"Don't get your dander up again, friend. She did love him, too, but wouldn't accept him until she put him clearly in his place—which, by the way, provides a good segue into the information I wanted to share with you from the friend I was asking you to help."

"I am all ears, Bea, and I will try to help her in any way that I can. I actually discussed her situation with my father. He didn't want to talk about it, but he reluctantly admitted that her life could very well be in danger if she returned to Ethiopia, or if her family here finds out that she has converted. Can you think of a safe place for me to meet with her?"

"I already found one. A friend of mine has a suite of offices right here in town. It's not far from where you live, actually. We could meet her there whenever you have an opening in the evening. She gets off work at five p.m."

"We'll have to wait until Ramadan ends. Her family will expect her home for that. How about sometime after the Easter break?"

"I will make it happen. Thank you, Aida."

"Don't thank me yet. I'm not sure that I can do anything."

After lunch, Aida returned home with a lighter heart knowing that she had made things up with her friend. She kept ruminating about whether she should bring up some of her own problems to Bea. She absentmindedly checked her phone for any missed calls. Her mother usually expected a call during Ramadan, but Aida was determined to wait and see whether, for once, her mother would call her. Aida saw twenty missed calls, but none were from her mother.

CHAPTER 14

FRAZ AND OMAR

Fraz had only seen Mr. Wafi once before, and the experience had not been pleasant. It was when Fraz stopped by to pick up the keys to Aida's apartment. It did not take Fraz long to figure out that his father was using the imam to keep an eye not only on Aida but also on him. At that time, Mr. Wafi had spared no words exhorting Fraz to live a holy life and upbraiding him for his many indiscretions with women. He also said over and over that Fraz was to influence Aida but must not touch her. Fraz had replied disdainfully that he could do much better than "that woman." Mr. Wafi had not been amused. He had his own well-being to consider. There would be no more funds coming from Egypt to his personal bank account in D.C. if he failed to keep Fraz in line. He also knew that the sums of money were too large to have all come from Fraz' father, Omar Abbas, but he had no idea who else was behind this project. Wafi had a very comfortable standard of living as he kept a tidy sum for himself and used only a small portion for the mosque's education program and for funding the emergency needs of the Muslims in his district. He had no intention of going back to the lean years.

When Fraz called him for a second meeting, he was delighted. He knew something that Fraz did not. Fraz' father was in town and they both already knew Aida had rejected Fraz. Omar was present at the appointed time and planned to make Fraz squirm. When Fraz walked in he was thrilled that his father had come to see him. He loved his father and his visits were rare. Fraz had been adopted by the Abbas family. He had no memory of his birth parents. All that his adoptive parents had told him was that he had been a hungry and dirty four-year-old street urchin when they took him in. Since they already had three sons of their own, Fraz was especially grateful to them, though they had treated him differently than their biological sons, more like a servant. He was expected to obey not only his parents but also his older brothers and even the actual servants. He had been told so often how fortunate he was to be in a good home that he stopped complaining. He had grown up in a house full of secrets. Men he did not know came to the family home for meetings in the dead of night. He was never included or informed. He knew none of their names. As an adult, Fraz was still trying to earn his father's respect, but it always seemed just out of reach.

He was so happy to see his father that he forgot he did not have good news to share. In the imam's office, Fraz started to reach out to embrace his father, but the frown on the older man's face deepened as he approached. The atmosphere was charged with anger.

"The imam has been telling me that he has not heard from you in weeks," Omar Abbas said. "You are supposed to be reporting to him. Where have you been? What have you managed to accomplish with Miss Aida Adams?"

Neither of the older men was happy with Fraz or his efforts to handle Aida. They wanted to make him admit the fact and that he could hardly handle Aida from Florida.

"Father, Imam Wafi, it is such a blessing to see you both again. I have had to travel back and forth to Florida, but I returned yesterday and have a report ready to give to you both."

"Just send me an email," his father said with a wave of his hand. "We have more serious issues to discuss. Imam Wafi has told me that he has information that you have been lying with several unclean infidel women. I have told you repeatedly that you cannot commit such acts and expect the mercy of Allah. Your brothers have all married, which you refuse to do, and they don't do such things."

He fell silent when the imam's secretary brought in a tray of tea. After she left the room, he seemed to have forgotten about the issue of women. Instead, he quickly turned the conversation to Aida. "Son, you have got to get back into that woman's good favor. I want you to be wherever she is. I want you to know who she is talking to and what bills are up for consideration. We need every vote we can get to advance our causes. She's liable to do anything. I heard that she even rides the Metro unescorted! What kind of Muslim is she? I don't have this problem with my women. They do what I tell them to do. How can you have so many women in love with you and not this one?"

Fraz opened his mouth to reply, but his father again waved his hand dismissively. "Don't interrupt me. I'm going to help you. I know women." Omar reached into his pocket and pulled out a pair of tickets.

"Here is the way back into her heart, son."

He waved the tickets in front of Fraz with a knowing intensity in his eyes. "The opera!"

Fraz looked confused. He thought it unlikely that Aida would agree to attend a concert with him.

"Uh, father?" he queried.

"*Aida! Aida!* The opera, son! Verdi! An Ethiopian princess falls in love with a handsome Egyptian. It will help her fall in love with you. Who is a more handsome Egyptian than my son Fraz, no?" Omar grinned and nudged the imam, who grunted. He had no admiration for Fraz Abbas.

"But father," Fraz protested, "I know nothing about opera, except that I can't stand it."

"Who cares?" Omar snorted. "She will love it, that's what's important. The music, the costumes, the smell of the theater!"

It was no surprise that *Aida* the opera was special to Aida the congresswoman. Fraz remembered her telling her staff about it on the campaign bus and actually singing one of the melodies. He realized that his father might be right, that she might not turn down the coveted tickets even if it meant having to attend the event with him. He felt sick to his stomach. This job was really becoming distasteful to him, and not just because he absolutely hated opera. He tried to hide his misgivings. "Um, thank you, father."

Omar was smiling now. "Listen; there will be a substantial amount of extra money available in your account. Spare no expense wining and dining Aida and you will soon be back in her good graces. Trust me!" He gave Fraz an unexpectedly warm embrace after the chilly start to their meeting and sent him on his way, remaining behind to continue talking with the imam.

Fraz left in a state of great agitation. He was now paranoid about being followed, being shocked to learn that someone had been spying on him to report his indiscretions in Florida. However, his thoughts quickly turned to the women he would call to help him forget about this additional source of worry. First, however, he had to find out who was following him and how to put a stop to the surveillance. He peered around furtively. On his way back to his car, he walked past a white Corolla without noticing it; there were hundreds of them in D.C. This one had tinted windows. He paid no attention to it, but, if he had, he still wouldn't have been able to see inside. There sat Beanie Man, hiding in plain sight again and shaking with silent laughter at Fraz's expense.

CHAPTER 15
AN INVITATION TO THE OPERA

Aida picked up her phone to listen to the dozens of voice messages. Only a few family members and close friends had this number, yet there were nearly fifty calls to sort through. She let out a heavy sigh. She had to listen to her messages every few hours, or the backlog would become completely out of hand. She clicked on the first one just as a new call came in and, by mistake, answered the call.

"Tickets! Don't hang up! I have tickets to the opening night of *Aida* at the Met!" the voice on the other end said.

Aida was confused. Her first thought was that a telemarketer had gotten her number.

The voice continued, "Tickets to the Metropolitan Opera, Aida."

Then she realized that the caller was Fraz, but she still wasn't sure whether it was a message or a live call. A glance at her phone confirmed her fear: it was, indeed, Fraz on a live call. Disgust welled up in her along with a fierce, almost uncontrollable hatred, and she instinctively hit the hang-up icon and took two deep cleansing breaths. She wished that she could just blow him away. Then, however, what he had said slowly registered. He had his hands on tickets to *Aida*. She wondered how he had managed to accomplish such a feat. Somehow, it had escaped Aida's notice that *Aida* was on the Met's repertoire this season. It registered

with her that he had said "opening night"—opening night perfor-
mances at the Met were nearly impossible to attend because most of the
seats were held by patrons with season tickets. She did a quick Google
search and confirmed it. Not only was *Aida* opening at the Met, but the
part of Radames was being sung by Lawrence Brownlee. Aida's eyes
shone at the thought of his rich tenor singing "Celeste Aida" as if to her.
She couldn't understand the Italian lyrics but had memorized the
English translation.

> *Heavenly Aida, form divine,*
>> *mystical garland of light and flowers,*
>> *of my thoughts you are the queen,*
>> *you are the light of my life.*
>> *I would return to you your lovely sky,*
>> *the gentle breezes of your native land;*
>> *a royal crown on your brow I would set,*
>> *build you a throne next to the sun.*

Then she caught herself, and her thoughts returned to Fraz. She felt
a strange anxiety come into her belly, unsure as she was of his motives.
She was certain, just based on his personality, that he did not like opera.
Then she stopped herself, reflecting that she did not really know him
that well. Perhaps he did like opera after all.

Aida was a lover of classical music but not really an opera fan. She
liked some of the famous arias, but there were plenty that she could not
stand. She had first heard about Verdi's *Aida* in college, as it happened,
when she and Karen first met. After they had introduced themselves.
"Your name is Aida as in the opera?" asked Karen.

"Umm, Aida as in that is my name. What do you mean, 'in the
opera'?"

"Are you kidding me? Didn't you say your family is Ethiopian?"

Aida nodded silently, totally confused.

"Well, Aida is an opera based on the true story of an Ethiopian
princess captured and enslaved by the Egyptians. She is made to serve an
Egyptian princess who cherishes her at first but then turns on her. The
reason is because the princess, Amneris, is in love with a great military

officer named Radames. All is well and good until Radames falls in love with Aida and Aida falls in love with him."

"Karen—you said your name is Karen, right?—is this true? How did I never know this? Tell me more!"

That was all it took. Before the week was over, Aida knew all there was to know about the tragic story of the star-crossed African lovers who died together like Romeo and Juliet.

Aida was still going through her voicemails when her phone buzzed again. Checking who it was, she took a moment to steady herself and then answered. "Fraz, how did you ever get tickets to *Aida*?"

Fraz smiled on the other end. He hadn't expected her to pick up. He quickly gathered his wits and assumed his most innocent persona. "Aida, I'm so glad I caught you! A friend of mine has season tickets, but his wife is sick, and he didn't want to go without her so he offered the ticket to me. You were the first person I thought of who would really enjoy this masterpiece."

"Oh, Fraz, that's so thoughtful of you! When is it?"

"It's a month from Saturday."

"That would be May 20? Perfect! I can't believe it. That's the only Saturday that I have free all month. It'll be a little awkward to sit with your friend, but you know me—I get along with everyone. I hope he likes politics."

Fraz paused; surprised that she had not understood his offer. "Aida, unfortunately for him, he has to stay home with his wife and their small children, but, fortunately for us, he gave me both tickets. I have one for myself, and I have one for you. We can go to the city together and have a wonderful evening."

Aida's smile quickly faded and her eyes narrowed. She wanted to kick herself for getting sucked into this trap. Disappointment swept over her. She wanted to go so badly, but not enough to go with him. There was no question of it. Sadly, she prepared to repeat what she had told him formerly, that their relationship was strictly professional. It was a hard line that she swore she would never let him cross again, and that is just what he was trying to do now. Anger flared up inside her as she remembered the first time he crossed that line, when he had stolen something from her that could not be returned. He clearly did not respect her boundaries and clearly had not changed.

"Fraz," she started her voice shaking, her tone cold as ice. Then she stopped abruptly. An idea had popped into her mind for a way out of the situation that would also give her a little satisfaction in the process. Her eyes reflected a steely resolve that he felt but could not see.

"Okay, Fraz, I accept, but on one condition."

Now Fraz was even more on edge. "Of course," he answered cautiously. "What is it?"

"I want my driver, Tony, to take us and drop me off at home later. That way, I won't have to be embarrassed by my spying landlord seeing me with an eligible bachelor such as you."

Fraz felt the hair on the back of his neck stand up. His jaw clenched, and his face reddened. He had to pause and take a slow breath to calm himself back down. This woman was so infuriating. He thought for a minute, though, and realized that from her point of view she did have to be concerned with her reputation. Perhaps she was starting it get it. He told himself to let it go and figure out the rest later.

"Your driver—you mean Tony? Isn't he from New York? What a good idea. He can take us right to the door."

"It's settled, then. What time do you think we should leave?"

"The opera starts at seven-thirty, so I think we would want to be in the city by five for dinner."

"OK, we'll pick you up at your hotel at four sharp."

Now Aida was grinning broadly. She could hardly hold back chuckles. Fraz could hear the joy in her voice. He stood up straighter, pleased at his success. His father knew women better than he had realized, but perhaps that wasn't so surprising since he had had five wives.

"Thanks again, Fraz. See you then!"

"Aida, just another moment, please. I have some information for you."

"Yes?"

"Remember that you asked me to make a connection for you in your district to inquire about the evangelical vote?"

"Yes, did you have any luck?"

"Well, I contacted a lady who fits the—"

Aida cut him off. "Just email me the information. I'm going to Gainesville for Father's Day weekend, and I'll have Roger set something up." Aida had planned a long overdue visit with her father to talk to him more about Muslim cultural practices in Dearborn, Michigan. She thought perhaps she could also squeeze in an interview with the person Fraz had contacted. "Bye for now!" Aida said and hung up before he could reply. She couldn't stand to talk to him a minute longer. She was very pleased about her plan for the opera, however, and hoped that she hadn't annoyed Fraz so much that he would change his mind.

Fraz let out a long sigh after the call ended. He really hated opera. He was glad that she had consented to go, but also upset that he would not have privacy in the limo for the ride to and from the city. He consoled himself that at least Tony wouldn't be at the dinner. He would make sure that they had a quiet, secluded table at the best restaurant in the city. He would take plenty of cash for the evening, and he would use it if necessary to make sure that they were undisturbed during the meal.

CHAPTER 16
A NIGHT AT THE MET

F raz had not spoken to Aida since she agreed to go to the opera. A month had passed since then, and she hadn't answered his phone calls or texts. Fraz had to resort to contacting Roger to confirm the evening's plans. Fraz spent the day quietly in D.C., giving himself extra time to get ready. He had his own tuxedo, and it was freshly pressed. He was always fastidious about his dress and person, but this occasion called for extra care. He chose each item of clothing carefully, down to the engraved gold cufflinks. He felt the excitement of the challenge more keenly than ever before. He was trying to gain the affection of a woman whom he had already alienated. He didn't think of it that way, of course. In his mind, she had foolishly turned against him because her pride was offended when she realized that he had no intention to marry her after their one night of intimacy. In fact, he had no intention to marry anyone, at least not until he was much, much older.

He glanced toward the window, which looked out over the entrance to the hotel. Headlights caught his eye, and he recognized the short black limo that Tony drove for Aida. The vehicle turned into the hotel's covered entrance and stopped. Tony emerged and stood behind it. Fraz could not see Aida through the tinted window. He wondered what she would wear that night. He hoped that it would be something appropriate and that he would not have to be embarrassed to be seen with her. He leaned closer and looked out again. Tony was wearing a tux. "What is he thinking?" Fraz asked himself. He wished for the hundredth time that there was a privacy window in the little limo, but he knew there was not. Tony would be hearing every word that they said. It was no wonder Aida had insisted that Tony drive, Fraz reflected. He hurried from his room to the elevator and soon was on his way out the door.

Tony opened the rear passenger door and made a grand gesture toward the back with a sweep on his hand. "Good evening, sir."

Fraz didn't even glance at him. He leaned into the car and then backed back out. "Where is she? I thought you would pick her up first. This is going to cost us some time."

"Where is who?" Tony answered innocently.

"You know who I mean, you idiot! Aida! Where is she?"

"Oh, the congresswoman? Didn't she tell ya? She has a headache tonight." Tony cracked the gum he was chewing. Fraz grimaced.

"What! And she didn't even call me?" Fraz was shocked and then angry in the blink of an eye. "I can't believe it. A headache—what a lame excuse! Then what are you doing here? Did she send you out in a tux just to tell me she couldn't make it?"

"Oh no, she said she knew I love opera—which I do, by the way—and she said she figured, since she couldn't make it, the two of us should just go ahead and enjoy it. You know, kind of a guys' night out!"

The veins in Fraz's neck stood out, and his fists clenched reflectively, but he didn't say a word. The very thought that he would attend a public event with another man infuriated him. "Why didn't she send Karen, then?"

Tony had to work to keep a straight face. He could tell that Fraz was beside himself with humiliation. "I guess Karen doesn't like opera. Go figure. Who doesn't like opera?"

Fraz started pacing back and forth. At length, he pulled the tickets from his pocket, looked intently at them, and ripped them in half. Turning abruptly, he started walking away. He passed a garbage receptacle and forcefully threw the tickets in on his way back through the front doors and into the lobby. Tony saw him enter the building and immediately head toward a neon sign blinking *Envy Lounge*.

"Hey, what's th' matter wit' youse? You gonna throw away the best night of your life?" Tony called after him. "Does this mean we're not goin'?"

As soon as Fraz was out of sight, Tony hurried to the trash can and gingerly retrieved the pieces of the tickets. "Thank you, Mr. Fancy Pants, for not throwing these babies into any rotten stuff. These will do just fine!" He climbed back into the limo and headed to Aida's apartment.

It was nearly two in the morning when Tony delivered Aida back to her door. Mr. Wafi was at the window as usual. The sound of Aida and Tony laughing had woken him. Tony was trying to sing and producing quite a unique sound. The imam at first thought that the man was in pain. He hit an exceptionally low note that sounded like a growl, and Aida burst into a loud belly laugh. He hit the note again and she couldn't control herself, bending in half and holding her stomach, but unable to make a sound for several seconds. She gasped for breath, but then burst out laughing again.

"Oh, Tony, stop it! The cats will be singing with you in a minute. If you wake up my baby, I'll—if you wake up *our* baby, I mean—" Tony took a hold of her arm as she tottered on her heels.

"If you insist. But why would you deprive the poor felines? What a night! Thank you so much, my lady, and please send my regards to our favorite patron of the arts, Mr. Fraz Abbas!" Tony's voice echoed off the brick buildings, and Mr. Wafi heard every word. His eyes in the window narrowed and he scowled, hissing to himself, "*My* baby!"

"What a night indeed!" Aida replied. "I didn't realize how much I miss classical music. It's been ages! I haven't been out like that since Emmit was—since Karen had Emmit!"

Tony looked puzzled, but he didn't miss a beat. "Well, that's been too long. I hope you will remember tonight and get a little culture now and then. The government won't shut down if you do, I promise!"

"Thanks again, Tony. You made my day. I wish I could have seen Fraz's face when you told him I expected the two of you to go together."

"Let's just say he didn't show his best side. But if I woulda known it would make you happy I woulda taken a picture of his ugly mug!" They stood there laughing a moment longer. Neither of them wanted the fun evening to end. Aida looked up at Tony and realized that he was staring at her. His expression had turned serious. She started to step forward and hug him. He was becoming such an important part of her life. Just then he took a step backward. He cleared his throat.

"Well, here you are, back at home, safe and sound."

"Yes, here I am." She wanted to make a joke and get back to the easy camaraderie they had been having but couldn't think of one or of anything else to say but "Thanks so much for taking me, Tony."

"The pleasure was all mine." He bent in a bow with one arm held against his waist and the other behind his back. "Goodnight, Aida." He stood back up but didn't turn away. Aida didn't move either. She felt as if her feet were made of lead.

"Tony," she started. He took a step forward and looked deeply into her eyes.

"Yes?"

Aida sighed deeply. "I wish I could hit a replay button and start this evening all over again."

"That's two of us." Tony reached out his hand and Aida gave him hers. He lifted it to his lips and kissed it.

Aida gave a small gasp and took a step closer, holding his hand tightly. "How gallant," she whispered.

Tony cleared his throat. "I guess I'll go now."

"Have a good day off, Tony."

"Call me if you need anything."

"I will."

"See you Monday."

"Yes." Neither of them moved. They were still holding hands. A thin cry caught their attention.

"Sounds like the cats did decide to join in," murmured Tony, still looking deeply into her eyes.

Aida glanced up at the second-floor window. "That's not cats, Tony, that's an unhappy baby boy. If I hurry, I may get to him before he wakes Karen." Aida turned quickly toward the door and hurried inside. She leaned back out and gave him a huge smile and said, "Thanks again, Tony! This was just what I needed."

"Bad timing, kid," Tony grumbled after the door closed. "Or I should thank you. I came pretty close to making a move on your mama. I'm not at all sure she wouldn't have liked it, but I'm not at all sure that she would have, either." He turned sadly back to the limo. "Goodnight, imam," he called over his shoulder.

CHAPTER 17
THE DIMPLE

Tony was eager to see Aida again after their good time at the opera. He arrived early on Monday morning and kept his eye on the front door of the brownstone. As soon as he saw the door open, he hurriedly placed his coffee cup in the cup holder and opened the car door. Determined to get the back door open for her before Aida opened it herself, he practically raced around to the other side of the car. He knew that it was a silly game but didn't care.

He pulled the door open and, with a flourish of his arm, bowed as he turned to grin at the woman emerging from the brownstone. She was still at the door, struggling with something. He left the door open and jogged up the steps. The morning sun that had just topped the building and he could hardly see her. "Need a hand there, lady?" he called.

She said something over her shoulder, but it was drowned out by the wailing of a baby. She gave a final yank and pulled a baby stroller through the doorway.

He reached to hold the door open. "Let me give you a hand," he called.

She turned around and yelled furiously, "Back off, creep!"

At that moment Tony found himself uncomfortably close to what turned out to be, not Aida, but Karen. She was not happy to be

103

approached from behind. Her face was red, and she looked distressed. He could see her struggling to make a plan to protect herself and the baby. She grabbed her purse and reached inside.

"I've got a—" she started. At last, she realized who it was. "I—I—Tony!" she yelled. "You about scared me to death! What's wrong with you?" The baby screamed louder.

"Karen! I thought you were Aida. Let me help you, please." Without a moment's hesitation, he picked up the stroller and jogged down the steps with it. As he set it down, Karen followed, placing a hand on the railing to steady herself. Tony started pushing the stroller back and forth and shushing Emmit. He had never seen the baby before, but he had heard about him. Aida was constantly telling him how cute he was and how sweet and giving him updates on his development.

"There's certainly nothing wrong with your lungs, little guy. Come on now. What's the trouble? You got sore chompers or sumpin'?"

Karen stood there watching him nervously, trying to compose herself and wondering what she should do. Aida didn't want anyone to get a good look at Emmit. Hopefully, Karen thought, with the baby's thrashing around, Tony would only see a blur. She took hold of the stroller handle and pulled it back toward herself.

"Yes, he's teething. I'm going to walk down to the drugstore and get some Orajel for him. I mean, we're going. Um, the congresswoman is on the phone with the Speaker, and I had to get him out of there so she could hear." Karen was mortified. She still had on the lightweight jogging set that she slept in.

Suddenly, there was blessed silence. The baby had stopped crying. Tony straightened up and looked at Karen.

"I'm sorry I scared you like that, Karen. I thought you were Aida. You two look kind of alike, from the back anyway. I mean you're about the same height and—" he stopped and just looked at her for a moment. She was so pretty, though her hair was a mess, and she had no makeup on. He started to say, "You're cute when you're angry," but stopped, whispering to himself "My mama didn't raise no fools!" and just smiled.

Karen realized that she hadn't even combed her hair. Luckily, or maybe unluckily, Tony had turned his attention back to the baby. His eyes were all soft, and he started to reach in.

"You wiggled your way right out of your hat, little man," he said. "Man, what I wouldn't give for a head of hair like that!"

Karen jerked the stroller back, trying to turn it in the other direction so that the hood of Emmit's stroller would block Tony's view of him.

Emmit made a sweet little baby noise, and Tony chuckled and looked up at Karen with a question in his eyes.

Karen turned the stroller around and started quickly down the block. "Thanks, Tony," she called over her shoulder. "Gotta run! Aida should be right out."

Tony straightened slowly and turned his eyes to the sky as if searching for something. He wondered whether he had seen what he thought he had seen. He looked after Karen as she hurried down the sidewalk. She turned and waved with a worried look on her face. Tony just stared blankly. He was deep in thought.

"Darn, darn, darn!" Karen repeated to herself. She was a mess. She was terrified that Tony had recognized Emmit's resemblance to his father. She felt so guilty, worried that he would let his suspicions slip out.

Tony was not the only one who had had a look at the baby. Mr. Wafi was at his usual post at the window. This time, he had a camera with a telephoto lens aimed through the blinds. He lowered it just before Tony turned around to scan the doorway for Aida. When the driver saw the imam looking down the street after Karen, he yelled, "Get a life, old man!"

The blinds quickly closed. Tony's cop instincts were on high alert. He started wondering whether the imam had any connection to Beanie Man. He resolved to do some detective work and see what he could find out.

Just then, the door opened, and Aida stepped out. "What are you doing up here, and what did you just say?" she asked.

"Just a few choice words for the imam, who is the worst busybody I have ever met!" Tony answered loud enough for the imam to hear clearly. "I was up here helping Karen with the stroller. It got stuck on the threshold."

"Oh boy, Karen must have been frustrated. Emmit has been crying all morning." Aida answered. "Come on, let's get going. I'm running a little late because the Speaker called to be sure I hadn't changed my mind about the vote. It's going to be close."

Tony jogged down the stairs after Aida, a little upset that she was going to get to the car before him. He reached around her to open the door and inhaled a pleasant wisp of her fragrance. It was familiar to him, and he started searching his memory for what it was. It had very pleasant associations for him. While she was settling in, he stood looking down at her, hoping to see that special look in her eyes that he saw the night of the opera. She had her phone in her hand and started to make a call but then stopped to see why he was still there. She definitely caught the intensity in his gaze because she blushed and then stammered, "Uh, we better get going, then." Tony saluted with a grin. "Yes, ma'am!" The blush was all the answer he needed for now.

After they were on their way and Aida was off the phone, Tony asked what the vote was on this morning. "Oh, it won't be this morning. There will be lots of speeches and comments and interviews before we finally vote tonight. It's the government spending bill. If we pass it today, it will go to the Senate tomorrow, where, hopefully, it will pass after a couple of days of speeches and posturing and then go to the president for signing. "

"Didn't you all vote for that a couple of times already?"

"Yes, and we were unable to pass it. We're having trouble because of all the earmarks. We started off with nine billion in earmarks."

"Holy smokes! How much is the total bill?"

"With the earmarks, the total budget for the second six months of this year would have been one-point-five trillion. There was no way the president would sign that, though, so we've been debating the relative merits of all kinds of stuff in the earmarks."

"Pork, you mean?"

"Yes, earmarks are commonly called pork barrel spending."

"Didn't the president promise to get rid of those?"

"Oh yes, he did, within his first term. Right now, he's over a barrel; excuse the pun, because he wants to avoid the expense of a government shutdown. He says that he is willing to compromise, but then he keeps saying earmarks have to stop. That's why everyone is fighting so hard to get what they can while they can."

"Did you request anything for your Florida district?"

"No, Florida is in such good shape budget-wise I wouldn't dare. I am using my political capital for a worthy cause, though. I really don't have much choice. Telly has been coaching us since the day we got elected that every Egalitarian should advocate for Palestinian reconstruction aid."

"Really?" Tony queried. "I had no idea that Egalitarians wanted to invest in any foreign nation. Isn't it out of the norm? I thought your party's platform was all focused on the USA minding our own business and rebuilding America."

"It's strange really, because you're right. When I first read the platform information I could find nothing relating to foreign aid. Fraz is the one who explained it to me. As you know, after The Great Exposure a great clean up began. We had to identify and vet the immigrants who came in through the months of open borders. Thousands of innocent refugees came in and we have extended a path to citizenship to them. Thousands of bad actors came in as well, including many with ties to radical Islam, whether it was Al Qaida, the Taliban, the E.I.J., Isis or Hezbollah and other smaller groups. Many of them were found to have extensive criminal records in this country and others. Some of them managed to get lighter sentences when they agreed to become state's witnesses and began to testify against each other."

"I remember the news coverage of that. Oh, how I loved hearing those jailbirds sing," Tony put in. "But I never heard of the E.I.J." Tony said. "What do those letters stand for?"

"Empire of Islamic Jihad," Aida answered. "They are the most radical of all. Thanks be to God, they were apprehended. Several of them are at Gitmo. Unfortunately, they are holdouts. Not one of them would turn state's witness. They all had taken vows to die first rather than betray their cause."

"I remember that the U.S. government used the information from the more cooperative terrorists to find and go after extremists not just in the United States, but also in other countries. For example, the United States cooperated with Israel in operations that decimated Hamas and Hezbollah," Tony offered.

Aida picked back up, "Well, yes, but we do have to give our current president credit for schooling Americans in the difference between the citizens of Iran and Palestine, for example, and the radical elements that held power there who ruled through intimidation and violence. Each time they incited war the common people were the ones who suffered most. Many of the recent Muslim immigrants, legal and illegal, have family still living in war-torn areas. The Egalitarian Party embraces Muslims and all minorities. Fraz said that Telly believes that the president and congress would be favorable to helping some of these nations rebuild and form new governments."

"I'll believe when I see it," Tony commented. "I only know what the rest of the public knew about these operations," Tony continued, "but I didn't know that anyone was considering rebuilding these nations."

Aida picked up her story. "It's such an amazing time. Everyone is so much more open- minded. Our budget is balanced for the first time in decades. The funds seized from the deep state traitors have stabilized our economy. We no longer have a simple two-party system. Those who were allowed to stay after the mass open border immigration have made us more of a melting pot than we have been for decades.

"That's who you were focused on helping with Melting Pot Justice, I believe."

"Yes, Tony! It's exciting, really, to help innocent people start a new life here free of oppression and injustice, especially Muslims. They have suffered so much to get here. All they want is to live a peaceful life of freedom. We Egalitarians are hoping to get the ball rolling by insisting on aid for Palestine. This cause is near to my heart because my mother is married to a Palestinian. They live in Israel currently. She's told me quite a bit about his family history."

"Ya don't say," Tony replied. "So this is why the spending bill has been held up?"

"Yes, I'm fighting for my people." The limo arrived at the Capitol and Aida prepared to jump out. "See you later, Mr. Romano!"

"Oh, so we're all formal now! See you later Ms. Adams!"

"I'll be glad to get this bill passed because next on the agenda is term limits."

Tony drove away shaking his head. He muttered to himself, "Where was she born? Under a cabbage leaf? Can she really believe those groups are no longer active? They're just underground. Palestinian aid?" The car in front of him braked suddenly. Tony laid on the horn and shouted out the open window, "What is she thinking? And what are you thinking, moron?"

The spending bill did not pass that day. The president decided to take his case to the public. He broadcast a prime time message and read a list of the House members who refused to vote for the bill. The president declared that he would not sign the budget unless all of the earmarks were removed. The public supported his decision. Telly refused to budge, and Aida kept voting no. Her approval rating suffered significantly. After nine days. Aida was one of the last holdouts. She was bombarded with demands from her constituents that she back off from earmarks and vote for the bill. She felt she had no choice but to capitulate. She did not really care that much about forcing Palestinian aid through this early in her term of office. She had no idea what the real reason was behind Telly's stance. It was an ugly standoff. It took an additional ten days and the threat of an imminent government shutdown before the House had finally come together to agree on the federal spending bill for the second half of the year. She finally gave in—against Telly's orders. No one really understood why the Egalitarians were so invested in the plight of the Palestinians, not even Aida. She was finding politics very stressful and wondered whether she had any chance of retaining her seat for a second term. She was fairly certain that she didn't want to.

CHAPTER 18
FRAZ AMBUSHED

Fraz frowned at his phone. There was a text from Imam Wafi insisting that he meet him at the mosque first thing the next morning. Wafi said that the order came from the top. Fraz frowned. He wondered who "the top" might be, how far up in the organization's hierarchy. He knew next to nothing about his father's many business dealings. He had been left completely out of the loop. He had asked about it many times and been told to mind his own business. Fraz rushed to make last minute travel arrangements yet again. He caught the last flight to D.C. late that night. On the way, he plotted how to explain away his failure to handle Aida and her voting.

Back in Washington, when Fraz dutifully arrived at the mosque the next morning, Mr. Wafi's secretary led him into the imam's study. Fraz was shocked to again find his father there. Omar and the imam were looking at a document. When Omar heard the door open, he quickly turned the document over and laid it down on the table in front of them. He looked slowly up at Fraz. Omar crossed his arms and gave Fraz a dark look. Fraz was immediately filled with dread when he sensed the mood. Fraz reached out to give his father the customary kiss on each cheek, but Omar waved him off. "Sit!" he barked. There was no coffee, no small talk, just this command to sit.

The imam held his phone in his hand. He stared coldly at Fraz as he hit send.

Fraz was puzzled. His phone was in his jacket pocket on mute, and he was giving the two men his full attention. At that moment, it vibrated, but he ignored it. However, the men looked pointedly at him, so he pulled the phone from his pocket to discover that he had just received a text from the imam with a picture. Fraz quickly scanned the image, which was of a baby. Fraz looked up, confusion in his eyes. "Okay, it's a baby. Why would you send me this?"

"Look closer, fool!" the imam hissed.

Fraz stared intently at the image, the holy man's tone having filled his belly with dread. The baby had a full head of black hair and a face red and shiny with tears and a runny nose. Fraz wondered whether he was supposed to notice something in the background. The infant was in a stroller on a perfectly normal empty city street. A hat was perched just above the baby's head. Fraz found the profoundly unhappy grimace comical, though it seemed unlikely that the men across from him simply wanted to share a humorous moment. Fraz couldn't help smiling, but his father was as serious as he had ever seen him. Fraz looked down again, smiling at the child almost against his will. "I like this kid's attitude," he said. "He looks like I feel today." He looked up again to see if there was any reaction to his attempt to lighten the mood.

The two older men turned quickly to each other, and the imam whispered, "Like father, like son."

"Give him a chance to defend himself," the elder Abbas demanded.

Fraz wasn't paying attention to their words, though, but was focused on the photo, intent on solving the puzzle. His ability to solve puzzles was part of what made him successful. His lips started to turn up at the corners again in an involuntary grin. It felt good. A genuine smile was unusual for him. Though he could paste on a fake one at the drop of a hat he was tired of having to do so.

"This looks like it was taken outside your building, Imam," Fraz remarked thoughtfully.

Suddenly Fraz's jaw fell slack. Recognition, horror, and rage played across his countenance in rapid succession as he figured out the mystery. The baby had a distinct dimple in the middle of his little chin.

That was the moment that the other men were waiting for. Wafi jumped up in his excitement. "Now you know what we know! This baby is your seed!"

"Father—" Fraz began, hanging his head to avoid his father's eyes.

"I am not your father!" Omar growled. He stood up abruptly and the papers in front of him scattered onto the floor. "Get out!" he shouted. "I never want to see you again."

Fraz hastily bent and started picking up the papers. "Don't touch those! You will never be one of us now!" Fraz dropped the papers onto the table and only got a glimpse before Wafi swooped them up. He saw the letterhead for E.I.J., Empire of Islamic Jihad. He looked up in stunned silence.

"Get out!" Omar screamed. "Get out, you spawn of infidels! Get out before I kill you! I should have killed you when I killed your worthless parents!"

Omar was shaking with rage. Fraz froze at those words. His mouth hung open. His head was spinning. He couldn't move. "What did you say, father? My parents? Father, what did you say?" he asked again.

"You heard me! I should never have let you live!"

"Not here, brother. Calm yourself," the imam urged. "Not here!" The older man held Omar back and screamed at Fraz, "If you value your life, get out of here, you filthy infidel!"

Fraz's heart nearly pounded out of his chest. Fear exploded in his belly. He was shaking but barely kept control of himself. He slowly stood, his eyes trained on his father. He knew Omar always kept a pistol under his robes. He wanted to turn and run but knew that doing so would further enrage him and increase his risk of being shot in the back. He backed slowly to the door, sensing that he could be shot before he could leave. As he backed out and closed the door gently behind him, he heard the last words that he would ever hear his father say.

"We have no further use for this infidel and his whore."

Fraz had always feared this day would come. No matter how hard he tried, he had never been able to please his father. It seemed that his brothers could do no wrong in their father's eyes. It was different for Fraz. The fear in his belly kept growing. The imam must have taken that picture from his post at the window. For all Wafi knew, it could have been Karen's baby, but Fraz knew that it wasn't. Fear competed with feelings of rage as he realized that Aida had kept her pregnancy a secret from him. He had a right to know. This did not have to happen. Why would she do this?

He rushed through the mosque complex and headed toward the exit. He burst out of the door to the street and hailed a cab. He directed the driver to his hotel, his thoughts racing. He had to figure this out. He had a right to his son, and he knew it. He also knew that his father might decide to take the child and raise him as he did Fraz, as a fully observant Muslim. His father's words echoed in his head, "I should have killed you when I killed your infidel parents."

When Fraz arrived at his hotel, he had the cabbie wait while he hurried in to gather his belongings. By the time he returned to the cab, he had formed the beginnings of a plan. He decided to stay in Washington, but he knew that he would have to go undercover. His life was in danger, and so was his son's. He would find a way to get to Aida and talk some sense into her. In the meantime, he would hide out. He scrolled his phone for one of the most recent texts. He found one from a woman he had met the night Aida stood him up. He would stay with her.

CHAPTER 19
LUNCH AT ZARA'S

I t was the day after Father's Day. Aida was in Gainesville to visit her
father and also to meet with the contact Fraz had recommended.
Tony and Aida drove to the Hotel Eleo at the University of Florida to
pick up Sandra Moore. Sandra, a media representative from Tallahassee,
had volunteered for Aida's campaign. She was a Christian, and Aida
hoped that she could provide some insight into the thinking of her
Christian constituents. Aida's goal was to discover ways to correct
misunderstandings about Muslims. She also hoped that Sandra would
write something favorable about her as a Muslim politician to help
ensure that Christians wouldn't associate the acts of militants elsewhere
in the world with the Muslims she knew and loved. This was the first
time the two women had met. She was waiting outside the hotel as they
pulled up. She stepped forward quickly when she saw the car and waved
to Tony, though she couldn't see Aida through the heavily tinted
windows. As Tony stepped out of the limo, she called out, "You must be
Tony! I'm Sandra," and bustled toward him with an outstretched hand.

Tony took the small hand in his and was surprised at her firm handshake. He quickly sized her up. She looked to be about fifty-five or sixty
years old. Her dark hair had beautiful grey highlights around her face
and was swept up into a loose French twist. He felt nothing but

straightforward good-heartedness in her. Tony turned to open the back door and found Aida already standing there, her hand stretched out to greet her guest. It startled him and he flinched. "Whoa! Didn't see you there!" Everyone laughed and the ladies introduced themselves. After a firm handshake they climbed into the back of the limo.

Sandra and Aida exchanged pleasantries as they drove to the restaurant, saving serious discussion for later. Soon, Tony pulled into a small, nondescript shopping strip. Sandra was about to ask whether something was wrong, but Tony announced, "Ladies, we have arrived at your destination!"

Sandra saw a Laundromat, a nail salon, and a small market called Zara's, but no restaurant.

"What a fancy joint," Tony wisecracked.

Sandra turned to Aida with a confused look.

"Don't you diss our yummy Florida strip-mall restaurants, Mr. New York," Aida replied. "You know it's the little hidden away mom-and-pop places that have the best food, don't you?"

"Don't even get me started," he replied. "What I wouldn't give to be in Alterie's little greasy pizza joint or Lou and Hy's deli back in NYC!"

Zara's was a small Middle Eastern market that also served meals. It was located not far from where Aida's father used to live, on Thirteenth Street. Aida had lived there with him in the neighborhood during her high school and college years. Tony dropped off the ladies and headed to the nearby Natural History Museum for a quick look at the giant sloth exhibit he had heard about. Aida and Sandra entered the store and were assaulted by the competing aromas of many spices.

"Oooh, smells just like I remember," Aida breathed.

"What is that smell? It's wonderful," asked Sandra.

"Too many spices to list, Mrs. Moore," replied Aida.

"Aida!" A short, stocky middle-aged man called out and hurried toward them. His hair was dark but sprinkled with gray. He wore a long white apron over dark pants and a white shirt. Sandra could see that he worked there.

"My favorite congresswoman is here to bless my humble establishment!" he said when he reached them.

Aida's eyes lit up as she answered, "Ozzy! I can't believe you'd—"

"Remember you? You're breaking my heart!" He gestured toward the window. "Look, I still have your campaign poster in my window! I told all my customers to vote for you or else." He made a fist and shook it. "How could I forget you?" He put his hands on his hips. "And how could you forget me? It's been one whole year since I saw you. I can't believe you came to Gainesville all those times to campaign and didn't come in here." He tried to look serious with lowered eyebrows, but his twinkling eyes gave him away.

"Ozzy, I'm so—" Aida started, but Ozzy interrupted her again.

"And I know for sure that they did vote for you, too. We were thrilled to have Glenn Adams's daughter go to Washington to straighten things out. You have always had a smart brain, a level head just like your father. I remember when you were in the volleyball finals." He smacked his forehead with his palm. "What is wrong with me?" He shook his head. "Forgive me; forgive me! Who is this"—he paused dramatically and turned to Sandra before continuing—"lovely lady you have brought to me?"

"This is my friend, Sandra Moore. She's an editor for the *Tallahassee Newsline*, so be careful what you say!" Smiling, Aida turned to Sandra. "This is my friend, Ozzy, the owner of this wonderful place. I've known him since I was a child. He's a friend of my father's, and he practically kept me from starving to death during my college years."

Ozzy turned to Sandra and smiled. Sandra smiled back and joined in the banter. "Don't worry, Ozzy. We are off the record on this visit but look out next time!"

"Two lovely ladies at the same time," Ozzy said and patted his heart. "I don't know if I can take it!" They all laughed again. "Sit wherever you wish, Aida." He gestured toward the table by the window. "I see your favorite table is free." He turned again to Sandra and smiled. "And you come back whenever you wish - on the record or off. I will be happy to see you."

"Oh, perfect," Aida said. "Is this okay, Mrs. Moore?" she asked Sandra.

"Yes, yes, of course, but it's not okay for you to call me 'Mrs. Moore'! That's my mother-in-law's name." She jokingly shook her finger at Aida. "I'm Sandra!"

Aida was a little shocked but didn't miss a beat. "Yes, Mrs. Sandra!" She raised her hand to her forehead and gave a salute.

"That's more like it, missy!"

Aida had to stop herself from rolling her eyes. It rubbed her the wrong way for a casual acquaintance to chide her.

After their beverages arrived—sweet tea for Sandra and water for Aida—the two ladies settled in to talk.

"Thank you again for accepting my invitation and being so flexible about the day and time," Aida offered. "My schedule is packed every time I come down here to the home office. Today is rushed, too, because I have to leave by four at the latest to get to the airport. That gives us a good hour, though."

"Too bad you have to rush! Are you staying with your father?"

"Yes, I came yesterday for Father's Day and got to spend an evening with him catching up. I said goodbye to him already. The visit was much too short!"

"Well, let's get right to it, then. I can talk fast if I have to." Sandra chuckled as she smoothed her napkin on her lap. She seemed to Aida to be a very happy lady.

"Ms. Adams, I was so surprised when Mr. Abbas called me. I didn't understand exactly what he was asking me to do except to have lunch with you and, of course, whenever there's food involved, you can count me in! I don't see any fried catfish on this menu, though, do you?"

"No, I'm sorry, it's all Middle Eastern—" Aida started.

"Don't be silly, honey," Sandra interrupted her. "That's just my lame excuse for a joke. I just love a good falafel sandwich." She flashed Aida a big smile.

Aida was confused. "You do? That doesn't sound like a typical Southern dish."

"No, it's not. Even hummus is a stretch for many of my friends." She stooped down to retrieve her napkin, which had slipped off her silky skirt to the floor. "Shoot, now I'll need a new napkin!" She returned her attention to Aida. "Yeah, I first had falafel in Israel when we took a tour of the Holy Land with our church."

Aida's eyes darkened, but Sandra didn't seem to notice, and Aida wondered whether she was a typical Christian, always siding with the Israeli oppressors.

"It was the trip of a lifetime," she enthused. "Anyway, we were blessed to make the trip when there were no hostilities going on at the time, so that was a relief."

The server arrived, and Sandra asked, "Could I have another napkin, please, honey? I dropped this one on the floor. Oh, and I think we're ready to order, too. This important lady has a deadline to get to the airport." She looked at Aida.

"Yes, I'm ready. I always get the falafel plate. You'll find quite a difference between these and the Israeli ones," she said pointedly. "Ozzy is from Palestine." She turned to the waitress and said, "This will be on me. My friend will have?" She turned to Sandra with uplifted eyebrows.

"The falafel plate, of course," Sandra announced. She spoke a little too loud for Aida's taste, and the other patrons turned to look at them over their shoulders.

"Two falafel plates and I'll put a rush on that, Miss Aida," the server added.

"Thank you," both ladies said in unison. Aida laughed, losing her serious expression.

Sandra leaned in a little. "Ms. Adams, I'm so happy that your friend is from Palestine! Did he immigrate here recently?" She caught herself. "No, of course, not too recently if you knew him as a teenager."

"He came here with his parents when he was three. He's an American citizen," Aida replied.

"How wonderful! And it looks like he's successful, too. I can't wait to taste his version of the falafels!"

Aida looked at Sandra again. She seemed so genuine that Aida was ashamed of herself for jumping to conclusions. She reminded herself how natural Sandra had been with Ozzy and with herself. The fact that Sandra had enjoyed a trip to Israel, she decided, was not enough reason to conclude that she was anti-Arab.

After they had finished their falafel plates, Sandra leaned back and rubbed her stomach. "Oh, that was so good! I think those were even better than the ones we had in Israel. Why did you make me eat so much?"

Aida was about to protest, but she saw the twinkle in Sandra's eyes and tried to match her mood. "Oh, yes, I made sure you ate every last bite, and now I'm going to order some baklava for you!"

"Noooo! Have mercy!" Sandra pleaded.

"Okay, you're off the hook, but I do demand something in return for all this wonderful food I'm paying for."

"What's that?"

"I want you to tell me why the conservative Christians did not vote for me. Our platform is pretty conservative, yet I only got 1% of their vote. Why is that, do you suppose?"

Sandra leaned forward again and cleared her throat. "I knew you were going to ask me about this, and so I did a little informal research. I asked some of my friends at the city-wide Bible study I attend if they voted for you. If they said no, I asked them why.

"Really? Thank you so much," Aida said. "What did they say?"

Tony walked into the restaurant, looking from his watch, to Aida, and then back again. She could see the car through the glass door, illegally parked in front of the restaurant door and with flashers on.

"Oh no, there's Tony!" Aida said. She looked at her own watch and jumped up. "I'm so very, sorry Sandra, but we are going to have to leave right away, or I will miss my flight."

"I understand completely!" Sandra answered. She laid a hundred-dollar bill on the table and jumped up herself. "Please let me cover this meal for you. We can finish the conversation on the way back to my hotel."

"Oh Sandra, that's not necessary," Aida protested.

"We don't have time to fight over it, do we? You can get the check the next time. Now go say goodbye to your friend and I'll get settled in the limo." She promptly turned and followed Tony out the door.

Aida soon hurried out herself. She apologized again, "I'm so sorry we had to rush. Can we pick up where we left off? You were just going to tell me what you found out from Christian voters."

"Right, well, I'm just going to give it to you straight in the interest of time. I'm ashamed to admit this, but some of them plain out said they'd never vote for a Muslim."

Aida smiled. "That's what I thought."

"Yes, but that was just a few. They just couldn't understand how someone could follow Mohammad."

"Why is that strange?"

"Aida, I don't understand why anyone would follow Mohammad either. I just don't see the benefits. I see a lot of rules and threats of hell, but I don't see any benefits."

Aida explained, "Observant Muslims believe the rewards come later, in Paradise, for people who follow the rules and live a holy life."

"Here's the deal," Sandra broke in, "We Christians believe in the Pentateuch, the first five books of the Bible, as do Muslims. However, we see the love and relationships in it, while Mohammad seemed to only see rules."

"How can you say you see love when the Old Testament is full of warfare, and where God Himself told the Israelites to kill every man, woman, and child of some of the native peoples? The Jews were occupiers even then!" Aida was shocked at her own vehemence, especially since she did not even practice her faith. She quickly grew angry when reminded of the way that the Israelis treated their Arab neighbors.

Sandra was not about to get herself pulled into a discussion of the Israeli-Arab conflict. She had seen the flicker of anger in Aida's eyes earlier when she referenced her trip to Israel. She continued her line of thought. "The first place I see love in the Bible is in Genesis Chapter One, where God stooped to create mankind with His own hands. Then I see more love when He created a woman and gave Adam and Eve the blessing of marriage."

"But then they sinned, and He cast them out."

"Yes, they had wanted to be like God. Isn't that what Satan himself wanted, that caused him to be cast out of heaven?" Sandra thought to herself that Mohammad wanted to be like God, too, but thought better of saying it. "Well, it was what Satan wanted. Anyway, when they sinned, God still made a way for them. He killed an animal and took the skin to cover their nakedness. It was the first sacrifice, the first death. God Himself became their priest and made a way for them."

"But He cast them out."

"Yes," Sandra continued, "He did cast them out of the garden, but not out of a relationship with Him. Sin has a penalty. Sin has no place with God. They had to leave that perfect environment and, from that point on, had to seek Him by faith. He never changed, though. He always loved them. He loved them so much that He gave His only Son, the Lord Jesus Christ—"

"John 3:16," Aida interjected, eager to show off her knowledge. "I remember that Tim Tebow used to write that on his face when he got geared up for the playing field."

"You know Gainesville well!" Sandra replied.

"I was curious. I knew he was a local hero, and, when I did research on him, this John 3:16 thing kept popping up. It says, "For God so loved the world that He gave His one and only Son, that everyone who believes in Him shall not perish but have eternal life."

"I'm glad you brought that verse up because, as I was saying, God loved mankind so much that He sent part of Himself, His perfect Son, Jesus Christ, to die on the cross and take our punishment, the sins of all of us, the whole world through all of history. God's love caused Him to find a way, not to send us to hell, like Islam seems to want for every infraction, but to make a way for us to have eternal life with Him in heaven in spite of our sins."

Aida was surprised at the passion in Sandra's voice. She was used to passion in religious people, but Sandra seemed to be especially concerned that Aida understood her point. Aida really had no clue, however. She struggled to relate to what the other woman was saying and to defend Islam, but she was unsure that she could. After all, she had paid little attention to her faith herself. "We believe that Mohammad was a prophet and Jesus was a prophet."

"Are you putting Jesus and Mohammad on the same level?"

"Well—"

"Did Mohammad die for you to have life, or did He kill and lead warfare? Every nation has wars to defend itself," she continued, "but Mohammad's battles were aggressive. The conversions he got were made of fear. Jesus never led a war. He said that His kingdom was a spiritual kingdom. Did Mohammad die for you?"

"Well, no, he died and is buried in the tomb at Mecca. He instructed us to make Hajj, the Pilgrimage to the Sacred House, at least once in a person's lifetime, if they are able."

"And what good does that do?" Sandra's intense gaze was unnerving Aida like no fierce debate or interview with a rabid journalist had before. "Mohammad wanted glory for Himself; Jesus wanted glory for His Father, Almighty God."

Aida felt confused. She looked up and saw Tony's eyes in the rearview mirror. He raised his eyebrows. She realized that she had no idea what his spiritual beliefs were. She hoped she wasn't sounding like an idiot to him.

She sighed. "At least we have God in common—"

"We do not have God in common," Sandra declared. "Almighty God is a God of love, mercy, and forgiveness. Allah is nothing like that."

"Are you saying there are two Gods?"

"No, I'm saying Allah is not God."

Aida actually gasped. Even though she did not practice her faith, she considered Allah to be God. She actually stuttered as she tried to bring the discussion to an amicable conclusion. Tony pulled up by the entrance to the hotel and stopped. Glancing at her watch, Aida said weakly, "S-S-S-Sandra, this is um, well I don't, because—" She looked helplessly at the other woman. "I really do have to go now, but, but thank you for—"

A gentle tone came back to Sandra's voice. "Aida, I don't know if I will ever see you again. That's why I have been so intense. I'm sorry, but I'm not sorry. Everyone has a right to hear the gospel of Jesus Christ. Everyone has the right to make up their own mind and their own choices, but what kind of choice can they make if they don't know all the facts?" She put her hand on Tony's shoulder. "Thank you so much, Tony, it was a pleasure to meet you." Tony nodded his head and winked at her. She smiled in recognition that he shared her faith in Christ. She turned again to Aida as Tony came around to open the door for her. The fire was back in her eyes. "I just have to share one last thing. Muslims claim that Mohammad was lifted up to heaven, yet his body is still in the tomb at Mecca." She raised her eyebrows and asked pointedly, "Jesus died on the cross for my sins, your sins, even Mohammad's sins five hundred years before Mohammad was born. Why did we need Mohammad? What else could he do for us that Jesus did not already do? Why did he not follow Jesus' teachings if they both were prophets?"

Sandra hopped out of the car and bustled inside. Tony closed the door of the limo. He turned his eyes toward heaven and chuckled. Inside the car, Aida was lost in a tangle of emotions and confusion. They drove in silence until they were on the expressway and then Tony looked at her in the rearview mirror and asked, "Did they have anything good in that joint? I ran up to Panera for something I could identify."

Aida didn't answer but stared absently at her cell phone. She turned her gaze out the window; her thoughts were racing a hundred miles an hour in response to Sandra's comments. Tony accelerated to almost that speed trying to get her to the airport on time.

CHAPTER 20
TERM LIMITS

Because the public outcry was so furious against the House members regarding earmarks, the Speaker immediately sought to distract the public. He decided to push forward with term limits. The proposed amendment would affect all members of Congress, representatives, and senators alike. The process went forward swiftly. A two-thirds supermajority was required for passage. A mere thirty days after it came out of committee, the first vote was to be held.

When the big day arrived, Aida was waiting on the curb for Tony when he pulled up. As soon as he stopped, she opened the rear door and hopped in. She started chattering about the vote without as much as a "good morning." Tony smiled at her in the rearview mirror and shook his head.

"Tony, I entered the office knowing that much of my job on Capitol Hill would be tedious, but so is law practice. I thought I was ready for it. Boy, was I wrong. I can't believe how long it has taken for a significant piece of legislation to reach the chamber. Eight long months of tedium and stress before finally, just two weeks before the summer recess, I truly get to participate."

"Don't count your chickens before they hatch. The House members aren't the only ones who have to approve this, right?"

"Oh, I know. It will have to go to the Senate and get a supermajority, but they claim to have more than enough votes. Of course, the president will sign it then."

"And then the states have to approve it, too," Tony chimed in. "That's the part I like. New York is a question mark on this one, but I made sure all my family up there is going to support it."

They hadn't gone far before the traffic slowed, and then it was stop-and-go, all the way to the Capital mall.

Tony peered ahead. "Looks like demonstrators."

"Oh, good; people care about this. I like to see citizens participating in our process, but I can't be late. Not today, of all days. The Speaker would have my head on a platter!"

"Easy, tiger! Did you forget that you insisted I pick you up a whole hour earlier than normal?" Tony grumbled through a stifled yawn. "Didn't even get my second cup of joe yet."

"Oh, right. Thanks again, Tony. You're the best."

"Ah, forgetaboutit."

Aida looked at him again. They were both grinning from ear to ear, but he didn't see her smile. He was dutifully scanning the crowd ahead. His eyes narrowed and he scowled. Aida saw his shoulders tense.

"Oh, great!"

"What is it, Tony?"

"This is getting bad. I can see some of the signs now. One says, 'NO MORE PORK.' Oh boy, I see Palestinian and Israeli flags, too." He looked up into the mirror and met Aida's eyes. "I think these guys are still hot under the collar about the earmarks. I don't like the looks of this. Maybe we should go around the other way."

Aida was oblivious, as often, to Tony's security concerns. She replied, "No problem, we are so close I'll walk!" She unbuckled her seat-belt and flung the door open. "It's only two blocks. Bye, Tony!"

"Aida, wait! It's not safe! I'm supposed to—" he said, but the back door slammed before he could finish, and he threw up his hands. "Aida! Aida! What's wrong with you? You wanna get me fired?" he yelled out the window at her retreating back. "What's wrong with that dame, anyway?" he continued to himself in a quieter voice. "All those nuts out there!"

Tony quickly scanned the area. What he saw made his stomach drop into his shoes. Beanie Man was right behind Aida, and the two of them were disappearing into the crowd. Tony pulled over, turned on the hazard lights, and jumped out of the limo. He knew that it would probably be towed, but he could not let Beanie Man get to Aida or miss this chance to put him behind bars.

Aida was wearing her running shoes as she had taken to doing every morning on her way to her office. She was very glad to have them on now since she was in a hurry. She would change into the pair of low-heeled black pumps that she kept in her desk drawer once she reached her office. Some of the other female members were too proud to be seen in casual shoes, but Aida thought that they were being ridiculous. She had half made-up her mind to start wearing her lowly Reeboks all the time to speed into the building before anyone recognized her—or, at least before certain people recognized her. She loved to stop and talk with the visitors to Capitol Hill, but she always tried to avoid the press. Today, though, she didn't want to stop for anyone. She had to take care of the usual morning issues with her staff, have a quick chat with Telly and the caucus, and review her brief speech about the term limits bill before it was time to start the session. The Speaker had actually conceded to let Aida say a few words. She knew that it was only for show, just to highlight the unity on this bill, but it was a thrill for her all the same. She started going over her speech in her head as she rapidly closed the distance to her destination.

When she rounded a corner, however, she nearly barreled into a news crew. The journalists were scanning the crowd and almost failed to notice her. A shapely red-headed journalist froze when she noticed Aida and then tugged on the sleeve of a cameraman and pointed. "Isn't that somebody?" she whispered. The journalist was Lucinda Moran of the Reeltime Network. Aida remembered her from the ambush at the courthouse in Orlando when she had learned about being chosen for *We Are America*. The cameraman, Jack Virkner, was the photographer who had taken that horrible photo of her when they surprised her. Apparently, the reporter had forgotten about Aida. Her hesitation gave Aida time to rush past her. She was determined not to stop and let history repeat itself.

"Somebody?" he shouted. "Lucinda, that's Representative Adams, remember? Held up the budget trying to get earmarks for the Palestinians. Go after her!"

She gave him a puzzled look.

"Go, go, go! Just go! I'll follow." He trained his camera in Aida's direction and started walking.

Aida hitched up her skirt and took longer strides, widening the gap between them until the journalist, in her four-inch heels, had no hope of catching her.

"Ms. Adams, Ms. Adams, how are you going to live with yourself after abandoning the Palestinian cause?" The gap between her and Aida widened, but she kept calling out. "Ms. Adams, your Muslim constituents deserve an answer!"

When Aida reached the building, she turned to smile broadly and wave as she opened the door. She saw the journalist hopping on one foot with one of her shoes a few feet behind her. The cameraman still had his camera focused on Aida. She just had to do something.

"I hope you're okay!" she shouted. "I'll go get someone to help." Smiling sweetly for the camera, she silently congratulated herself on having just avoided giving them an opportunity to characterize her as callous. As soon as she was inside, she burst out laughing, and she kept chuckling all the way up to the fifth floor.

Lucinda Moran was furious. She wasn't usually so slow on the draw. She was hopping mad that she had not landed an interview for what would have been the perfect human-interest angle to attach to the term limits story. She turned around and faced the cameraman with a scowl. Tony arrived just as Aida entered the building. He stopped and bent over with his hands on his knees to catch his breath. Beanie Man was nowhere to be seen. Lucinda grabbed her other shoe and stalked awkwardly back toward them. She ignored Tony and turned on the photographer.

"Darn it! Jack, that was Aida Adams. We surprised her with the *We Are America* announcement! How could you let her get by?"

"Me? I didn't miss a thing," he answered. "I've got her on film. What I don't have is my partner, Lucinda Moran, interviewing her. Guess that wasn't important enough for you." Lucinda shot him a deadly look and then stalked off in the opposite direction. She spent the rest of the day in Starbucks drinking strong coffee and watching the House proceedings on C-SPAN. As soon as she saw the vote wrapping up, she returned to the Capital to try to catch Aida on her way out.

Throughout the day in the House chambers, Aida and many others made speeches. The Speaker arranged the event so that the final voting was during prime time. The last vote was cast around six p.m. The count was taken, and the term limits bill squeaked by with barely the supermajority necessary for Constitutional amendments. Aida was beside herself with joy. She found Bea as soon as the final results were clear, and the two friends hugged and squealed and did a happy dance right on the floor of the House.

"Oh, Bea, stop and let me catch my breath!" Aida gasped and held her side as she bent over laughing. "Where do you get all your energy?"

"From climbing those West Virginia hills all my life, darlin'," Bea replied. "We are gonna be a C-SPAN sensation, just wait and see. After that, we'll probably be a YouTube sensation, too."

"I don't care," Aida replied. "Nothing can spoil my mood after this victory!"

"You deserve a good celebration. Everyone knows that this bill never would have passed without the votes of the Egalitarians."

Aida felt that all of her sacrifices had been worthwhile. She was filled with a hope that her public service really could make a difference. "I'm going to call Tony and get home to celebrate with my little family. Are we still on with your friend for Wednesday?"

"Yes, she's getting desperate, too. But our time was so dominated by this amendment that we've had no choice but to reschedule," Bea replied.

"Third time is the charm, though. Be there or be square," Aida quipped, laughing as she turned toward the exit. The women parted. Aida's phone buzzed but she was too happy and distracted to notice the caller ID. She was eager to share the celebratory moment with anyone on her private calling list.

As it happened, the caller was Fraz, who hoped to catch her at this opportune moment. He had watched the drama unfold on C-SPAN. The sight of Aida's happy dance with Congresswoman Gainer had caused a visceral reaction in him. He considered her celebration to be disgraceful conduct. He had his phone was in his hand, finger poised over the speed dial contact for Aida. As soon as he saw Aida and Beatrice part on the House floor, he hit the green call button, considering this his best chance. His hopes were rewarded.

"Aida, congratulations! This is why we do what we do, right?"

Aida registered that she was talking to Fraz, but, even so, her euphoria was not dampened. "Oh, Fraz isn't it wonderful!"

"They couldn't have done it without you, either!"

"Fraz, thanks but I—" Aida was interrupted by her phone blowing up with texts, calls, and notifications.

Fraz had counted on the predictable deluge as a distraction to help him convince her to agree to his plan to get her alone. "Aida, I know everyone wants to talk to you, so let's postpone our talk. Let me buy you a drink to celebrate. We started this together, and now it's all worth it. I'm going to let you go. I know everyone wants to congratulate us. Let's take our moment to celebrate too. How about eight p.m. at The Embers? Just drinks, just a half-hour."

Still high on success and eager to hang up and talk to her true team members, Aida answered reflexively, as he hoped that she would. "Sure, why not? See you then." Dread immediately started to creep into her belly. She shook it off, telling herself that she would figure a way out of this trap. She turned her attention to her next call. She had no intention of meeting Fraz.

Lucinda Moran was waiting for Aida at the door where she had last seen her. Aida knew better than to go out that way. She purposefully varied her routine unless she did want to talk to the press. This particular reporter was still on Aida's naughty list, however, and would be getting no exclusives from her if she had anything to say about it. Lucinda's stakeout did pay off, though. She overheard a comment from two of Aida's staff about a party that they had been asked to arrange for eight that evening at The Embers. "Be sure to let Congresswoman Gainer know," the young intern had added.

CHAPTER 21
THE EMBERS

Aida raised her glass in another toast and took a tiny sip. She had to keep her wits about her. She was not used to drinking and knew her limits. She frowned as she remembered what had happened the last time she overindulged.

"Aida?"

Startled back to the present, she looked up to see her entire staff gazing at her expectantly. Everyone was in a celebratory mood, and she was glad that she had taken advantage of the opportunity to invite her staff and several friends to The Embers. Her intention was twofold. She did want to celebrate, but she did not want to be alone with Fraz, now or ever again. The large party would shield her from any unwanted attention from him when he arrived. Of course, her guests did not know that. She quickly scanned the crowd, wondering what she'd missed. "Yes?" she answered. "Earth to Aida!" Beatrice laughed as she waved her hand in front of Aida's face and flashed her best Gainer grin. "Where did you go?" she teased. "It looked like a pretty dark place." Aida's eyes filled with tears. "I'm sorry; it's just that some trips down memory lane—"

"Have potholes!" Roger finished her sentence for her. "But today, we have—"

"We have turned those bumpy roads into a smooth highway—" Tracy chimed in.

"By filling those potholes with power-hungry old codgers!" a young aide added.

"Wait just a minute, you young whippersnapper!" Bea said jokingly. "I resemble that remark!"

Everyone laughed heartily at the offending aide. He blushed furiously, opening and closing his mouth like a codfish before stuttering, "C-C-C-Congresswoman Gainer, I'm so, so, so sorry. I didn't m-mean you, of course! You're different. You're—"

"Wonderful!" Aida sang out as she hugged her friend. "I never would have survived these past hundred days without you. I don't even know if I'm willing to stay in these shark-infested waters without you."

"Easy there, tiger, I'm not going anywhere until the end of the term. And no apologies are necessary, young man. Please be advised, though, that not every public servant wants to stay in office forever. I've had my turn, and, when this term ends, I'm looking forward to civilian life. Time for me to take off my congresswoman hat and put on my Grammy hat. If I get bored, though, I might just join your staff, Aida. It looks like you guys have way more fun than some of us in the conservative caucus."

"You know it!" Telly shouted from the doorway. All eyes turned toward the party leader, and everyone broke into loud applause and rose to their feet. Telly laughed and launched into a surprisingly skilled victory dance in time with the band, sashaying across the room to join the party. Everyone hooted and hollered. Aida ran into her wide-open arms, and they rocked back and forth in a tight embrace. Telly ended her dance by spinning Aida to the point of dizziness, and the band ended the song with a heady drum solo. The whole place erupted in applause. Aida fell into a giggling fit and actually snorted.

"We fight hard, and we party hard! Next round is on me!" Telly shouted, and cheers erupted anew.

Lucinda Moran observed the event from a table in the far corner of the room. She'd already had a couple of drinks and was not shy about accepting another since everything was on Telly Gavin's bill. She had been writing notes. She looked up as the front door opened and a gorgeous man stepped in. The maître d' called out, "Mr. Abbas!" Fraz took two steps into the room and stood there in shock. He had come expecting a private meeting with Aida, but her whole staff was there and most of the Egalitarian representatives, too. He turned abruptly and walked back out without hearing the bartender call to him, "Mr. Abbas, sir, your table is ready."

"Too bad," Lucinda whispered to herself. "I could have looked at him all night."

Fraz stalked outside, crossed the street, and prowled up and down the block, power-walking with his eyes fixed on the doorway of The Embers. His fury was turning into desperation. Aida had completely ruined another of his plans. He had no idea what to do now, but he had to do something since, he believed, his life and his influence over his son depended on what he did next. He resolved to get to his son before Omar did, being filled with a strong protective instinct that he had never felt before. This puzzled him because he had never felt protected himself. With each lap in his power-walk, he passed a popular gay bar, and the handsome greeter never failed to offer an invitation. This grated horribly on Fraz's nerves, and his mood grew increasingly dark until he flashed a look at the greeter so murderous that he fell silent. One gay man after another heading into the bar seeking companionship looked at Fraz with hope in his eyes, but each quickly discerned that he was too hot to handle. Fraz was in no shape to confront Aida now, but his desperation held him there, causing him to linger and imagine that he could still convince Aida to turn over their son to him. He convinced himself that he could make her see his point and surrender the child to him if he could only get her alone. He decided to keep waiting until she had parted company with her companions.

Five minutes before midnight, Aida finally emerged, laughing and accompanied by Telly. Lucinda Moran exited just after them and stepped back into an alcove in the building. She planned to write a story about the party and did not have the pictures she wanted. She had seen several of them take pictures, though. She looked over the stragglers, trying to decide how drunk each was. Aida was clearly sober, and Lucinda wouldn't dream of asking Telly. Her plan was to charm one of the men into giving her his number, which she could then use to hack his phone to obtain the pictures.

Aida had just called to ask Tony to pick her up, and she still had her phone in her hand. Someone shouted "Aida!" and everyone looked to see who. Lucinda noted that it was that handsome man again. As she watched he abruptly darted into the street, oblivious of the traffic and focused solely on Aida. The street was nearly empty at that moment, but, suddenly, tires squealed and the smell of burning rubber filled the air as a taxi driver floored his idling cab into motion. Fraz turned at the sound. He jumped involuntarily as he saw the approaching vehicle and adrenalin poured into his system.

Telly's head whipped around at the sound of the commotion, and she screamed, "Look out!" Others on the street cried out as well, raising a crescendo of alarm for the pedestrian now in harm's way. Aida recognized him first. "Fraz!" she tried to scream, but her larynx, frozen with tension, refused to produce a sound. Closer to him than any of the others on the street, she exerted all her strength to try to save the life of a man she had repeatedly wished dead. Her legs felt like rubber, but she lunged toward him and reached out her hands to help, dropping her phone in the process.

Fraz turned his head toward the car. Through the windshield he saw dark eyes, filled with fury and a shape hunched over the wheel, gripping it with both hands. Fraz' horror increased as the driver screamed and turned the wheel sharply toward him. His vision narrowed and became blurry at the edges. A commanding voice spoke loudly in his thoughts: "Everything that is covered up will be revealed, and all that is secret will be made known to all."

As if observing from outside of his body, he saw, in rapid succession, the countless selfish, empty choices that he had made over the years. He saw dark, grotesque specters swirling around him and the cab and realized that the cabbie was being used by dark forces. He realized that he had served these forces as well. He saw his birth parents begging for mercy as their home was breached by militants. He heard them cry, "No, no, no, not our son!" He saw his infant self ripped from their arms and his father falling under heavy blows from the soldiers. They grabbed his sobbing mother and held her back as she screamed, "Fraz, Fraz, never forget that we love you, son! God is with you," as she reached out for him.

Somehow, Fraz knew that this was his history. He saw scenes in the militant jihad school where he had been educated. He saw his adoptive father approving the harsh punishments he endured there. Only then did he recognize fully the darkness that he had always excused behind the eyes of his mentors and adopted family. The scenes flashed back and forth between his youth and recent history as an adult. His heart was crushed with regret as he saw a seemingly endless parade of women crying, fully aware that his callous treatment of them caused their tears. He saw tiny, unborn Emmit safely cradled in Aida's womb. He desperately wanted to go back and relive his choices. He desperately wanted to know who his real parents were. A bright and shining light filled his eyes and captured his full attention. "I must be dying," he thought as a white-robed man appeared. Pure love filled the man's eyes. He reached out his hands to Fraz. "Do you want to receive your father's Savior?" the figure asked.

The rear end of the cab fishtailed and careened in Aida's direction filling her field of vision. Telly grabbed Aida's arm with both hands and yanked her back so hard that she felt her shoulder come out of its socket, and the two of them fell into a plate glass window. At that moment, Aida heard the sickening thud of metal hitting a body like the heavy stroke of a mallet against a bass drum, and she glimpsed Fraz's body flying through the air. She even thought that she heard the air whooshing out of his lungs. In quick succession, the cymbal crash of his head against shattering glass punctuated the end of Fraz's trajectory even as Aida's head smashed against the window behind her.

Lucinda was shaking and leaned against the building to catch her breath. This would be another huge story. She cursed herself for not bringing Jack with her, but she was still mad at him. She focused on the sidewalk and took deep breaths. Her eyes slowly focused on something on the ground before her. It was Aida's phone. Lucinda could not believe her luck.

CHAPTER 22
TELLY VISITS FRAZ

Telly's phone went right to voicemail. She glanced down when she heard the notification but then quickly turned her attention back to Fraz, who was still in the ICU. Through the window into his room, she could see that his face was a swollen purple balloon crisscrossed with more stitches than she had the stomach to count. He was surrounded by IV poles, tubes, machines, and medical equipment. His face looked horrible, but it was the just the beginning of his injuries. He had broken both of his legs and several ribs. He also had serious internal injuries. Miraculously, none of the glass shards from the windshield had gotten in his eyes. He was heavily sedated because of the pain and because he became extremely agitated every time he woke up.

Telly had given the medical team Fraz's emergency contact number from his employee files, which named Omar Abbas as his emergency contact. The members of the hospital staff had Fraz under close observation and wanted to notify his family. The secretary for the ICU made the call. A few minutes later she approached Telly. "A man answered in a language other than English. When I asked if he spoke English, he demanded to know who I was and how I had obtained his private number."

"Really?" Telly replied.

"Yes, I explained the situation, and then there was silence on the other end of the line. I thought that he hung up on me, but then finally, he said, 'I have no son in America named Fraz!' Then he did hang up on me."

Telly checked the number again and confirmed it with the secretary. "I'm as much in the dark as you are," Telly said. "I knew that Fraz had no family in the United States, but now it seems he has no family at all! I feel some responsibility for him as his employer." Telly gazed at the broken man in front of her. "I hardly know him, really."

As the painkillers wore off, Fraz started mumbling and shaking his head. The machines started to beep, and the nurse hurried in with more drugs.

"What's he saying?" Telly asked when she came back out.

"He does this every time the meds wear off," the nurse explained. "It's always the same thing. All I've been able to understand is 'so sorry,' and then it sounds like he's saying 'I eat a.' Doesn't make any sense, though, does it?"

Fraz continued mumbling and shaking his head for several more minutes until the drugs took effect again. Telly finally understood that he was saying "So, so, sorry. So sorry, Aida, so sorry."

She watched as tears slid down his cheeks and he made some choking noises. His heart rate on the monitor increased rapidly.

"Oh Jesus, yes! Yes, I do, yes!" Fraz blurted out. He was full-out sobbing now. His eyes opened, but he did not seem to be able to focus. A red light on the wall began to flash, and a team of medical personnel swarmed into the small room. On his way in, one of the doctors glanced at Telly and then barked at the guard, "Get her out of here!"

CHAPTER 23

CONCUSSION

Aida was in a different hospital. She was conscious and very upset. She had watched in horror as the cab hit Fraz and his body flew through the air. It landed atop a car twenty feet away. He had hit the windshield face-first and gone right through it at the same moment Aida's head hit the front window of The Embers. The scene kept playing in her mind and when she closed her eyes, she saw it again. She felt desperately guilty for misleading Fraz about the meeting at the bar. She realized that she had gone too far. She never imagined that he would lose control to the point of charging into traffic.

She had been incredibly angry at him for the past couple of years, so much so that she had forgotten he was only human. What upset her more was that now, perhaps, Emmit truly was fatherless. Silent tears ran down her cheeks. She wiped them away angrily. No one would tell her anything. She didn't know whether Fraz had survived or, if so, how badly he had been injured. One thing she was sure of—he would never be devastatingly handsome again.

Tony stood observing her from the doorway, glancing away every few seconds to scan the hallway. Aida had given his name as the one person who could come in. She didn't want Karen to bring the baby to the hospital.

139

Aida's head was still pounding from the concussion caused by her skull striking the heavy plate glass. Her shoulder was throbbing from being dislocated and then shoved back into place. "Tony, do you know where my phone is?" she asked urgently. "I want to call Fraz and see if he's ok."

Tony turned wearily back to her. "Aida, your phone is missing. We got your handbag, but it wasn't in there. The police are still collecting evidence at the scene of the accident. I'm sure they will find it."

She felt bruised everywhere, confused, and so tired that she could barely keep her eyes open. She was horrified to realize that she wanted her mother by her side. Even so, she answered every question that the medical staff asked about her symptoms with a negative: "No, I don't have any pain. No, I don't feel dizzy." She was desperate to get out of the hospital. She kept telling the nurse that her husband was a doctor and would be more than competent to watch and assess her through the night. She continued to ask Tony where her phone was.

The doctor on call reviewed Aida's chart, trying to decide whether to discharge her.

"So, your husband is a doctor?" he asked Aida. "Would I know him? Where does he practice?"

Tony was standing in the doorway shaking his head. Obviously, the man did not follow politics or read the news. Tony looked like a thundercloud as he mouthed, "No!" to Aida.

The doctor turned and looked at Tony skeptically. "Are you the husband?"

Aida jumped in quickly. "No, doctor, Tony is my driver and also a cherished friend." The words poured out unbidden, but she did not care. He truly was a cherished friend. She felt so emotional. She opened her eyes briefly to meet Tony's. Suddenly, both of them were on the edge of tears. "Thank you, Tony," she whispered. "You're always here for me."

Emotions rose to the surface. Tony was nearly undone as he lost himself in her tender gaze. She was looking at him with something more like pure love than any look he had ever seen apart from his mother. Her expression changed then to a silent pleading. He could almost hear her willing him to get her out of this hospital.

The doctor missed this exchange since he was busy entering information into his tablet.

Tony, still undecided what to do, asked, "How bad is she, doc?"

The doctor did not look up. "This young lady has suffered a very serious blow to the head. Although she is conscious, and her CAT scan shows no bleeding, she really needs to stay for close observation. I wish that her husband were here and I could talk to him directly. We doctors tend to stay very busy, but if he's too busy to be here when his wife, well —" he stopped talking abruptly, realizing that he had said too much. He looked at Aida's hand and saw no ring. He shook his head sadly. He was unwilling to say that he knew firsthand, that doctors were often obligated to put their patients' needs ahead of their own families. He was thrice-divorced himself. He knew that Aida was lying.

"Doctor, is Mr. Fraz Abbas here?" she asked him.

"That's protected health information, Ms. Adams. You know I can't share that." He looked up from his tablet. "Congresswoman, I am going to write your discharge orders, but I want to promise me that you will stay still for at least twenty-four hours. Absolutely no work. Is that understood?"

"Of course, doctor. My husband will take care of me."

After the doctor left, Aida got out of bed and started gathering up her things. She wanted to be ready the moment the discharge nurse came in with the papers. She shooed Tony out so that she could change back into her street clothes. He stayed right outside the curtain. Her outfit was not fresh at all. She made a face as she pulled on her blouse.

Aida paced back and forth the rest of the morning, waiting for her discharge. She asked everyone who came into the room about Fraz. Tony kept telling her that Telly had visited him and that he was alive at a different hospital, but she never remembered and kept asking the same question.

CHAPTER 24
HOMECOMING

When they arrived back home at Aida's apartment, for the first time, Aida allowed Tony to help her up the stairs. She was weak and light-headed and leaned on him heavily. The imam, for his part did not disappoint. His beady eye reliably scanned the scene from the peephole in his door.

Karen flew down the steps with the baby on her hip the minute she heard the front door open. "Aida, thank God!" she cried. "You look like hell! How are you feeling? Are you sure you should be home? Tony, just let me put Emmit down, and I'll help you!"

She turned and ran back up the stairs, the baby bouncing and giggling all the way. She called over her shoulder, "Telly has been blowing up my phone. She'll be so relieved." Back inside the apartment, she placed Emmit in his crib and headed back, almost bumping into Tony in the doorway. He was carrying Aida in his arms like a baby; her head slumped against his chest.

"I can walk, Tony," she protested weakly.

"Yeah, and I can leap a tall building in a single bound." He quipped. "You're not Wonder Woman, Aida."

"Oh yes she is!" Karen leapt to her friend's defense.

"Whatever," Tony replied. "Karen, listen up. She should not have left the hospital. She fed the doctor a line about her husband being a doctor who would sit up with her all night. It's a serious concussion, Karen. Call back Telly and telly her, crap, I mean, *tell* her that Aida needs a home health nurse for at least the next forty-eight hours, and they need to get here stat!"

Karen's face clouded over with concern. "Oh, Aida!"

Aida responded with a retching sound as her stomach convulsed again.

Tony gently placed her in front of the kitchen sink. Her legs were shaky, so he held her up with one hand and her forehead with the other. "She hasn't stopped puking since we left the hospital. I'm about to call an ambulance to take her straight back there."

"No!" Aida protested weakly. "I'll fire you if you do!"

"Yeah, and who else is going to put up with all of this?"

Karen could tell he was joking.

Aida was oblivious. "My husband will sit up with me. He's a doctor," she mumbled.

"So that's your story and you're sticking to it, huh? Great line." He looked up sharply at Karen. "I said stat!"

Tony stayed with Aida and Karen for the next two hours until the home health nurse arrived. The nurse was young and plump. She was much taller than Aida and dressed in plain navy scrubs. Karen was relieved to see that she looked strong and fit. She still did not trust Aida on her feet, and she had no medical background herself. Emmit demanded so much attention lately, too. He was teething again. She wondered whether it would ever stop. He was also crawling and getting into everything. The nurse introduced herself as Sally and laughed along sympathetically at Karen's stories about teething, flashing a pair of adorable dimples in her round cheeks. Tony played with Emmit while Karen ran to the drugstore to pick up the prescription for nausea that the hospital had sent home with Aida. When Karen returned, she gave the nurse the medications and then turned to Tony and the baby.

"Tony, please don't let Aida know that I left Emmit with you. She's very strict about leaving him with anyone."

Tony looked up with a pained expression. "You think she'd be mad? Believe me, he's not the first little rug rat I've looked after. I have more nieces and nephews that you can shake a stick at and more coming all the time. My sisters are always begging me to come and watch them so they can have a break."

"Tony, I wish I could confide in you, I really do. It's just for the best. She and I go way back. We have this agreement, and that's all I can say. Please promise me."

Tony nodded and got to his feet. "Looks like everything is taken care of here," he answered tersely. "Guess I'll get back to enjoying my day off." He handed Emmit to Karen. The baby immediately started fussing. "The little dude loves me, see? They all do." Then he turned and slowly walked out the door.

Karen had no idea what to do or say, so she said nothing. Tony closed the door quietly, considerate of Aida's headache. Emmit had no such regard. His fussing quickly escalated into a high-pitched wail.

"Aida and I are going to have to renegotiate a few things," Karen said under her breath. "Emmit! What's wrong with—wait—oh, no, did I forget to feed you? I did! Oh, I'm so sorry, baby. I'm so sorry!"

After she took the anti-nausea medication, Aida felt her stomach settle down, and she slept off and on for the next several hours. In her waking moments, she kept saying over and over, "My husband is a doctor, and he is more than able to sit up with me. You can go now, nurse."

After Aida became more alert, Nurse Sally gave her some clear broth and watched her closely. After Aida kept it down for twenty minutes, she let her sit up on the edge of the bed. Aida tolerated this movement well and proceeded to stand and walk into the living room with the nurse close by her side. Aida sat on the couch and watched Emmit playing on the floor. She reached for him, but the nurse stepped between them.

"Congresswoman, you are not strong enough to pick up the baby yet."

"Well, he's strong enough to come to me. Hey little buddy, roll on over," she coached. "Come see your mommy. Come on, come to mommy."

Mindful that Aida was being indiscreet, Karen jumped in. "Heh,

heh, that bump on the head! Emmit, your Auntie Aida is still a little confused."

Aida realized what she had said and bit her lip. The nurse looked concerned. "I need to get home and let my children's babysitter leave. My replacement should be here by now. She stood to peek outside between the curtains. "I don't know what's going on. She's never —oh no!"

"What is it?" Karen asked.

"Take a look," Sally said, pulling the curtain further back.

A dozen reporters crowded the cul-de-sac in front of the building along with two vans topped by satellite dishes. Mr. Wafi was out there, too, shouting and waving his arms.

"How is the next nurse supposed to get through that?" Sally asked.

"What in the world!" Karen said. "Why is the press here? What's going on?"

As if in response to Karen's request, there was a gentle knock on the door. She hurried to the door and looked cautiously through the peep-hole; she was relieved to see it was Tony and immediately let him in. As he stepped past her, Sally sat up straight in her chair, smiling and flashing those dimples again. Tony didn't notice.

"I was listening to the news on the way," he explained. "There is a story going around the talk shows about Aida that has gotten a lot of interest."

Karen and Aida both stared at Tony without speaking. The nurse broke the silence.

"Well, it was a terrible accident to happen to a congresswoman."

"Tony," Karen asked. "Why are the reporters here at our apartment? How do they know where we live?"

"I don't know, but I'm gonna find out. I don't like this at all."

Aida added, "Well, if they're not blocking the street, they have a right. It's a free world."

"Aida, you're a genius! They are blocking traffic. I'm going to call this in and let the men in blue clear them out of here." He stepped out into the hallway to make the call.

Aida was preoccupied with the baby. Karen and the nurse exchanged worried glances. Tony came back in and looked back out the window. "Don't worry ladies; they should be disposed of shortly." He leaned closer to the glass. "What does the imam think he's doing, talking to those bums?"

Mr. Wafi was off to the side talking with one of the journalists.

Tony turned back to the ladies. "I have to leave, but, as you can hear"—for the sound of sirens just then became audible in the apartment—"D.C.'s finest have nearly arrived, and I believe you're gonna see this crowd disperse pretty quick."

Tony turned to Sally. "Your relief nurse should be right behind them."

Aida muttered, "I don't need a nurse anymore, anyway."

Everyone looked concerned. Aida was still not herself, and none of them knew when she would be.

Tony looked back at the nurse pointedly. "I trust that you will manage to win the medical debate you're about to have with the congresswoman. Stand firm, Florence!" Then he was out of the door before Sally could reply.

"Her name is not Florence," Aida mumbled, "and I don't need a nurse. My husband will sit up with me. He's a doctor."

"I think he's referencing Florence Nightingale, ma'am," said Sally. "It's a compliment, really. At least I think it is. What a nice man he is—and not hard on the eyes, either. What a build on that guy!"

Tony, meanwhile, had raced down the steps and out the front door. The journalists surged toward him and started shouting questions. They stretched microphones toward him though they had no idea who he was.

"Sir, how is Ms. Adams?"

"Have you seen the baby?"

"Does he look like Fraz Abbas?"

"Why did she keep her child a secret?"

Tony muscled his way through them to Mr. Wafi, who appeared to be wrapping up his conversation with the journalist. Tony noted the *Washington Post* insignia on the man's jacket as he jogged up to them. The imam turned away and ducked quickly back into the building. Tony made no move to pursue him but grabbed the journalist by the arm. "Just a minute, buddy, I wanna word with you."

"Get your hands off me, I warn you," the man replied. "I'm armed!"

"Easy, tiger, I just wanna know what you and the imam were kibitzing about."

"I'm sure you do, but you'll just have to wait until the morning. You can read about it with all these other chumps. Now get outta my face!"

Tony glared after the man. While he had his head turned another reporter stepped up to him.

"Mr. Romano, I'm Lucinda Moran with Reel America News. How is Congresswoman Adams today? We are all so concerned about her." Tony turned and sized up the redhead. "I bet you are concerned about her," he answered. He couldn't suppress a little smile.

Lucinda's smile faded, but she pressed on. "Mr. Romano, you are Congresswoman Adam's driver, isn't that correct? I understand that you are a close friend as well. Has there been a paternity test?" Tony just stared at her. She tried again, "What do you think about her love child with Mr. Abbas?" There was still no response from Tony. She continued, "Were they fighting the night of the accident?" Jack came up behind Lucinda, his camera focused on Tony's face. She took another stab at getting a rise out of him. "How did Ms. Adams keep her pregnancy secret during the campaign?"

"Hey, Jack, are we gonna be live?" Tony asked.

Jack looked up with surprise when he heard Tony use his name. "Yes, sir, we are." Jack responded. Tony noted the red light blinking on the camera. Lucinda picked up the cue. "This is Lucinda Moran live with Reel America News. We have an exclusive here with Mr. Tony Romano, an intimate friend of Congresswoman Aida Adams. Mr. Romano, Aida Adams has pulled the wool over the eyes of her constituents and the eyes of the whole nation, in fact, by hiding her love child with Mr. Fraz Abbas. Can you tell us what really happened last night? What may have caused him to run into traffic like that?"

Tony cleared his throat. "Lucinda Moran, right? Reel America News? Live? Wow, that's great. I just want to thank you for giving me this chance. I'm Ms. Adams driver, not intimate friend, by the way, and I'd love to tell you about my employer, Ms. Adams."

Lucinda lit up and Tony knew he had her. "Miss Lucinda, you are quite a journalist, it's just such an honor to meet such a fine-looking lady." Tony was beaming as he looked Lucinda up and down.

"Mr. Romano," Lucinda interrupted, "Aida Adams fooled the voters in Florida. Would you agree that she doesn't deserve to be in public office?" She leaned toward him as she spoke. Tony slowly leaned back and waved his hand in front of his nose.

"Well, that's an interesting thing for you to bring up. I'm sure the public would like to know the answer to that. I bet they would like to know this, too. Miss Moran, have you been drinking on the job? I seem to smell alcohol on your breath."

Jack put down the camera and Lucinda gave Tony a look that could kill. She was really going to be in trouble now.

PART THREE

CHAPTER 25
SAD SECURITY SOLUTIONS

Telly was overwhelmed. The forty-eight hours since the House passed Term Limits had been a tidal wave of events and emotions. She felt out of control but had to keep herself together and stabilize the situation. She paced around her office grumbling. The morning's *Washington Post* had landed like a bomb on her desk. Aida was on page one above the fold, but the story wasn't about term limits, the press outside Aida's apartment, or Aida's health. The headline read, "Rep. Aida Adams' Secret Love Child." There was a beautiful, full-color picture of Aida holding an adorable baby against her cheek. Both were smiling broadly. The baby's face was partially blurred because he was a minor, but a deep cleft in his chin was clearly visible. Telly was shocked and saddened. She had heard of women hiding their pregnancies, but Aida must have done so in the middle of her campaign for public office. Front-page coverage like this was every politician's dream or nightmare, depending on the situation. Telly had no idea how this situation would play out. Without question, Aida would soon be the most talked-about politician in the nation's capital.

Telly had received a phone call from the Speaker of the House at four that morning. The speaker had seen the *Post* story just before it went to the newsstands and was kind enough to give Telly a heads-up—

if it was really kindness rather than gloating. Telly was unnerved by all the reporting on Aida Adams. What if more came to light? She was not worried about skeletons in Aida's closet but those in her own. She was terrified that the illegal campaign contributions from the E.I.J. would be discovered, leaving her to deal with a great exposure of her own.

Her young assistant, Megan, cracked the door open and peeked in. Megan was short and stocky and was wearing a plain brown suit.

"Come on in," Telly said. "I won't bite your head off. Sorry about earlier."

Megan was used to Telly's temper. She shrugged off the apology. "Ms. Adams is on her way, ma'am. She should be here momentarily."

"Is Mr. Romano with her?"

"Yes, ma'am, he's driving. They should be here in five minutes, more or less." Megan quickly ducked back out of the room.

Telly reviewed all that had happened over the past two days. The party had racked up an amazing accomplishment with the passage of the term-limits amendment in the House. She had gloried in the positive news coverage, which credited the Egalitarian party with standing together to create the necessary two-thirds majority. She had been on TV for the rest of the day until the time came for the big celebration that Aida had organized at The Embers. It was the pinnacle of her career. The joy had been so sweet. That evening at The Embers, she had let her hair down and thoroughly enjoyed herself. She couldn't remember the last time she had had so much fun. She cared about her party, the causes that its members embraced as well as the members themselves. She longed to regain the feeling that she had had at the celebration again, the hours from six p.m. to twelve a.m., when everything had been wonderful and full of possibilities. But, of course, she could not. She was still having flashbacks of Fraz flying through the air like a rag doll, the taxi careening toward her and Aida, and the crack of Aida's head against the glass. She had been immensely relieved when Aida regained consciousness and, eventually, seemed to be intact mentally.

Telly was still shaken. She had never had such a close brush with death nor had to watch others whom she cared about suffering in that way. She felt responsible for Aida, having lobbied her hard. She did everything but physically twist her arm to convince her to run for office. Now Aida was experiencing a feeding frenzy from the media. The story was just the sort of click-bait fodder that they loved. Fraz's handsome face was everywhere on social media. The story was a hot topic for all the morning news shows. The worst thing, though, was the picture of Emmit that was popping up everywhere. His face was mostly blurred, but the newspaper had placed a circle around the deep dimple in his little chin. Of course, Fraz was not the only man in the country with a dimple in his chin, but the press continued to describe him as the "alleged" father. Telly's thoughts circled back to Fraz. She felt guilty about him, too. He hadn't wanted his job either. Her stomach did another flip-flop as she remembered how he looked in the ICU. She could not get over his face. She had found it difficult to accept the nurse's repeated assurance that the battered person truly was Fraz Abbas. She wondered how the most beautiful, vain, and proud man she had ever seen would be able to live with himself now. Her stomach turned again at the memory of the swollen red and purple landscape of his face crisscrossed with stitches. She held back a gag as five cups of coffee fought a noisy war with her stomach acid. She wasn't sure when she had last eaten. Her mind was a blur, cycling through the recent catastrophic events. It seemed that the term limits victory had been swallowed up immediately, first by the accident, and then by the revelation of Aida's baby. The whole nation now knew something that Telly would have known first had she been more attentive. She had noticed when Aida started wearing long, loose gowns but didn't press her for more information. She had been furious when Aida took two weeks off just before the home stretch of the campaign. Sure, she did blow up Aida's phone and demand that she communicate with the campaign, but she was disappointed with herself for failing to put two and two together. She could have come up with a better plan than this. Now, anyone who was computer savvy could find out where Aida lived, including many who had threatened her life. Telly wished that she knew who had leaked that information. She would love to wring his or her neck. It was probably that Lucinda Moran, she thought. Those kinds of dirty tricks in the media had largely stopped after The Great Exposure, but apparently not completely. She had worked feverishly, as had her aid, Megan, to get Aida and her little family into a safe house as soon as the police had dispatched the crowd in front of her house.

It had been no small task to convince Aida to leave the apartment. She regained her mental clarity slowly over a period of around forty-eight hours. Her stubbornness had been in full force continually. She did not want to move until the whole situation was clear to her and she could understand it. It took all the persuasiveness of Karen and Tony to talk her into leaving. In the end, Karen had to resort to pulling down the neckline of her tee-shirt to expose her "Semper Fi" tattoo. She made Aida focus on her eyes and said, "Aida Adams, am I gonna have to pull up your shirt and show you your matching tat in front of God and Tony, or are you going to remember that I am your true friend forever? Are you going to trust me? You have a concussion, for heaven's sake. For once, let me make the call." Aida slowly pulled open the front of her shirt and checked for herself. The tattoo worked when nothing else would, and Aida agreed to leave.

For the hundredth time that day, Telly rued the cruelty of politics and regretted her decision to make it her life's work. When she was a young woman, she held an idealistic picture of public office. *"What a fantasy!"* she said to herself. The truth was often a nightmare. Aida had called Telly early in the morning from the safe house. She had been up all night talking to Karen and finally felt confident that she had all the facts straight about the past two days as well as the sequence of events. The more she understood, the more upset she became. When she finally grasped the situation, she was more eager than anyone to move her family to a safe house.

"Telly, I'd like an appointment with you as soon as possible." she had said.

"Of course, Aida, I'll clear my schedule and come whenever you want."

"No, I don't want you to come here; I'll come to the office. I want to resume my normal routine as soon as possible." Aida was not yet ready to let anyone, not even Telly, get close to Emmit and examine him. She had not yet acknowledged that Fraz was Emmit's father. She was desperate to regain some sense of privacy.

"Aida, how are you really doing?" Telly asked.

"I'm fine," Aida answered. "I'm just concerned about," her voice choked as she stifled a sob, "my family!"

Telly sat down for the first time that morning just as Aida burst into her office, ignoring protocol. A frazzled Megan trailed helplessly behind her, and Tony served as the caboose of the train. Aida looked as if she had not slept. Her face was blotchy, her eyes were red, and her normally neat bun was leaning to one side with loose strands on both sides of her face.

"Oh, Telly, I shouldn't have ignored your warnings!" Aida wailed. "I just didn't think I was important enough for anyone to bother with. They found out where my home is, where Karen and the baby live! We can't stay in that cramped little safe house forever. I have got to get them out of town. It isn't safe for them here. I'm moving them back to Florida tomorrow."

"Whoa, whoa, whoa, Aida, take a deep breath," Telly said, trying to sound soothing. "They're secure in the safe house now, and yes, you will move them to Florida."

"Oh, how I don't want to, but I have t-t-too!" Aida sobbed. "I can't take any chances with them!" She gasped for air and then fell into a fit of coughing. "They are so precious to me, and I will not—I will not—I will not put them in any more danger!" The pitch of her voice kept increasing, and she barely squeaked out "I just don't know how I can bear to be away from them!" before the tears started again.

Telly glanced at Tony, who was obviously in abject misery. "And what are you so glum about?" she snapped.

Tony didn't answer but straightened his back and put on a blank expression. Telly continued to soothe Aida by promising to take care of everything and see to it that she, Karen, Emmit, and Tony were booked on a private jet to Gainesville. She also promised an increase in Aida's expense account to cover extra trips to Florida whenever the House schedule permitted. Then she told her, "Aida, I have some good news and some bad news. The FBI has recovered your cell phone from the scene of the accident." Aida instinctively reached into her pocket for her phone. She kept forgetting that it was missing. "Oh, good, I was just—" she started to say.

Telly interrupted, "The bad news is that they insisted on keeping it to examine for information and evidence." Aida paled and quickly started a mental review of the personal information and messages on her phone. "That's where they got the pictures of Emmit!" she exclaimed. She reached for the edge of the desk to steady herself just as Tony stepped forward and took hold of her arm. She looked up at him sadly.

Telly handed Aida a new cell phone and a slip of paper with the new phone number. "All of your contacts have been ported over, but nothing else," she explained. "All of your other information is on a hard drive that we want you to use only when you are in the House. This is only until the investigation is concluded."

"And how long will that be?" Aida asked. "I guess probably as long as it took to get term limits passed," she answered herself.

Telly ignored her and continued, "I want you to consult with Tony about who will be safe to call or to give the new number to."

Aida shocked Telly with an awkward hug before she left, fresh tears springing up as she thanked her for the fifth or sixth time. Telly closed the door and looked out the window after her. She appeared so small and defenseless. When Tony opened the rear door of the limo for her, she saw a look pass between them that surprised her. Aida had been steadfastly resistant to having a driver, much less a bodyguard, yet she seemed to have warmed to Tony. He obviously cared about her as well. Telly was glad. That would make him even more vigilant in watching over her.

"Oh, by the way, congratulations on the birth of your son," Telly whispered, realizing she had not even broached that topic with Aida.

CHAPTER 26
GLENN

After they returned to the safe house Tony opened an umbrella over Aida and kept pace with her as she walked slowly to the entrance. She looked as tired as she had on the night of the inauguration. She didn't say anything and neither did he. He stood there with her until a security officer unlocked the front door and Aida hurried inside.

She heard the door lock behind her and scanned the house quickly for Karen and Emma. She found them napping in the room that Karen had claimed. The tears flowed as she looked at them lying there, so beautiful and innocent. Aida quickly turned and went into the bathroom, turned the shower on, and sat down on the toilet, still fully clothed. She started to shake and sob and grabbed a towel to muffle the sound. She cried from exhaustion. She cried from grief over Fraz's accident. She cried to release all the pent-up stress that she had carried since she discovered that she was pregnant. She cried for shame over all the deception and for hiding the baby from her parents. She cried from embarrassment over the revelation of it all. She cried with sorrow as she thought of Tony's sad face. Then, finally, she cried for the first time over the rape that had precipitated it all. She cried until she couldn't anymore, and the shaking stopped. Once she regained some control of herself, and some of the pressure in her chest subsided, she went to the sink and splashed cold water on her face, all the while muttering what she could remember of her childhood prayers. She felt the full weight of all the secrets and deception that she had endured since Fraz had forced himself on her. After several minutes, she straightened up. Wiping the steam from the mirror with a towel, she looked at her blurry reflection and said out loud, "Wow, you look like hell."

Digging through her purse, she found her phone and called her father.

"Hello, who is this?"

"Abeh," Aida choked as the tears threatened to resume at the sound of her father's voice.

"Aida, my heart!" her father exclaimed. "I didn't recognize this phone number!"

"I had to get a new phone, Abeh," she choked out.

Glenn Adams immediately sensed the distress in his daughter's voice. "Of course, of course! What is this all about? Are you well?" Aida breathed a sigh of relief. Her father hadn't heard the news. She thanked Allah that he had sworn off the news since the Great Exposure when he and the rest of the nation found out that the media had been controlled by globalist powers. He was determined not to be spoon-fed propaganda. He swore off listening to the major news sources, no longer listening to or watching any of it. He had not even known that Aida had won the nomination or that she had been elected until she had called him herself. That night of the primary was the most impactful of her entire life. She had experienced a great accomplishment and a great trauma on the same day. Each had changed her life forever. She hadn't been herself enough even to call her father until late the following day to tell him that she was officially going to be on the ballot in November.

"I must talk to you," Aida said. "Would it be convenient for me to come tomorrow and bring Karen and Emmit?"

"Aida, what is wrong? Can you not tell your Abeh?"

"I'm fine—I mean, I will be," she replied. "With your love and with the help of Allah, I will be, but I can't talk about it over the phone. Please put this number in your contacts. I have to go, Abeh, and make the preparations."

"Now my heart is troubled for you."

"I'm sorry, Abeh, I am just so, so sorry," The tears were falling again, and Aida knew she had to end the call before she lost control again.

"Aida, why are you sorry? You are my innocent child!"

She took a deep breath. Her knuckle was between her teeth.

"Aida! Are you still there, daughter?"

She forced herself to reply, "I'll be there soon. We can talk then."

"If you must go, go. I will cancel everything and wait for you to be here."

"Thank you, Abeh, I will text you the time of our arrival. I must go now, Father," she whispered. "And please, pray for me."

CHAPTER 27
FLIGHT TO DAD'S

Aida spent the whole flight from Washington to Florida typing an email with instructions for Roger. She hadn't been to the office since the car wreck, but she had let him in on the news about Emmit just hours before Telly held a press release to discuss it. The media sharks were hunting for information relentlessly. For once in her life, Aida had no idea what to do. She looked across the aisle at Tony. She felt her face flush. They hadn't talked since everything broke loose. She took a deep breath and wiggled out of her seat to slide into the empty seat beside him.

"Looks like the little guy finally quit fighting and fell asleep," Tony said as he looked behind them to where Karen and Emmit were dozing.

"Tony, I don't know what to say." She looked down, and tears again rolled down her cheeks and made wet spots on her blouse.

"You don't have to say anything. I know you haven't been yourself since that accident. You've been through a lot."

Aida looked miserable. "Tony, I owe you an apology, and I don't know what to say about all of this. All I can think to do is to just tell you the truth."

Tony turned and peered into her face. She was looking down at her clasped hands.

"Tony, I am Emmit's mother. When I found out that I was pregnant during the campaign, I just didn't know what to do. I went to Karen's place, and we talked for hours. She was the first one to suggest that I could hide my pregnancy. She volunteered to pretend to be Emmit's mother. At first I told her no, that she was crazy, but I just couldn't come up with any better idea. Of course, everything is so much clearer now. If I had just been honest, I could have prevented a lot of trouble for everyone—but I just couldn't stand for a man like his father to be part of his life." She dug around in her purse for a tissue and then blew her nose noisily. "Excuse me," she murmured. Only then did she peek up at Tony's face and then quickly looked away.

"Aida," Tony answered softly. "I already knew. I figured out a long time ago that Emmit was your baby. You had all the signs."

Aida inhaled and turned her head sharply. "What do you mean, 'all the signs?'"

"After growing up with five sisters and watching them become mothers with all the ups and downs that come with it—let's just say I could tell and that I'm smart enough to not say how I could tell, okay? That's a no-win. Cops notice a thing, that's all."

"I'm sorry. What you must think of me!"

"Well, you pulled a fast one on a lot of people, that's for sure. I'm pretty sure they'll forgive you, though. Lotsa single moms out there."

"I haven't told you everything yet." Aida twisted the tissue in her hands.

"Oh, I'm sure you haven't. You don't have to either, ya know. None of my business, really."

"I want you to know who his father is. No one else knows for sure except Karen. My own parents don't even know that I had a baby. I couldn't imagine telling them without telling them how and who and," Aida spoke through tears that were falling fast now.

Tony was surprised that Aida still thought that no one else knew who the baby's dad was. He wondered whether she thought it would only be real when she said it aloud. "Take your time," he said gently.

Karen was not really asleep and was listening with closed eyes. She had urged Aida to take advantage of the privacy of the flight to talk to Tony. He was the only real friend Aida had besides herself and Beatrice

Gainer. Karen knew that she had wanted to talk to Beatrice about it but just hadn't been able to open up and regretted it keenly now. Beatrice's wise counsel could have prevented or solved a great many problems. Karen heard another stifled sob and saw Aida's shoulders shudder. She reached up and put her hand gently on Aida's shoulder. Tony was stoically keeping his hands to himself but wanted with everything in him to wrap his arms around her.

Aida finally blurted out, "Tony, Fraz really is Emmit's father." She looked at him again, this time with a little defiance in her tear-filled brown eyes.

Tony was relieved to see this glimmer of spunk return; it was one of the things that he loved about her. He suppressed the smile that was tickling the corners of his mouth. He cleared his throat and put on a more serious expression. "Well, about his father, I uh, I didn't want to say anything, but I kinda ran into Karen and the baby one day when I came to pick you up. Once I saw that dimple in his chin, it didn't take a genius to figure out who the father was."

"You did? Why didn't you say anything?"

"Deadbeat dads like Abbas are a dime a dozen. I have no issues with this. It's your business, water under the dam. As far as apologizing to me, on the other hand, I do have an issue. There's nothing to forgive. My job is not to get into your personal life. If you ever need to share sensitive stuff like this, though, I hope you know that I would never, ever let it go further than the empty space between these two ears."

Tony pulled his ears out in a comical gesture and Aida couldn't help but giggle. She was still emotional, though, and more tears quickly followed.

"Oh, Tony, you're the greatest."

"Ah, forgetaboutit." He held out the napkin that he received with his beverage and winked at her.

Aida reached out to take it and their fingers touched. She was a little startled as her stomach felt a little jolt of something that she did not understand. He held her eyes for a moment, and then she quickly looked away. She loved his kind, blue eyes.

"Who knows?" he said hopefully, "This might just boost your poll numbers."

"Poll numbers! What a joke. I'm ready to quit this wretched job." She looked down at her hands and the napkin that she was now twisting into shreds. "I wish I had never agreed to get into politics."

Tony looked at her intently. "Yeah, lots of things would be different right now. Some things I kind of woulda missed, like having the honor to know you," he said.

Aida looked up at him quickly. "Really?" she asked.

"Really," he answered quietly. "Don't let it go to your head, though." Now he was grinning broadly.

"I won't," she whispered. Her eyes never left him.

"You wouldn't have Emmit, either, if you didn't get into politics." His voice was very quiet. Karen leaned forward in her seat and turned her head to hear the conversation better. There was a peaceful smile on her lips.

"That's right!" Aida exclaimed loudly and slapped her hand on her knee. "I wouldn't trade him for anything!" Her spunk was even more evident now. Karen was startled and jumped a little before settling back into her seat, content now to mind her own business.

"Of course, you wouldn't!" Tony answered.

"And now he's in danger because his, his, his you know, his—"

"Father," Tony supplied.

"Well, I don't like to say that."

"Can't say that I blame ya."

"I sure hope the paparazzi aren't waiting for us down here."

"Well, they might be, but they'll have to go through me first, not to mention the Gainesville Police Department. Aida, thanks for trusting me enough to tell me all of this."

"Tony, I do trust you, and I don't think I ever thanked you for all the ways you have helped me."

"I seem to remember a time or two that you did."

"Well, maybe, but not enough!"

"Ah, forgetabout it."

"No, I won't forget. You're the greatest. Next to my dad, you're the best man I ever have known. I just want you to know that I'm sorry I dragged you into all this."

"Like I said, no apologies necessary, but, if it'll make you feel any better, I accept your apology. There, now that's enough of that."

They were quiet then, lost in their own thoughts. Behind them, Karen was deep in thought about her own future. She was feeling very nervous about the big reveal to Aida's father, Glenn Adams. She knew him very well from her college years, but, like Aida, had seen very little of him since Aida entered politics. She knew him to be unfailingly kind. She smiled as she recalled Aida's account of his response after she told him that she, Karen, had a baby without a husband: "He just calmly looked at me and said, 'Well, she's a nice girl. I'm sure she will be a great mother'." Karen had reminded Aida of this reaction several times in the hours leading up to the trip. Karen was fairly confident that Glenn Adams could handle finding out that Aida had a baby. She figured that the deception would be harder for him to accept.

The flight attendant approached Aida and said, "Ms. Adams, we are about to descend and make our final approach. I understand that you asked for advance notice so you could visit the lavatory before the captain turns on the seat belt sign."

"Yes, thank you so much." Aida stood up and pulled a carry-on out of the overhead compartment, then proceeded down the aisle and entered the lav. Karen started giggling. Tony turned around and looked at her, thinking the baby had awakened, but he hadn't.

"What's so funny?" he asked.

"You'll see," she answered. "And Tony, I hope that you don't mind, but Aida and I decided it might be safer and easier if we reserved the rental in my name, which is—"

"Dawn Karen Rizzo," he finished her sentence.

"How did you know that?"

"Well, Dawn, I make my business to know the skinny on the folks close to my charge."

"Then do you know that I don't like to be called Dawn?" she retorted.

"Oh, yes, I definitely know that, Dawn." Now Tony was chuckling, but Karen was getting a little annoyed. She liked being called Dawn even less than being called Squiggy. Tony, caught up in the moment, started singing, "Dawn, go away, I'm no good for you" in a falsetto like Frankie

Valli's in the hit single from 1964. He grinned at Karen, who simply glared back at him.

"Now, now Dawn, are you practicing that unhappy grumpy wifey look on me? I understand that we're meant to be a married couple with an adorable baby and a much older auntie on a vacay to Florida. He grinned wider. "Yep, that's good and grumpy. I think you've got it!"

Karen was trying not to smile now. She wanted to hold onto the anger for fortitude with Glenn during the reveal, though. She settled back in her seat, still focused on her view of Tony. She had had daydreams of being Tony's wife starting the first time she laid eyes on him. Aida had told her it was because Tony was the only man she ever saw apart from Wafi. Over the past few months, however, it had become increasingly clear to Karen that Tony had eyes only for Aida. She didn't tell Aida that, though, being fairly certain that she had no use for romance at this point in her life when she was busy with one crisis after another.

The private jet landed at the Gainesville airport and the flight attendant and pilot helped them deplane and gather the mountain of luggage that the women had considered essential. They were met by a porter, who piled it all high onto his trolley without a word. Tony slipped him a large tip and said, "We're in a hurry, pal, so don't stop for anything, okay? We're heading to the rental car kiosk."

Aida could tell that Tony was in full-out professional mode by the look in his eyes, but he acted casually. He turned and looked at his supposed family. "Everyone ready?" he asked. Karen nodded. She looked completely normal in her jeans and tee shirt. She was carrying Emmit in a baby carrier strapped around her chest. He was facing her and wearing a little bucket hat that she kept pulling lower over his eyes. The Florida sunshine was blinding, but, in addition, they did not want him to be seen or photographed. They had even filled in the dimple in his little chin with some heavy pancake makeup. Tony surveyed the area and then offered Karen his arm. She accepted readily and enjoyed it tremendously. It was very hard for her to not take the opportunity to feel his bicep, but she managed to restrain herself. Aida took a position behind them, but Tony kept turning around to look at her, not only to assure that she was safe, but to gawk at her appearance. She was wearing a long, loose moo-moo dress with a bright tropical print, a gray curly wig, and a wide-brimmed straw hat. Tony couldn't stop chuckling, and Karen gave him a sharp elbow in the ribs to stop him.

"Ow, honey, what was that for? He grunted in mock alarm. He turned around and told Aida, "Hey, Auntie, wifey here is giving me a hard time. I'm gonna walk with you!" Aida was wearing huge sunglasses that covered most of her face, and her tiny feet shuffled along in a pair of old flip-flops that were two sizes too big for her. Tony couldn't see her expression, but he imagined that she might be having trouble walking in that footwear and wanted to be able to see whether she fell behind. He nodded to the porter and said, "Lead on, McDuff!" The porter gave him a strange look but then shrugged and headed off to the car rental area.

Karen kicked herself all the way to the car rental for losing Tony's arm so quickly. When they arrived, she stepped up to deal with the paperwork for the van and then handed the key fob over to Tony. The van that she had reserved was waiting for them with the engine running and the AC on full-blast. They all piled into the van and breathed a sigh of relief. As far as they could tell, they had attracted no attention. They continued to act out the charade as Tony took the wheel with "Dawn" beside him. Karen was really enjoying herself but couldn't help feeling pretty pathetic at the same time because this was the closest that she had been to an eligible male since they had moved away from Florida. Aida sat in the back enjoying her baby. Since the windows were tinted, she felt safe to pull off her wig and hat.

"Tony, do you mind if we just park here for a minute while I prepare a bottle for Emmit?" Tony caught her gaze in the rearview mirror as he had so many times before.

"Not at all, Auntie. Can't have the little man starving now, can we?" he answered with a smile. Karen looked hopelessly on, aware again that Tony seemed smitten with Aida.

Having confided in Tony, Aida felt a little more confident about facing her father. She and Karen had made a plan, and she decided to run it by Tony on the drive to the house. She waited until he had successfully navigated the congestion around the airport and was on the main highway.

"Tony, could we please talk to you about how we are going to tell my dad all of this?"

Tony's eyes darted back to the rearview mirror. He suddenly looked concerned. "Aida," he answered, "How much does Mr. Adams know so far?"

"Well, he knows about Emmit. He's already met him once. He loved him right off."

Tony gripped the wheel and then consciously stretched and relaxed his fingers. He glanced in the mirror again and asked, "And he thinks Emmit is Karen's baby, right?"

"Yes"

"Okay, what's your plan?"

Tony listened patiently while Aida, with frequent interjections from Karen, outlined what they planned to tell Glenn Adams. They decided to give Aida practice role-playing and had Tony pretend to be Glenn. Aida practiced her big reveal speech, and Tony gasped and scowled and yelled, "Oh no! How could you?" Before long, the ladies were in stitches, and much of the anxiety had melted away. Before they knew it, they were turning into the long drive leading to the gated community where Glenn lived. Aida grew quiet as they passed through the security gate.

The next morning, Tony arrived at six a.m. to pick up Aida for the return trip. As he rolled up to the front door, she came bursting out and ran to the rental van without looking back. She was slightly out of breath as she climbed into the back seat. Tony turned around and placed his right hand on the passenger side headrest beside him. "Just go, Tony! Go!" she said. He took one look at the thunderstorm on Aida's face and quietly turned back around and started driving. They had driven several miles before she spoke, and then what she said was nothing more than a disjointed string of expletives that made little sense. He stopped listening and focused on the road until she felt her hand on his shoulder shaking him.

"Tony, I'm talking to you!"

"Sorry, ma'am, I have a habit of tuning out when others have a need to, uh, you know. Were you speaking to me?"

"No, of course not, until now. The rant is over for now. I have just been so angry that I have to vent." She gulped and went quiet.

"You do have some pretty good reasons to be angry." Tony offered. Aida looked up gratefully into the mirror where most of their communication took place.

"Tony, I wanted to thank you for listening to my practice speech and preparations to tell Dad."

"My pleasure," he replied, "How did it go?"

"Well, looking back, it would actually have been hilarious if it wasn't so serious. My dad, he just kept opening and closing his mouth. He looked very confused. He listened without interrupting, and then he sat in silence for what seemed like years. Dad is like that; he processes everything internally. Then, he got up and walked over to the portable crib where Emmit was sleeping and looked at him very closely. Just about then Emmit stirred and stretched out his little arms and made some baby lip-smacking noises. Dad started chuckling, and then Emmit opened his eyes. They looked at each other for the longest time and then in unison, I'm not kidding, Tony, in perfect unison, the two of them slowly began to smile." She sat back for a moment with a slight smile on her face as she remembered the scene.

Tony's eyes kept moving from the road to her face, and he also started to slowly smile.

"He's going to be okay, Tony," she said. "He's still in shock, but he's going to be okay. He said that Karen and Emmit can stay with him as long as I need them to. We were up all night talking. He really wants me to resign and get out of Washington."

"Is that why you were so angry?" he asked.

"No!" she shouted the anger returning. Tony flinched. Aida frowned. "I want the same thing. I had to literally force myself to come out the door this morning." She stared out her side window. They were driving in heavy rain punctuated by frequent claps of thunder. "This weather matches my mood. If we weren't so close to the summer recess, I would have resigned today."

Tony's eyebrows rose as he asked, "Ok, then, what now?"

"I am just so mad at this whole situation! No one has a right to mess up my life like this! If I could just get my hands on Beanie Man and whoever is behind him, I'd—" she stopped abruptly, took a deep, cleansing breath, and continued. "I'd do all those things I just said earlier in some words I regret using in front of one of the finest men I know, which happens to be you!" She looked up sheepishly to see Tony's reaction. Tony felt relief wash over himself to find out that she wasn't upset with him and quite happy inside to have been called a fine man. He chuckled.

"What's so funny?"

More thunder and sheets of rain made talking impossible for a few minutes. When the storm let up, Tony said, "Oh Aida, you are something else! I think that you are the first person I have ever had the pleasure of knowing who has found it necessary to apologize to an NYC police officer, even if I'm only a former one, for swearing. No one else has ever apologized for swearing in front of me." He grinned at her in the mirror, and she grew more flustered.

"Well, I just wanted to let you know that I don't make it a habit."

At this, Tony broke out into a full deep-throated laugh. When he could speak again, they were nearing the airport, so his eyes didn't leave the road. "Apology accepted," he simply stated. He was all business again.

CHAPTER 28
BACK TO WORK

B ack in Washington, Aida entered her empty apartment with a heavy heart, waved a sad goodbye to Tony, and slowly closed the door. She was sorely tempted to invite him in. She wondered how he would have reacted. Tony lived alone, and he seemed happy all the time. If he could do it, she could too. He didn't have a baby, though. Emmit was always on Aida's mind, but even more so now that he was nine hundred miles away from her. She realized for the first time that she had no other real friendships, no girlfriends other than Karen to call and pour her heart out to or to go out to a meal. Not that she actually could go out to a meal—Tony had made it very clear that she was to go nowhere without a security detail. All the fine dining would be taking place in the house. Her stomach rumbled, and she realized that she hadn't eaten since breakfast. She wished that she had asked Tony to stop for take-out on the way home. Trudging to the kitchen, she pulled open the fridge and saw several carry-out boxes of old food and an open half-gallon of almond milk. She picked the almond milk up and sniffed it cautiously. It smelled fine, so she used it to make a bowl of cereal for her dinner, a meal that she often turned to.

After she had eaten, she changed into her pajamas and sat down at her laptop to review the schedule for the next two weeks. She was counting down the days until the summer recess, thirty glorious days she could be in Florida with her family. This time was not really a break for representatives since they were usually busy campaigning for the next election at fairs, festivals, and meetings with local leaders, and some dealt with their legal issues. Others had brief vacations to become reacquainted with their families.

Aida's office had received numerous requests for her to attend events back in Florida during her summer recess. She had instructed Roger to put them all on hold, hoping that she could be out of office by then.

She turned her attention to the next day's appointment schedule. She saw that Roger had arranged a meeting with Telly at eight a.m. "Good," she said to herself. "Time to get the ball rolling." She saw several committee meetings at the Capital for the rest of the morning. She was pleasantly surprised to see an appointment with Bea for lunch. "Good," she repeated. "Maybe I do have a friend." She wondered how they would manage a meal without a lot of attention from the media. She decided Roger could reserve a conference room in her office building and arrange for sandwiches. She sent him a message and then looked around the apartment for a cozy place to relax and think.

Aida hadn't even explored the house since their hectic move there and hardly remembered it. She walked into the living room and spied an old leather recliner in the corner. She was exhausted but didn't want to go to bed. The empty apartment just felt unnatural, as if she were trespassing in someone's hastily abandoned residence. The leather chair was worn, its big cushions broken down. She sat down. An old crocheted throw was draped over one arm of the recliner. It felt a little scratchy, but she wrapped it around herself anyway. It was covered with stars and stripes. She wondered how long it had been since it had been washed, but felt grateful for the warmth. The leather was chilly. It had been raining all day in Washington. A chill in the air had cooled the house down but not enough for the heat to come on. She shivered as she looked around the empty room. They had taken all of Emmit's things with him to Gainesville, but she saw something on the floor that she couldn't quite identify. She got up and looked. It was a stuffed animal, one that she did not remember. She hoped that it wasn't important to him. She started to call Karen to ask but then noticed the time and thought better of it. "They'll be in bed by now," she said to herself. She held the cuddly toy up to her nose and inhaled deeply. She smelled nothing; not a trace of her baby's fragrance remained. She looked into its black, shiny eyes. It was a teddy bear about the same size as a six-month-old baby.

She kissed it and gave it a tight hug. "Not the same at all!" she complained and held it to her stomach as she shifted around in the leather chair, trying to get comfortable. She felt something hard and found that she was sitting on a remote control. "Hmmm, recline, heat, massage..." She pushed all three buttons and leaned back to elevate the footrest. She quickly fell asleep and slept fitfully until the gloomy night gradually gave way to weak daylight from a new day.

By the time Aida woke up and dragged herself into the shower, Telly had already been at work for some time. She always arrived at her office an hour before her first appointment. She started things off with a brief meeting with Megan, her admin, and then caught up on some of the hundreds of emails that she had received overnight.

She read each subject line and deleted ninety percent of them before proceeding with the tedious job of reading the ones that needed her attention. Repeatedly glancing at the clock, she had worked her way through most of the messages when she came upon one from the FBI and saw that it contained the communications collected from Aida's phone.

There were hundreds of emails and texts. She scanned them quickly and stopped when she saw that there were several text messages from Aida's mother and several from Fraz.

"Why the hell am I getting these?" she wondered. She saw that she had about ten minutes before her appointment with Aida. She knew that she shouldn't read Aida's private correspondence, but she did anyway.

Monday 10:00 a.m. Gloria Adams

Aida, you were supposed to call me back
when you made your arrangements to come
here. There is someone I want you to meet.
You know how the Jews are all crazy about
what tribe they are in, etc. and genealogy.
Your step daddy gave me a full genealogy kit
for Ramadan. I sent it in just for laughs and to
humor him. You'll never guess what I found
out. It's hilarious. I met this person, Malcolm,
when he called because we'd been matched.
You just have to meet him. Fly into Eliat. It will
be more convenient for us to meet you there
at one of the resorts. You know I don't like
house guests.

Monday 11:00 a.m. Fraz Abbas

A da so sry so so sorry fraaz
Cant test good but so so sry cabt text

Tuesday 10:00 a.m. Gloria Adams

Aida, shame on you for neglecting your
mother. Call me at once.

Tuesday 11:00 a.m. Fraz Abbas

Representative Adams, this is Betty Roberts,
a volunteer from the Park Place Rehabilitation
Center. Mr. Fraz Abbas asked me to send you
this text message on his phone. He is making
steady progress but is not able to speak very
clearly or to control his hands enough to type.
This is what he has been asking me to say for
him, "Aida, I am so very, very sorry for
everything. It's my entire fault. I know that we
have a son. I am so sorry."

Wednesday 10:00 p.m. Gloria Adams

Aida, I expected to hear from you by now.
Surely you have nothing more important than
honoring and respecting your mother. I'm
going to contact your father and get an
explanation.

"Wow!" Telly muttered. "How warm and nurturing!"

Wednesday 11:00 a.m. Fraz Abbas

Representative Adams, this is Betty Roberts again, on behalf of Mr. Abbas. I hope that you are not disturbed by these messages. If you are, please reply "STOP" and I certainly will. Please be assured that, as for me, I hold all this information strictly confidential. Mr. Abbas says, "Please read this. If you don't want to ever talk to me again, I understand. I just want to do everything I can to admit and confess my sins against you and against my son."

The next messages were garbled and must have been typed by Fraz himself. Next, she saw a lengthy email from Fraz that was intelligible.

Thursday 11:00 a.m. Fraz Abbas

Aida, they have removed the wires from my jaw, and I am now able to speak to text. I must know that you get this message. I am so very, very sorry for how I have treated you and my child. Let these texts be evidence of any charge you want to bring against me. I deserve it all. I have been a pig of an infidel and I am sick at heart at the way I have lived my life. Now that I know I am a father I am doubly ashamed of myself. Aida, when I was hit by that taxi, I experienced a personal Great Exposure. I had such an amazing spiritual experience and I really, really would like to tell you about it. I pray that you will find that I am a different man than the Fraz that you used to know. I must talk to you about how to keep our son safe.

The first thing I want to admit is that I have used and misused many women in my life. It became not only a habit but an addiction. I used women, and having sex with women, to calm myself down and to make myself feel superior. I cringe with shame as I dictate these words, but they need to be said. I know that you never would have accepted my advances unless you were compromised in some way, so I looked for an opportunity. Every time I tried to charm you and you did not respond made me more determined. I found my chance when we were all celebrating the night you secured the nomination. Everyone was toasting you and I counted the sips of wine you took until I was sure you were under the influence. I saw you call an Uber driver and I went out ahead of you to find him. I bribed him to go away and then pretended to be helpful and insisted on driving you home. When we got there, I insisted on coming in. What I insisted on after, that I am too ashamed to say in writing. I am so, so sorry.

There was a quick tap on the door and Megan, Telly's administrative assistant, stuck her head in. "Congresswoman Adams is here, ma'am," She announced.

"Give me a moment," Telly barked. She quickly saved and closed the emails, trying to decide how to proceed. "So that's why she hates him so much," she whispered aloud. She stood up, straightened her jacket, went to the door, and opened it with a smile.

"Aida, good morning!" She looked Aida over and decided that she looked only marginally better than the last time she had seen her. Her hair was neat, and her jacket and skirt were freshly pressed, but her expression was grim. She had a large legal envelope in her hand. Telly hoped that it didn't contain what she thought it did.

Six hours later, Aida was sitting in the conference room that Roger had reserved for her lunch with Bea. Aida recognized the same small room with a low round table and two small, upholstered side chairs where she had met with Fraz at the beginning of the year. The memory of that meeting did nothing to improve her mood. She turned her thoughts away and focused on what she had done that morning.

First, she had finally visited her office upstairs and brought the customary tray of coffees from Dunkin. There was no "March of Triumph" playing this time. Everyone had been so nice, though, and that lifted her spirits a little.

Tracy, the intern, had been the first to break the ice, meekly venturing, "Congresswoman, I have a little one about the same age as yours. She doesn't sleep through the night yet. Does yours?"

Aida had been taken aback by the question but answered quickly. "Not very often! Does yours?"

Tracy had smiled, "No, but I don't mind. It's the only time I can have her all to myself. Aren't the nighttime snuggles the best?"

Now, Aida smiled as she remembered the conversation, which represented the first "mom talk" that she had exchanged with anyone other than Karen.

"Well, my friend, it's so good to see you, and to see you smiling," Bea announced as she rushed in the door. "I hope you haven't been waiting long."

"Bea, it's so very good—" Aida tried to speak but felt her throat tighten and just looked up pitifully at her friend, her eyes filled with tears. "Bea, what must you think of me?" She had not seen her friend since the accident, except across the wide expanse of the House chambers. Bea sat down across the table from Aida and reached out her hands.

"Aida, give me your hands," She ordered, and Aida obeyed. "Aida, you and I have been friends for only a short while, but, where I come from; we don't turn against our friends when they stumble. We reach down and take hold of their hands and help them back up." Bea held eye contact with Aida in silence until Aida started dripping tears on the table and reached for a tissue to wipe her eyes. "Oh Aida, I sure wish that we could have had a few more lunches so that you could have gotten comfortable enough to confide in me before this all broke loose."

"Me too," Aida cried. "I wanted to tell you so badly, but I just couldn't."

"Aida, you aren't the first woman in government to struggle with an unplanned pregnancy. We don't give out scarlet letters anymore, you know."

"Well, it is totally unacceptable in Islam," Aida answered.

"And yet it happens," Bea answered. "As for what I think of you, I'd like to tell you."

Aida stiffened and sat back a little. "Okay," she replied tentatively.

"Aida, I think that you are a remarkable woman. You were recruited to public service at a time when many older and more experienced candidates refused to get involved or to take a risk. You are brave, and competent, and—"

"But what about the immorality, and the lies, and the cover-up?" Aida sounded miserable. Tears started falling again.

"What about it?" Bea answered.

"Don't you think less of me?"

"No, I don't. I think only that you are human. I think that you are important, that you are lovable, and that you are forgivable. That's a foundation of my personal faith."

"I never asked," Aida replied. "What is your religion?"

Before Bea could answer, there was a quick rap on the door, and Roger opened it a crack. "Excuse me, please ladies. Your lunch order finally arrived. I'm sorry it's so late." He held a tall white paper bag. "Do you still want it?"

"No," Aida said. "Yes," Bea said at the same time. She turned back to Aida and said, "This young lady must have lost five pounds since I last saw her. I don't even want to stand beside her."

Aida looked up, still stricken with guilt. Bea patted her hand as Roger surrendered the bag and continued. "She makes me look like a Butterball turkey all fattened up for Thanksgiving by comparison. Thank you, Roger."

"You're more than welcome, ma'am," he replied as he backed out of the room. "And, for what it's worth," he teased, "I think you look great, Congresswoman Butterball, I mean Beatrice!" He winked and closed the door behind him.

"Roger, you're terrible!" she called after him. "That joke is as old as the hills!" She turned back to Aida. "That's what you need, Aida."

"What? Jokes?" she attempted a feeble smile.

"No, although I do recommend laughter yoga. It has lifted my mood on plenty of stormy days. No, what I recommend for you is a visit to 'Almost Heaven'."

"'Almost heaven'? What's that?" Aida asked as she made a note to investigate "laughter yoga."

"West Virginia! Don't you know that old song John Denver made famous?"

Aida stared blankly at her.

"Never mind, I keep forgetting how young you are. That was way before your time. I think you need a visit to my home state."

"West Virginia? Why is that?"

"Because, in my state, we accept each other, warts and all. No one is allowed to act big. No one is allowed to act small. We all act medium! Besides that, the green rolling hills and lakes and rivers are so beautiful this time of the year. Promise me you'll come home with me for a weekend and bring your sweet little boy. I'd love to meet him."

"Okay," Aida answered obediently. Her voice still quivered.

Bea opened the carry-out bag and started sorting the contents. "Here, eat this sandwich," she ordered as she pushed a wrapped package toward Aida.

Aida absentmindedly unwrapped the sandwich and lifted a corner of the bread to see what was on it.

"What kind of sandwich is this? I don't see any meat, just tomato and onion and mayo and—oh yuck! Is this what I think it is?"

"Is it peanut butter?" Bea asked.

Aida sniffed cautiously. "I think so."

"That'll be mine, "she commented as she pulled Aida's bundle back to herself and handed Aida the other one. "Have you ever had a peanut butter and tomato sandwich?"

Aida shook her head vigorously and shivered, "No."

"Didn't think so," Bea replied. "I grew up on them. They're much better with a thick slice of fresh tomato from my mamaw's garden and with Miracle Whip, not mayo, but, hey, I'm not too picky to eat this. It reminds me of home."

Aida checked her new sandwich and was relieved to see turkey and Swiss. She took a bite and chewed thoughtfully. Beatrice watched her carefully as she chewed a big bite of her own sandwich. "Excuse me for talking with my mouth full, but we don't have a lot of time. Aida, I seriously would love to have you come to Philippi with me sometime during the summer recess. I can guarantee you and your little one would be safe there. No one would think to look for you there. "

"I'd love to, "Aida answered. "Let's make it happen!"

"You've got it!" Bea replied.

"Bea, I'm sure that what I'm about to tell you won't surprise you, but I want to tell you before the press release. I resigned my seat today. I gave Telly my letter of resignation effective at the end of this week." She looked for her reaction, but there was none. Bea just continued eating.

"You're right, I'm not surprised," she mumbled at length around another big bite of sandwich. "Excuse me; this peanut butter is sticking—"

"To the roof of your mouth? That's what I hate about peanut butter!" Aida interjected.

"Exactly!" Bea answered, having managed to resolve the problem. Her expression turned serious. "I hope that you don't feel compelled to resign because of this kerfuffle, Aida."

"Well, moral failure is a good reason, and, in addition, the press attention and the danger to my family just make it sound like, well, almost heaven to get out of politics!"

"Ha!" Bea laughed.

"Besides," Aida added, "I don't feel effective in the House. I really believe that I can make more of a difference going back to full-time involvement in my nonprofit, Melting Pot Justice. It's still active, you know."

"So, in spite of term limits kicking me out of office at the end of the legislative year, you may be out of office before me?"

"I hadn't thought about it like that," Aida answered. "I guess so."

"How did Telly take it?"

"She didn't, actually. She refused to allow me to resign."

"I'm sure she did! It reduces her head count in Congress by ten percent."

"Oh, wow, I never thought of that."

"Well, you don't need to. Your reasons are your reasons, and they are valid because of that."

"She must have resigned herself to my resignation, though, because I got an email attachment from Megan, her admin, soon after I left. It was reams of paperwork about the requirements before leaving office."

"Oh no! I got that, too! Who has time for all that drivel?"

"Apparently, me. I live alone now, and I'm not allowed out of the apartment except to go to work. I do get to go to Gainesville on the weekends." she sighed as she realized it was only Monday, so Friday was a long way off. "Bea, do you think I'm a quitter?"

"Nope, I think you're a starter. You are going to start being a proud first-time mom!" she smiled as she answered. "When do I get to meet the little guy?"

"Emmit, his name is Emmit, Bea."

"A fine strong name. If I'm not mistaken, it's Hebrew."

"Really? Are you sure?" Aida replied, shocked. "I had no idea!" She looked mournful again.

"I actually have a grandfather named Emmet. It means 'he who tells the truth.'"

Aida's bite of sandwich stuck in her throat, and she gagged a little. "Are you okay?" Bea asked. "You look like peanut butter is stuck to the roof of your mouth. Are you sure you have the right sandwich?"

"Yes, it's just that I just hope my Emmit does tell the truth better than his father and me."

"Ha!" Bea laughed. "He'll learn, just like you're doing. Life is much simpler when we just tell the truth. But really, I want to thank you for sharing all this. I'm honored that you trust me that much." Bea glanced at her watch and started cleaning up the paper napkins and wrappers.

"Bea, you are the only politician in this town that I trust."

"Thank you, Aida; that means a lot to me." She rose from her chair. "I've got to run, but I'm going to hold you to that trip to WVA. I'll have my admin work out the dates with Roger. Bye now!"

"Bye, Bea and thanks again." Bea turned and smiled before sweeping

183

out the door. Aida lingered a moment, feeling sad about Emmit's being so far away. She opened her emails and found another one from Telly.

Her stomach tightened as she worried that it might be a further effort to talk her out of the resignation. It wasn't. The message was brief and there were several attachments. Telly simply said, "I don't know why I got this email that should have been sent to you. Of course, I didn't open it."

Aida opened the first attachment and found a large file of pictures. She cried out with joy and started scrolling through her pictures of Emmit and Karen. "Oh, this is just what I needed!" she said to herself. After several minutes, she closed the photos and opened an attachment sent from the FBI. "What in the world?" she murmured. It was a list of text messages and emails that she had received on her old phone since she lost it outside of The Embers on the night of the accident. She saw several from her mother, and her stomach lurched. "Oh, she's going to be so mad I didn't answer!" Before she read them, she saw several others from Fraz.

She suddenly felt exhausted. If Karen and Emmit had been in town, she would have gone straight home to be with them. She didn't know how to comfort herself without her baby and her friend. She checked her watch. She had time for a short video call before her next appointment. She would talk to her family first and leave the text messages until she got home and had privacy. She told herself that, if she could just get through this week, she would have the weekend, and then it would only be one more week until she would have a whole month with them before needing to return to Washington again. The video call went through, and the screen filled with the face of her son. "Hi, precious angel, Emmit!" she cried. His smile in response to his name made her day.

CHAPTER 29
TO GAINESVILLE AND BACK AGAIN

Aida left town right after her last appointment on Friday. Tony was waiting for her, and they drove together to the airport for the flight to Gainesville. He shared some news with her on the way. "Aida, the police finally caught Beanie Man."

Aida gasped and leaned forward in her seat, her hand over her mouth. "You're kidding! When?"

"One of the detectives recognized him hanging around your old apartment last night. They pulled him in for loitering and started questioning him."

"Loitering! How about stealing mail, stalking, and attempted vehicular homicide?"

"All in good time," Tony answered. "This is a big case and a hot one. Everyone wants a piece of him. I wouldn't know this at all except I've been hanging out at police headquarters and pestering them every day for info. I knew one of the detectives back in NYC, and he passed this information to me. He said that several government agencies want to question the slime bag. Homeland Security has him now."

"What else do you know?" Aida demanded.

Tony took his time answering. He didn't want to upset Aida or for her to compromise the investigation in any way. He had learned the hard way how impulsive she could be. Also, he didn't want to spoil her week-end. He knew how homesick she was. Besides that, the detective had warned him not to tell Aida any more than he already had. Tony decided not to tell her that they had examined Beanie Man's cell phone and found that he had contacts with known operatives of the E.I.J., the Empire of Islamic Jihad. This violent terrorist organization had been building a presence in the United States. At this point they didn't know if they were behind the attack on Fraz or why. Tony was going to find out if he could. He decided not to tell Aida until he knew more. She was already under protection, but it would have to be beefed up if they had something against her.

Aida was watching Tony expectantly. "Tony, what else do you know?" she repeated.

"Isn't that enough? I was lucky to get that much out of my detective friend. We know enough for now. These investigations take forever. Beanie Man is off the streets, but we can't be sure there aren't others like him interested in you and Fraz. The police have questioned Fraz several times since the accident, just like they did you. I don't know if he knew anything or not, but apparently, he's not talking."

"They have asked me so many questions about him. I'm so glad I could honestly say that I haven't seen him or talked to him since the accident. I don't want to, either. They already know about the text messages he sent me with his apologies."

Tony eyed Aida thoughtfully, glancing back and forth from the road to her distraught face. He knew better than to bring it up right now, but he realized that Fraz did have some rights as a father. As a lawyer, Aida knew that better than anyone, except perhaps Fraz. Tony wondered whether Fraz would resort to legal action if Aida continued to shut him out of Emmit's life.

The weekend passed far too quickly, and soon Aida was back in Washington for the last week before the summer recess. The next few days were a blur of activity. To begin with, there was the endless paper-work associated with resigning her seat and numerous mind-numbing meetings to attend. She stayed in the safe house and arranged for a moving company to empty their former apartment and send everything to a storage unit in Gainesville. She decided to stay with her father when she arrived there until she figured out where to live next. As she checked off each task, she felt more relieved. She was so eager to get out of D.C. and back to Emmit.

Just as the gavel finally fell in the House marking the end of the session and the start of the summer recess, Aida's phone pinged a notification. She glanced quickly at it. It was from the office of the Speaker of the House. She looked up and saw the Speaker walking out laughing and surrounded by his associates. He turned and looked around the chamber one last time. He looked through Aida as though he didn't see her. Aida was startled but quickly realized that the email had come from the Speaker's staff rather than directly from him. She decided to open it in case there was something pressing that she had to do before she left. Inside the email, she saw a brief statement reading "Please amend your resignation date per the regulations on the attached document." Aida looked up in confusion and saw Roger weaving through the crowd like a fish trying to swim upstream. He didn't look happy.

"Ma'am, I just got a copy of a document concerning your date of resignation."

"Yes, Roger, I just saw it. Did you get a chance to read the regulation?"

"I'm afraid I did, Ma'am."

"Well, out with it. What did it say?"

Roger looked down at the floor. "A resignation can't be accepted until thirty days after all of the paperwork has been received and approved."

"That's no problem, Roger. That's been done already, and the recess is thirty days, so—"

"But, ma'am, there was also a second document attached that had not been completed. Unfortunately, it is one that you have not seen before, and it is required."

"What?" she shouted. Heads turned at her outburst, but then quickly turned away. Everyone was eager to get going. "What the hell?" she repeated. "No!" she howled.

Roger stepped back slowly. "Is there anything I can do for you before you leave for Gainesville?" he asked.

"Oh, Roger!" she exclaimed as she tried to get a hold of herself. "Oh,

Roger, thanks, you've been so wonderful. Would you just please pass this update along to the staff and let them know that I'll be in touch over the recess—and that I guess I'll see them in September after all."

During the flight to Gainesville, Aida completed the additional paperwork and sent it off as soon as the plane landed and was taxiing to the gate. She donned her disguise again before deplaning. Tony wore a casual shirt with a loud tropical print and Bermuda shorts. Each was amused at the appearance of the other. After they arrived at Glenn's house, Tony left Aida in his care and tended to the security personnel at the gate. Aida settled in and decided not to leave the house because no one trusted the neighbors to keep her presence a secret.

Aida loved every minute of the vacation and relaxed a little, though she was preoccupied with finalizing her resignation. She checked her emails frequently every day for acknowledgment that her paperwork was complete and had been accepted. When none was forthcoming, she called everyone she could think of and pestered Telly every day, but the situation remained unresolved. Aida was tempted to fly back up to Washington early to handle things face to face but, in the end, couldn't bear to give up one day of her precious time with Emmit.

CHAPTER 30
KAREN'S BOMBSHELL

The day for Aida's departure came all too soon. Tony arrived right on time and waited outside under the crepe myrtle trees. Aida noticed that Karen looked nervous, and her father was acting strangely, too. He approached his daughter cautiously, but Karen intervened.

"Glen, please, let me talk to her first."

He stopped and looked into her eyes for a few seconds and then nodded.

"I think it's better if I talk to her first," she repeated. "Why don't you go for a walk?"

He turned toward the door and took his hat from the table nearby. "Okay," he answered.

"Give us at least twenty minutes," Karen added.

He nodded silently as he placed the hat on his head. Tony looked up as he passed by on his way out and shook his head, unsure what was going on.

Inside, Aida patted the couch beside her. "Come here, Squiggy. You've been so nervous all morning. What's up?"

Karen burst into tears.

Aida scooted closer and put her arm around her. "It's okay, honey, you can tell me."

"I'm afraid you'll hate me," Karen sobbed.

"What in the world? Karen, that is not even possible. Semper fi, remember?" Aida felt relieved that Karen didn't seem to have news about some new danger but was instead concerned that she had done something that she thought Aida would disapprove of. As it turned out, she was right. Aida gave Karen a little shake. "Come on, out with it!"

"Ummm, Aida, you know, ummmm, you know how I always, I always liked your dad?"

"Uh-huh."

"You know he really keeps in good shape, too."

"Okay."

"He's speed-walking around the neighborhood right now."

They both looked out the window at his rapidly retreating back.

"So, Dad is healthy. Wait! Oh, my God! What's wrong with Dad?" Aida was suddenly terror-stricken.

"Nothing!" Karen immediately replied. "Nothing is wrong with your dad! That's just the problem. He's too fit —too attractive!"

"What the hell? Too attractive?"

"Yeah, for me! I think I'm falling for him!" Karen hid her face in her hands and bent over onto her knees.

Aida sat staring with her mouth gaping. "Huh? Um, that's gross, Karen!" She felt herself becoming angry. "He's thirty years older than you!"

"I know!" Karen cried pitifully. "But, but, you know, he has started acting a little funny lately, and I thought he might not like me being here, so I asked him if he wanted me to find my own place, but he said the opposite is true, that he's liking it a little too much!"

Aida had just taken a sip of Coke and, hearing this, snorted and sprayed it back out as she started choking and coughing. Karen reached out and patted her back. Aida gasped as she aspirated some of it. She was waving her hand and trying to get control and wipe her face all at the same time. Both of them were crying now. Karen was actually wailing. She turned her eyes toward the window and saw Glenn racing by on his second lap around the block and Tony bounding up the steps.

The door flew open, and both women screamed, "Get out of here!" Tony left as quickly as he had arrived.

Aida turned to see his sheepish expression as he backed out and closed the door quietly. "Tony is so sweet!" she gasped.

They both cried for a minute, and then Aida let out a huge belch. "That feels better, anyway."

"Congresswoman!" Karen said, trying and failing to hold back her laughter. She snorted, and then the real laughter began as Aida joined her. The tears flowed. Neither of them could stop. Tony could hear them howling now. Glenn rounded the corner a third time and heard them, too. Uncertain whether this development was good or bad, he broke into a jog. When she finally caught her breath, Aida turned to Karen and pulled up her shirt to reveal her own tattoo on one small, round breast. "Semper fi, sista! Semper fi!" Karen threw her arms around her friend, and the waterworks recommenced.

Once this relationship issue had been revealed and accepted, Aida began to steel herself for the departure.

CHAPTER 31
THERAPY

As Aida's plane touched down at Washington Dulles Airport, Fraz sat down to initiate a videoconference. He was about to face his most difficult therapy appointment since he had entered Park Place Rehabilitation Center in Bethesda, Maryland. After weeks of grueling surgeries and physical therapy, he was well enough to dress himself, sit in a chair, and walk with the help of a quad cane. He was desperate to be discharged, but had been told that he would not be discharged until he had started mental health counseling.

Dr. Sandra Henderson stared at her monitor. The man she saw was grotesque. His eyes were closed, and his face wet with tears and distorted with grief. His black hair was overgrown on one side and shaved on the other. Scars marked his face and scalp front to back on the shaved side. She felt her stomach turn. His agonizing grimaces stretched the partially healed scar tissue on his face and made it look even worse. Some of his teeth were missing. Her practice group had received his referral from his social worker at the exclusive Park Place Rehabilitation Center. Dr. Henderson had been warned by the social worker that the patient was disfigured, but she was still shocked when his face popped up on her monitor for their live video session. Though she kept her composure, she feared that she would be haunted by his appearance for days afterward.

The doctor was past retirement age. She was trying to decrease her caseload but had been coerced by her partners in the practice to take on this high-profile case. Despite her three decades of experience, she was still slightly insecure. She loved her work, but it tired her. She had only recently come into high demand as a therapist when clients started flooding the offices of mental health professionals in the aftermath of The Great Exposure seeking spiritual counsel. The doctor was unhappy with her own appearance on the screen in the corner of the monitor. Her short, naturally curly hair was streaked with gray, and she often wondered whether her younger clients would consider her to be relevant.

She forced a smile that first day as she looked into the camera and said, "Mr. Abbas, welcome to Better Life Counseling."

Fraz was physically incapable of smiling because of the extensive scarring but murmured quietly, "Thank you, doctor."

She smiled again and then focused on the intake protocol and required paperwork. She screened Fraz for suicide and homicide. She confirmed his emergency contact information; He named his attorney, Alan Atchison Esq., as his emergency contact person, and noted in his statement that he had no family willing to talk to him. She was startled when he then told her that some members of his family might even be plotting to kill him but said nothing, keeping the focus on his case history.

The account that Fraz gave of his life was unlike any that Dr. Henderson had heard, and she had heard many patients tell their stories. Sometimes, these stories of clients who were out of touch with reality were untrue. This story, however, was true. She had corroborated it based on what he had told a colleague of hers at the rehabilitation center as well as information that she found about the Abbas family online. She discovered that Fraz had, indeed, grown up in Egypt in the home of adoptive parents who told him that they had rescued him from the street when he was four years old. His adoptive mother was deceased, but his adoptive father, Omar Abbas, was still alive. These parents had three biological sons, all of whom were older than Fraz and highly successful, and from whom Fraz was now estranged, though it was unclear why. His father had encouraged and supported his move to the United States when he was only eighteen years old and paid for his college education and law school. Fraz had worked as a professional model to earn pocket money. The doctor's research before the session had caused her to gasp when she saw how beautiful he had been before the accident.

Having embarked on a successful law career, he then took part in Representative Adams's congressional campaign. His father had pushed him into accepting the job. He found out later that he was expected by his father and others to handle the congresswoman and influence her legislative decisions. Apparently, he had also handled her in the literal sense. His recently exposed relationship with Aida had been a widely followed story. The public was intrigued by Aida's ability to hide her pregnancy in the midst of a statewide political campaign and the fact that she had given birth one month before the election and then carried on as if nothing had happened. There were now Etsy businesses selling out of tee-shirts and other merchandise featuring her picture with the slogan, "Nothing stops a powerful woman!" Fraz seemed to have been in the dark about Aida's pregnancy and the birth of their child. Adding to the complexity of the situation was the fact that Aida and her best friend and roommate, Karen Rizzo, had switched roles and pretended that Karen was the baby's mother.

The doctor was naturally curious about her patients' personal lives. She was aware that she and most therapists were a bit voyeuristic. She consciously had to discipline herself not to ask this poor man probing questions just because of her own desire to know. She was captivated by him and wished that she could share his story with others, though, of course, she could not. She mused that Fraz's biography had the potential to be an all-time best seller. She wondered whether he had already been approached, but, somehow, she doubted that he would take any such offer.

She soon was able to see past his appearance as compassion flooded her heart for this desperate, motherless man. Despite his shocking behavior, she was touched by his remorse and relentless grief. By all accounts, he had been a conniving, manipulative narcissist. His appearance now, however, was not a show. It was real. She maintained her composure, but her armpits were damp, and she struggled to keep her breathing even. She thought that she had heard it all, but now she knew better. This was something else. The poor man had nearly died, now lived in severe physical pain, was crippled and disfigured, had no family, and, worst of all, in her opinion, was wracked with guilt over his previous behavior. Between her questions, he kept repeating some version of, "Dr. Henderson, I have been such a wicked man. I deserve the tortures of hell. I'm so sorry for what I have done! My son, oh, my son!"

Now, on top of all that, he had just shared a nightmare and flash-backs, not of the recent past, but from childhood, as if he were experiencing repressed memories, Unsure what she should do with this information, she decided to consult a former coworker who had had success using eye-movement therapy to treat post-traumatic stress. She had not yet formally diagnosed Fraz but was certain that he was suffering from it. Right now, though, her goal was to help this poor man find some relief from the guilt that was wracking him. She was praying silently throughout the session for insight into how to help him, perhaps by appealing to some tenet of Islam.

She interrupted his groaning. "Mr. Abbas, may I call you Fraz?"

"Of course, doctor," he answered.

Now, she looked at him with compassion. "Fraz, I can see that you have great remorse for the things that you have done. I know very little about Islam, but I have read the Quran because I truly respect the spiri-tuality of all of my clients, and I see quite a few Muslims here in D.C."

Dr. Henderson was watching him intently on the monitor. He was shaking his head back and forth, eyes closed.

"I know that the Quran says again and again that 'Allah is most merciful.' It teaches that anyone who has committed sin can ask forgive-ness directly from God. Fraz, in the Quran, doesn't the prophet say, 'God loves those who turn unto him in repentance, and he loves those who keep themselves pure?' From that verse, can't we conclude that, when people ask for forgiveness and repent, and then Allah will love them and surely forgive them?"

"Doctor, I am no longer Muslim."

Dr. Henderson leaned closer to the monitor. "You are no longer Muslim?" she repeated.

"I am not, but to help you understand your Muslim clients, I would like you to know that there is one condition for Muslims to be forgiven, and that is that the person should not commit that sin or mistake again. That is impossible. I know no one who lives without sin. I myself have sinned so many times that I could not begin to count." He waved his hand as if to erase the words he had just spoken.

"Doctor, I did not agree to work with you because you know a little about Islam. I agreed to work with you because your profile says that you are a Christian. I want to know what Christians believe about forgiveness. I must make amends. I cannot go on living if I do not."

She took a sip of water. She did not like to do so during sessions; it seemed like an indulgence when the whole focus should be on the client. She needed the water, though. Her mouth was dry, and her tongue was sticking to the roof of her mouth.

"Mr. Abbas, are you thinking of harming yourself?"

He made a grunting sound and shook his head. He gestured to his face and then pointed to the quad cane next to his chair. "How can I hurt myself more than this?"

She realized that she was going to need to be clearer.

"What I mean is, do you ever wish you could go to sleep and not wake up?"

"I wish I could see him again."

"Who, Fraz?"

"The man in the bright shining light," he replied.

"Mr. Abbas, I would be honored to talk to you about this experience. We can process it together. I'm afraid that I absolutely have to wrap this up for today, though, because I have another client waiting—"

Fraz interrupted, "Can we have another session tomorrow?"

"Mr. Abbas, your insurance would not pay for it, I'm afraid."

"That is of no concern to me. Could you please try to fit me in?"

"Let me look at my schedule, and I will email you a possible time. In the meantime, I will also contact your case manager at Park Place and let them know that you have completed your first session. You are clear now to finally go home."

Fraz didn't go home, however. He didn't really have a home. He didn't want to go back to the young woman with whom he had been staying, so he checked into the Willard Hotel on Pennsylvania Avenue so that he could pursue Aida and Emmit while he continued therapy with Dr. Henderson.

CHAPTER 32
TYING UP LOOSE ENDS

Tony and Aida were walking through Washington Dulles. She was not happy to be back in the Capital. She shuffled along in her too-big flip-flops while glumly scrolling her cell phone for messages. Tony looked over and cast a disdainful glance at her footwear.

"Ya know, Auntie, I think we can afford to buy you a better pair of shoes than that, don'tcha think?"

"I won't need them much longer," she replied without bothering to look up.

"Watch where you're going," he cautioned as she strayed toward a trash can.

"Oh my gosh, oh my gosh! Oh, oh, oh! Finally!" She turned to Tony with a radiant smile and whispered, "The Speaker finally accepted my resignation! I'm free! I'm free!"

Her voice grew louder, and heads turned. Tony reacted quickly.

"Hee-hee, yes, I'm glad you got out of jail, too," he said for the benefit of those around them. "Settle down now. You don't want your blood pressure to go up again." Aida looked up, still grinning, and then caught herself. "Oh, sorry! I wish that we could just turn around and go right back!"

"Well, why not?" he replied.

"I have one last item on my to-do list, and then we will be back there so fast it will make your head spin!" Tony looked slightly puzzled when she said "we." As far as he knew, his job would be ending. He was going to have to talk to her about that soon. He understood from Telly that, once Aida resigned, the government's responsibility to protect her would end.

"They sure had bad timing on that thing. If they just could have sent it earlier, you wouldn't have had to come back here," Tony groused. He was very displeased with how the government had treated his friend.

"Oh right, they have to jerk me around one last time. I would have come back anyway, though. I made a promise to Beatrice Gainer, and I intend to keep that promise before I leave for good."

Aida was referring to her promise to meet with Farah, the young Muslim woman whom Bea had taken under her wing. She and Beatrice had talked and scheduled an appointment for seven the following evening in an empty office building just outside the city.

When the appointed time came, Tony dropped Aida off and then left for an appointment of his own with Vince Piro, an old friend and former coworker. Aida planned on catching a ride home with Bea. Vince worked at the Department of Homeland Security and had insisted that Tony meet him at a secure location as soon as possible. When he arrived, Vince ran to his car and knocked on the passenger window. "Let me in, man!" he yelled. "I just found out from the guy tailing Abbas that he's heading to the location where you just left the congresswoman!" Tony unlocked the door and Vince jumped in.

Tony burned rubber as he turned around and sped back toward the office where he had left Aida. They blasted past a police car that was parked on the side of the road running radar. The officers were soon in pursuit, lights flashing. Vince turned around and looked out the back window. "Good job, fellas," he said. "We can use your help when we get there." Tony didn't slow down.

Aida knocked on the door at precisely seven. Bea opened the door right away. The lights were dim and the blinds closed. There was no furniture in the room. As Aida's eyes adjusted, she focused on a young woman standing in the shadows.

"Is all this drama really necessary?" she asked. "I feel like I'm undercover."

"That's because we are, darlin'," Bea replied. "I wasn't exaggerating when I said this young lady's life is in danger."

"Okay, well, let's get started," Aida said. The young lady stepped forward, and she recognized the lovely server from Dunkin Donuts. "Farah? Bea, is this who—?" Aida started to inquire, confused. She looked from one woman to the other and back again. "Farah—I know her, Bea. She prepares my coffee order every morning." She turned back to the young woman. "Farah, I had no idea Bea was talking about you. Why didn't you contact me directly?"

Farah looked down at her hands. She seemed so different in this context, lacking the confidence and energy that she displayed at work.

Aida shook her head. "Farah, I asked you a question." She heard a small sigh from Bea. Farah gave Aida a look of abject misery. "Farah," she continued, "are you an American citizen?"

"No, ma'am, I am Ethiopian," she answered quietly.

Aida had to stifle her irritation. She had no tolerance for weak, wimpy women who would barely speak above a whisper. "Speak up, please," she stated in a crisp, professional tone. "I can't help you if I can't hear you."

Farah repeated, a little louder, "No, ma'am, I am Ethiopian."

"And how is it that you are in this country?"

"I am here on a student visa, and it's about to expire. I graduate from the University of Michigan next week."

"Please tell me how I might be of service," Aida said tentatively.

"I felt a need to understand Islam. My friends had no such interest. They accepted the rules they were taught. I wanted to know what I was being asked to believe. I think that true faith requires more knowledge." Farah spoke rapidly and urgently. "As children, my brothers and sisters and I were forced to memorize the Quran in the original language, Arabic, but none of us spoke it or understood what we were reciting. We had to ask our tutor or our father what it meant. My brothers and sisters didn't care. They just wanted to get done and go on about their personal life." Her cheeks reddened, and Aida noticed her hands were clenched in her lap. "Must we always rely on men to tell us what is correct? Can we not find out for ourselves? Can we not think?"

Aida's heart began to soften.

Farah continued. "I found it very hard to believe that Allah really wanted us to be treated the way we were, which was lower than men. Unequal. My *ma'alim* taught me that God is merciful. If so, then why jihad? If He is just, why are Muslim women so subject to abuse? Many verses in the Quran say God is wise, omnipotent, just. Yet it also says, 'Men rule over women.' We were not allowed outside without being veiled. We were not allowed to go anywhere without a husband or a male family member. We were blamed for the lustful actions of men if they attacked us. We were shunned if we had sex before marriage, or even killed. No one cared if we were forced or not."

Aida had difficulty maintaining eye contact with this intense woman. She had heard these things before but never in such an open manner and never with the misused person right in front of her.

"I bought my own English version of the Quran and read it for myself. I found it said that women should obey their husbands and that women are worth half a man, that infidels should be killed. Husbands were allowed to punish their wives. Women were to be punished for being attractive to men; provocative, it was called. Purists like the E.I.J. want all Muslims to return to a pure form of the ancient faith." Farah continued, "They think contemporary Islam, like you practice, Ms. Congressman, is diluted."

Aida's stomach lurched with guilt as she wondered whether that was what she did; practice "contemporary Islam." She didn't know what the phrase even meant, but she did know that in reality, she did not practice Islam at all. She only identified with the group of Muslims, for this was her family heritage. She fell deep into thought. She knew that the strict practice of Islam in many countries, Ethiopia included, impacted every part of a person's life. In these countries, women had no social or economic rights. They remained ignorant and brought up their children to be just as ignorant. The boys were accustomed to seeing their mothers beaten and were quick to beat their sisters and, later, their wives. People don't submit without a good reason, and Aida considered fear of being beaten a pretty good reason. Her parents, however, never observed these practices. They were Muslim in name only. The religion was part of their ethnic origin but not their guide. None of those negative practices went on in the United States, to her knowledge.

Farah continued, "The passive *Insha'Allah* attitude so prevalent in Islam—'if Allah wills it'—affects the energy of women. I was born with an extra share of energy. I can't sit still. I don't fit into the quiet, submissive mold. My girlfriends in the community ask, 'Farah, why try to change the world?' They think that Allah predestines all, and so life is to be endured, because the good life comes after, if one can be good enough."

"Fatalism," Aida stated. "Farah, what you are telling me is not so unlike Christianity. After all, their Bible says that there is eternal life after death in a perfect place called heaven."

"No, it's not like Christianity!" Farah raised her voice and her cheeks flushed. "The Christ followers know that God is a loving Father and that He wants us to have what is called 'the abundant life in this world and the next'!" She grew increasingly agitated as she spoke. Aida began to think that she might not be as passive as she had first seemed.

"Well," Aida began cautiously, "you and I can debate what God is like, but, Muslim or Christian or Hindu, all are free to worship God as they see fit or to not believe at all."

"You may not know what God is like, but I do. I do know what God is like. I know Him."

Aida was blindsided with a blast of offense.

"Farah, no one can know God!" The offense that she felt was reflected in her sharp tone and sudden straightening of her spine. She did not know much about Muslim beliefs, but she certainly did agree with the teaching about knowing God. She knew how arrogant this girl was to think that she could know the unknowable God!

Farah continued with even greater intensity. She responded to Aida's last statement. "Muslims do not know God. He is unknowable, they think. What I think is that the one they think is God, Allah, is not God at all. The Jewish God is the true and only God. Allah is just a demonic imitation!"

"Blasphemy!" Aida shouted.

"I thought you said all were free to believe as they wished!" Farah retorted, refusing to back down.

Aida realized that her anger was not serving her well and struggled desperately to control herself. She did not care about these things. Why was she so angry? She looked in desperation at her mentor, who stood calmly and silently beside Farah. She was embarrassed for Bea to see her like this. In fact, just looking at Bea helped to steady her, though she did not understand why the older woman did not jump into this fiasco of a conversation.

"Ms. Adams, I say it again, Allah is not God! I have renounced him. The Hebrew and Christian God is the only true God."

"Farah, how can you turn against Allah? What has He done to you?"

"What has he done? What has he done? He is nothing. He has done nothing. The so-called Prophet is the one who has harmed me and every Muslim human being born female in this world."

"But you are in America, Farah. How has the Prophet harmed you here?"

"I am in America in an observant orthodox community. They serve as their own law. No one confronts them because they think it's politically incorrect, insensitive. They keep me nearly as captive as in my home country. I am graduating now and supposed to go back to Ethiopia. I am begging you to help me, to help me get asylum here. If I go back, I will be killed for my beliefs. My life is in danger already here."

"Farah, surely your mother and father will—" Aida started.

"Protect me?" Farah interrupted. "Do you mean my mother, the one who held me down on the kitchen table while my clitoris was excised and my labia sewn together to keep me clean?" Farah broke down, her face crumbling into a strained grimace of distress. Aida gasped at her words, but she continued between sobs. "Do you mean my father, who has already decided who I will marry when I return, a man forty years older than me that I have never met? What will it be like when he insists on consummating our marriage?" Farah was shaking like a leaf now. "I already have constant pain, constant yeast and bladder infections. My family does not care for me. They only want me to conform to this barbaric relic of a godless idea."

Aida was dumbfounded. She sat there, mouth agape. She looked to Bea, who simply nodded her head sadly in agreement with Farah's report. Aida had no idea what to do or say. She had heard of such things but thought they only occurred long ago and in small isolated rural communities. She had never talked to anyone who had actually experienced these horrors. She looked down and shifted uneasily in her chair. She unconsciously crossed her own legs tightly.

"We don't do this in America," she whispered.

"Oh yes you do!" Farah shouted. Her eyes flooded with tears that pooled and then overflowed. She wrapped her arms around herself and started rocking.

Aida's eyes widened as she looked at Farah. "What are you saying?" she demanded.

Farah pressed her lips tightly shut. The tears coursed down her cheeks and onto her clothes, but she was fully alert. She was the first one to hear a noise at the door. She sprang from her seat and began looking desperately for a window or door while the other two women looked at each other in confusion.

"Farah, what—" started Beatrice just as the door slammed open.

Fraz scanned the room as he barged in, moving as quickly as he could, limping badly while leaning heavily on a quad cane. "Everyone, quickly, follow me!" he ordered. All three women screamed when he approached and they saw his grotesque face. None of them recognized him. Finally Aida put the voice and the disfigured face together and it clicked.

"Fraz, how did you—?"

"No time! They're on their way! I have a car."

"Ms. Beatrice, do you trust this man?" asked Farah, her face pale with fear.

Fraz had crossed the room and was imploring Aida with his eyes while she stared back in confusion. Farah had gone to the door and peered cautiously around the jamb out into the darkness. She saw a white van with the motor idling and the driver's-side door open. It reminded her of kidnapping scenes she had seen in movies. She ran to Bea.

The congresswoman took charge. "Yes! I trust him. Come on, we're getting out of here!" She took Farah by one hand and Aida by the other.

A dark figure sprang into the room through the open door holding an AK-47 in front of him. Fraz sprang toward him and grabbed the barrel. A rapid burst of gunfire ripped through him and into the room.

Other dark figures rushed in. Farah was screaming loudly, and men were barking orders. It all blended into one deafening roar in Aida's ears. Her vision narrowed as she saw Fraz crumpled on the floor. Aida wrenched her hand out of Bea's grip and ran to Fraz, disregarding her own safety.

She reasoned that he had cheated death once and might be able to do so again. She wanted to call out to God, but she could not even form a concept of God after what Farah had shared and after she had seen pure evil pursue them all. Fraz lay in a heap in front of the door, and the assailant lay across the threshold, apparently knocked senseless by him. Two new arrivals grabbed the latter man roughly, rolled him over, and handcuffed him before dragging him off. Another pulled on gloves and picked up the gun. Aida remained on the floor beside Fraz. Others entered the room, stepping around them. "Give her a minute," one of them said. Aida heard sirens and saw the reflection of flashing lights. The last voice sounded vaguely familiar but strained in a way that kept her from recognizing it.

A paramedic knelt beside her and felt Fraz's neck. "His pulse is very weak," he said to one of the other people in the room.

Aida could see that his body was riddled with bullet holes. There was no way to staunch the bleeding from so many wounds, and a dark puddle was already forming under him. Aida gently turned Fraz's head and looked desperately into his eyes.

"Fraz—you saved our lives."

Tears were streaming down her face and dripping on him. She started to wipe them away but decided not to waste a moment. She could tell that he was fading, but he still returned her gaze. She saw love in his eyes for the first time. It was so unexpected that it caused her to gasp. His eyes were still beautiful—even more so now.

"Aida," he said, responding to her words, "Only Jesus saves people. Tell my son—"

Aida gasped to hear the name of Jesus come from Fraz's mouth. She noticed that Beatrice and Farah were being led quickly out the back door but paid it no mind.

"Yes, I'll tell him his f-father—" She could barely speak. She was so overwhelmed and confused.

"Tell him his Savior— Oh my! Oh boy! Oh my!" Fraz's eyes popped open in surprise. He stared over Aida's head.

"LORD Jesus," he whispered as his spirit slipped away.

"He's gone, Aida."

"That voice again, I know it," Aida whispered to herself. Through the fog and haze and blur of it all, she inexplicably suddenly felt safe.

Strong arms pulled her to her feet. She was hyperventilating, gasping, shaking from head to foot. She had no control over herself. She practically dangled in Tony's grasp. He picked her up like a sack of potatoes and threw her over his shoulder and carried her out of harm's way.

CHAPTER 33
TELLY'S TROUBLES

Telly yawned as she reached into her briefcase and pulled out a stack of mail. She took another sip of coffee and then pulled the belt of her bathrobe tighter. It was chilly for September. She slumped back into her chair and sorted through the mail. She rubbed her eyes and squinted up at the wall clock. It was midnight. She decided all of the rest of the mail could wait except one item. "What is this?" she asked as she stared at the official looking heavy weight envelope. "Megan must have signed for this. Why didn't she tell me about this?" She sat up straighter and quickly cut the envelope open. She scanned the document. She read it several times, trying to discover why she felt so uneasy about it. Her tired expression slowly changed into a mask of horror.

"Oh, God! Oh God! Oh God!" she cried. "What have I done?" It was midnight and she was alone in her apartment. She sprang out of her chair and ran to the window to close the blinds. She pivoted and ran to the front door. It was already locked, but she unlocked and relocked it just to be sure. She had no back door. There was only one way in and one way out. She set her security alarm and frantically began wondering who she could call.

"No one! I have no one!" she wailed. She wrapped her house coat more tightly around herself and grabbed a cushion off the couch. She hugged it to herself and rocked side to side as tears began streaming down her face. "Oh my God, how could I have been so stupid?"

She returned cautiously to her home office as if the document itself would spring at her throat and strangle her. She read it again, hoping against hope that she had misread it. She hadn't. It was report from the C.I.A. regarding the man who had stalked Aida and who ran down Fraz. One sentence glared at her as if it would burn her cornea; Hussien Amar Obidain has been found to have ties to E.I.J., the Empire of Islamic Jihad. What if this E.I.J. was the foreign donor to Aida's campaign instead of the Enterprise for International Justice?

The phone rang. It was right beside the document and Telly sprang away from it. Very few people had her private phone number and none she knew of would call at this hour. She let it ring until it went to voice mail. Only then did she lean cautiously toward the phone and look. The call was from Anthony Romano. "Tony," she whispered.

At seven a.m. the next morning, the door to Telly's office banged open and Tony barged in. Megan was not there yet and she couldn't have stopped him if she was. Telly jumped to her feet, startled.

"Why didn't you answer my call?" he demanded.

"Tony!" she exclaimed, fear turning quickly to anger. She staggered backward, woozy from no sleep and from standing too quickly. She grabbed the back of her chair for support. The flash of anger in her eyes suddenly dissolved in a pool of tears. She was breathing heavy. "Tony," she started, "I need help."

"You need help? Yes, you certainly do. Always thinking about yourself, aren't you? What about Aida? What about Fraz? Because of you and your cozy little arrangement with the E.I.J. two congresswomen were nearly murdered last night and, in the end, Fraz Abbas, of all people, was killed trying to protect them. The Department of Homeland Security is on their way here and they have lots of questions for you. I'm just here to make sure that you clear Aida, do you hear me?"

Telly let out a low groan and sank into her chair. She covered her face with her hands and started sobbing. "Oh no! Oh no! What happened? Fraz is dead? "

"Fraz is dead. He died in Aida's arms. I was there to witness it."

"Is Aida ok?

"Aida and Beatrice Gainer were there, as well as a young Muslim woman they were trying to help. They are all in shock, but in a safe location, not that it's any of your business. Look, I gotta get out of here before the place is swarming with feds. Look at me!"

Telly looked up, trying to focus through her tears.

"I don't care what you tell them about yourself. That's up to you. I suggest that you come clean and tell them everything and ask for mercy. About Aida, though, I want you to tell them over and over, she did not know about the illegal campaign contributions!"

"No, no she didn't. I'll tell them, Tony," she replied weakly.

Tony marched out the door without looking back. Megan was just arriving and started to greet him, but he didn't even see her. He had tunnel vision and was seething with fury.

CHAPTER 34
HAPPY BIRTHDAY, BABY

Aida had been back in Gainesville for almost two months. It was the first morning she woke up without her thoughts swirling with the recent horrific events. Fraz' funeral was over. She had met with his lawyers and been given a copy of his will to read. Telly had surrendered to the police and had given a full confession of her wrong doing. Miraculously, Aida had not been charged along with her. She had spent hours giving depositions, though, and still was not entirely convinced she was in the clear.

It was October 21 and she had a busy day ahead of her, but she took her time getting up. She had been dreaming. "Eleazar," she said aloud, "and Fraz. Finally, I have names to go with the faces."

Aida had been having what she thought of as the "father's dream" again. It had been recurring since she was first pregnant with Emmit. It was a dream about a baby and its forefathers. This time, she was able to identify the men in the dream, whereas, all the other times, she was left wondering. One of the fathers was Fraz. She had never seen him so calm. He had always been so tense and on guard. He was back to his original good looks, but the haughty air was absent. He looked soft, mellow, loving. He nodded at her. She turned her attention to the ancient father. He sensed this and turned to look at her full-on. He resembled her

213

maternal grandmother in some way that she could not quite put her finger on. She leaned in and asked, hoping to get an answer before they disappeared.

"Who are you?"

"My name is Eleazar, my daughter."

Thanks be to God," she whispered. "I finally know. Thanks be to God. Eleazar, you are wonderful. I still don't know who you are, but I know that you love me and that you love Emmit and that you are one of our fathers. Thanks be to God."

Aida loved that dream. She remembered the first time that she had it. It was during the primary election campaign, right after she had hit her stride on the campaign trail. Her unborn child had kicked and awakened her. She had quickly lost the peace of the dream as she realized for the umpteenth time that she was going to have to face the reality that she was pregnant.

Now, back in her father's house, she felt more peaceful than she had in years. She didn't open her eyes, but her mind clicked into motion, quickly reviewing where she was and what was coming on this day. She was with her wonderful little family, and today was Emmit's birthday. It was a happy day. Today, there was nothing on her agenda to disturb her reverie or for her to dread. She was in her old bed in her childhood bedroom. Emmit was still asleep in his crib beside her bed. She looked at him and felt waves of love pour over her.

"You are one year old today, Emmit. You have fathers. You don't have a daddy here on earth, but you have a grandpa who's pretty wonderful. This should be a pretty nice birthday."

She smiled and stretched, enjoying the moment. Soon, Karen slipped into the room to join her.

"Aida, I, um, are you awake?"

"Yes! Come in!" She patted the bed beside her.

"I was just wondering—I know your dad and I shocked you back in September with our relationship, so, um, what do you think about it now?" Karen looked down as she spoke, clearly embarrassed.

Aida slid up in the bed. "Squiggy, I was surprised for sure. I mean, I can't believe you didn't tell me sooner." She yawned and stretched her arms high above her head. "How have things developed in that regard?"

Karen looked at her friend, gauging her mood. She looked relaxed and actually happy.

"Well, now that you ask, I'd like to tell you about the date your dad and I had last night."

"Ok, sure, how was the new restaurant?"

Karen reached out and took Aida's hand. Tears formed in the corner of her eyes.

"Karen, what's wrong? He didn't break up with you, did he?"

"No! No!" Karen exclaimed. "Just the opposite. In fact, he—" Karen broke off, blushing a very becoming shade of pink.

"The opposite?" Aida reflected. She searched her internal thesaurus for a word the opposite of breaking up. Karen searched her face, waiting for the dots to connect. "Not break up but unite?" Aida said.

"In marriage!" Karen shouted, holding out her other hand, which had been hidden behind her back.

Aida pushed her long hair behind her ear and leaned forward for a closer look. Her mouth fell open, and she gasped, "He proposed? You said yes? This is your engagement ring?" She looked up with eyes full of questions. The situation clearly hadn't sunk in yet.

"Yes, yes, yes!" Karen answered. "Do we have your blessing?"

"There goes my inheritance! This rock must have cost a fortune. It's beautiful, though." Aida was still processing this news. She felt confused and rubbed her head. "I don't know what to say. I feel like I have another concussion!"

"Aida, are you grossed out?"

"Grossed out, no! My dad is a wonderful, manly, attractive man. I wanted to marry him myself until I was fourteen years old!" Both women laughed. "And I want him to be happy, and you, too. You're the best. He is one lucky, lucky guy!"

"It does kinda fix some problems, doesn't it?"

"It sure does! My two favorite people—aside from Emmit—happy and secure and with the best life partners ever! The only problem is—" This time, it was Aida who couldn't finish her sentence.

Karen looked at her with concern. "What's the problem, what?" she pressed.

"You'll be my stepmom, and I'll have to let go of one of my many non-Egalitarian biases!"

"And which non-Egalitarian biases are those?"

"That stepmothers are evil; but I know you aren't, so what do I do with that?"

Karen grabbed a pillow and hit Aida with it. That started a full-on pillow fight, which naturally woke Emmit and attracted Glenn's attention as well.

"Girls, don't make me come back there!" he called.

"Dad, you better come back here!" Aida cried. "Oh, am I going to rib you for robbing the cradle on this one!" She pulled her bathrobe on and tied it around her waist as her father slowly made his way down the hall. As soon as she saw him, she ran to him and threw her arms around his neck. "Congratulations! I'm so happy for you both. She stepped back, grinning from ear to ear and looking from her father to Karen and back again. Karen had picked up Emmit and was swaying back and forth and covering him with kisses. Her tears were splashing on his face.

Aida continued, "Hey, you guys, now Emmit will still have his other mom in his life forever—not that he wouldn't have anyway, but you know what I mean. If you had married anyone else, he would have wanted you to go to his family stuff, and it wouldn't be the same for us without you."

Both ladies teared up and then grabbed each other for a big hug, reaching around the baby.

"Oh, I'm so glad, Aida, I just couldn't be any happier," Karen said.

"Me neither, 'cause I have an announcement that I'm going to share later, and I want you to be the first one to know," Aida replied. Karen looked up expectantly.

"I intend to buy a house right here in Gainesville and continue my work with immigrants. At least, if my dad and stepmother will agree to watch their adorable grandson when I have to travel."

Karen's hand flew to her mouth. "Oh, Aida, that's the best. Oh my, I couldn't have worked out a better plan. You will be so much happier!"

"Being a representative is horrible, but that's not why I quit. I never wanted that job in the first place. I'm glad I did it, but even more glad that I'm done with it. I'm proud that I had a part in passing term limits, though. But it has been so hard!" Aida's eyes filled with tears. She held onto her friend, now sobbing and blubbering. When she was able to catch her breath, she said, "Thank you, Karen. I love you so much. You're the best friend-slash-mother I ever had."

"Just give me time, missy. I've only had the job one day!"

Beatrice Gainer was coming to the baby's birthday party. Aida was so grateful that she still wanted to be her friend. She had reached out to Aida after Telly was arrested and they finally had that long overdue talk that Aida had so longed for. She was honored that Beatrice would come even though it might result in bad press for her. They hadn't seen each other since Fraz's funeral.

Bea arrived early. It was wonderful to get together for a happy event. Nothing was ready, but everyone pitched in to help. Everyone wanted to do something nice for Aida because she had been through so much. Everyone laughed at Tony as he blew up one balloon after another, filling each in one long breath without even turning red in the face. Emmit loved the balloons and paid more attention to them than to the people or decorations or presents. Tony never tired of letting him bat the balloons around and then retrieving them for him.

Glenn excused himself to go pick up the birthday cake and the Middle Eastern cuisine that Aida had ordered from Zara's. Karen ordered a pizza delivery. It didn't take long for the decorations to be put up with everyone helping. Soon Glenn came back in the front door with his arms full of food. Karen ran out to the car and came back carefully handling the huge, car shaped birthday cake.

"Let's eat while it's hot," Glenn suggested.

"Not so fast, Grandpa!" Karen answered. "The pizza isn't here yet. I ordered it over an hour ago. Should be here any minute." As soon as they put everything down the doorbell rang. "There it is now," she stated as she ran into the living room to get the door.

CHAPTER 35
GLORIA

A puzzled Karen walked back into the living room with no pizza. A petite, dark-haired middle-aged woman bustled behind her and then quickly cut in front of her as soon as she saw Aida. A tall, dark-skinned elderly man followed her. Tony stood quickly, his hand on his sidearm, sizing up the new arrivals. He was shocked that Karen had let strangers into the house after all of the trouble. The woman who had just arrived had a lot of brass. He could tell that. The man looked embarrassed, keeping his eyes downcast, walking a few steps behind the woman, and peeking up briefly at those he passed. Tony decided that neither was a threat but scanned out the window looking for any others. The detail at the gate had received strict orders not to let anyone through who was not on that day's schedule of visitors or the roster of residents. Glenn's neighbor across the street, Mrs. Goldwood, had already come over twice to complain about having to show photo identification to enter her own neighborhood. The pizza delivery guy was on the list, but these two were clearly not from a pizza shop.

"Aida, I want you to have a word with that gatekeeper!" said the woman who had followed Karen into the room. "I told him I was your wife, Glenn, and he just kept saying I wasn't on the list. The nerve of him! I just busted on through that wooden gate anyway, that's what I did. It's a rental car, so who cares about a few scratches? Why haven't I heard from you? Who are these people?"

Glenn stepped over to Karen and put his arm around her. Karen had never much cared for Aida's mother and now that she was the future Mrs. Glenn Adams, she positively disliked this pushy woman standing in what was now her home. Tony noticed how she bristled and clenched her jaw. He did not yet know about the engagement.

Aida was speechless and stared at the woman for a moment before saying, simply, "Mother."

She spoke so quietly that Tony whipped his head around in surprise. She sounded unlike herself, completely devoid of confidence.

Gloria turned to the man she had in tow and pulled him forward.

"Come on in, Malcolm, don't be shy. Aida, this is who I wanted you to meet. Since you refused to come to me, I had to come to you. Have you forgotten your manners? Introductions! Whose baby is this? It looks like a party. You couldn't have known we were coming, did you?"

Aida froze in place, again speechless, though her mouth was open. Tony stepped forward and flashed his identification in front of them. He was no longer officially on the federal payroll, but Gloria did not know that.

Gloria peered at it and then said, "You work for the government, too, I see."

Tony turned to Aida and asked, "Is this dame really your ma?"

Aida nodded sadly.

"Do you know this other fella?"

"No," she mouthed.

"Hello, Mrs. Adams, my name is Tony. He turned to the tall stranger. "And you are?"

"He's my surprise, and you're spoiling everything!" Gloria snapped.

The man started backing up slowly and said in heavily accented English, "Sorry. Please, Gloria. Okay, sorry, no problem."

"Okay, you two, I am a federal officer," Tony said, "and the two of you have clearly broken the law. The gate was closed for a reason. Mrs. Adams, I'm afraid you may have put your daughter's and grandson's lives in danger. The security guards you blew off are surely right behind you, and you're going to have to talk really fast to make me call them off. I'm asking you to step outside and answer some questions."

Aida was beside herself. Still speechless, she sat heavily on the couch, lowering her head and shaking it back and forth. Karen sat stiffly beside her, eyes still flashing.

Tony led Gloria by the arm right back out the door. They could hear her outside, still talking. Her voice was shrill and an octave higher than usual. Mrs. Goldwood from across the street came out of her house and stood at the end of her driveway, arms crossed across her chest. Other neighbors emerged from their houses and stood gawking at the scene. The police arrived. Aida was relieved that they had not turned on the sirens, but then she heard the *whoppa-whoppa-whoppa* of helicopter rotors. Standing, she peeked out the window and saw her mother and the stranger being led to an unmarked black Suburban with their hands cuffed behind their backs. Gloria was now yelling at the top of her voice. Aida and Karen heard her last remarks.

"I am an Israeli citizen, and so is Malcolm! You don't want to cause an international incident, do you? Wait a minute, someone said 'grandson.' I don't have a grandson. Whose baby was that?"

Two hours later, Tony returned. They had waited for him to continue the party, and Emmit had napped in the meantime. When he walked in, Emmit grinned and squealed. He was on the floor and crawled over to Tony's leg and pulled himself up. The laughter all around dispelled some of the tension that they had all been feeling.

"Where's Mom?" Aida asked softly.

"She's safely at the spa where she has been staying the last few days," Tony explained, "and her friend is still in custody. She's been given strict orders not to contact you. You, of course, can contact her when and if you want to. They had to charge her for the destruction of property. She'll be able to handle the court stuff from home when she goes back."

"She deserves it," Glenn stated coldly. "What a drama queen!" He looked at Karen sheepishly.

Karen grinned and gave his arm a shove. "Ah, forgetaboutit. It will take more than that party-crasher to scare me off." She turned to Tony and the others. "We have a birthday to celebrate. It's our grandson's first birthday, isn't it, Grandpa?"

Tony looked thoroughly confused when she said "our," but he finally figured out what was going on when he saw Glenn squeeze Karen's hand.

"Tony, Squiggy is going to be my stepmother and Emmit's grandmother!" Aida announced. "Hot off the presses! Dad proposed last night, and they told me just this morning." Turning to Tony, she asked, "Can you believe it?"

"Well—"

Karen interrupted him. "Stop it with the 'Squiggy,' young lady! If I'm your stepmother, I demand a little respect. From now on, I decree that you and your son will call me the same thing. I am 'Grammy' from here on out!"

Everyone laughed, and Aida nodded in agreement.

"Grammy it is!"

Karen broke in. "Aida, if you'll get the little guy in his highchair, Grammy has some pizza for him."

"On it!" Aida replied. She picked up her son and smothered him with kisses until he wiggled so hard to get away that she had to put him down in the highchair. She turned and looked at Tony. "I guess he's too macho for that much mush, but he's just going to have to get used to it, 'cause I'm not letting up— oh no, I'm not!" She turned to give him another kiss but saw that he had just burped, and spit was flowing down his chin, so she stepped back and laughed.

"Well," Tony started again, "First of all, my congratulations to Glenn and Karen. Glenn, you got a good one there. She's a real keeper, and may I add that she can really keep a secret if you've got any! Karen, you are just one surprise after another. But Gloria said she was your wife, Glenn. What's up with that?"

"Ex-wife," Glenn replied with great emphasis on the ex. "She is Aida's elusive mother. We've been divorced for, let's see, Aida was just entering college. I guess it's been—"

"Ten years." Aida chimed in. "Hey, Tony, who was that guy with her?"

"Oh, right, gotcha." Tony continued. "So, Aida, to answer your question, I hate—not really—to steal Gloria's thunder, but that guy with her was the ancestor she wanted you to meet. His name is Malcolm something," Suddenly Tony caught movement out of the corner of his eye and was on his feet in an instant to look through the glass in the front door. He opened it quickly and rushed out.

"Now what?" Karen exclaimed.

Glenn positioned himself directly in front of Emmit and looked around the room for the baseball bat that he had placed at hand. He heard Tony laughing, though, and breathed a sigh of relief.

"What is it?" everyone called at once.

They all moved to the front door. They saw Glenn's neighbor, still in her pink chenille bathrobe and matching slippers, scurrying like a mouse into her house across the street. They looked at Tony for an explanation. He pointed at a sign, just planted in Glenn's front yard that read in large, red, hand-painted letters FOR SALE. Everyone had a big laugh about it.

Karen and Glenn looked at each other and grinned. "Good thing we were already planning to move anyway," Karen said.

"Poor Mrs. Goldwood! Guess that was one police event too many for her."

At last, the party began in earnest. After lots of good food, junk food, and messy cake, they helped Emmit open his gifts one by one. He loved them all and tasted each along with the paper that it had been wrapped in. They were all eager to see whether he would like the gifts that they had chosen, and no one was disappointed. After a while, Emmit started to tire, and he crawled to his grandfather and pulled on his leg. Glenn picked him up and was treated to a sweet cuddle. Everyone relaxed along with him and sat back to enjoy the strong Ethiopian coffee that Karen had served. Aida stood slowly, went to her father's desk, and extracted a large, white envelope that she had placed in the middle drawer.

"The gift-giving is not over, little man," she said to Emmit. "You still have some gifts from your father."

Everyone looked up in surprise. They knew that Aida had met the day before with the lawyers at Fraz's firm. She had not yet filled the others in about the meeting, though. Tony's eyebrows drew together. He still did not trust Fraz.

"Emmit, your father, may he rest in peace—" Aida had to stop and compose herself before going on. "Your father gave you something that you are really, really going to love." She reached into the envelope and pulled out a set of car keys. She handed them to the baby and warned Glenn, "Don't let him get the key fob in his mouth, Dad."

"What in the world?" Glenn asked.

Tony's jaw dropped. "The red Ferrari," he replied. His face was transfixed in a state of awe. He had noted the insignia right away. "Nice, real nice. It will be a priceless classic by the time he's old enough to drive it," he added.

"Speaking of a fortune," Aida continued, "there's another key in here. This one I won't hand over, Emmit. It's the key to your father's safety deposit box at his bank. He left you all his worldly assets." She held up a small, thin key. "I'm the trustee for this wealthy little man, who now has a net worth of over three million dollars."

"Now that's what I call an adequate first birthday gift, wouldn't you agree?" said Glenn.

Aida looked around the room through tear-filled eyes. Tony had been quietly circling the room with a tray of glasses of sparkling grape juice. He handed one to Aida and took one himself. He lifted it in a toast. "Raise your glasses, please. Sorry, this isn't champagne, but we'll expect this little tycoon to pay for some the next time, right, kiddo? Here's looking at you, kid, and to your father, Fraz Abbas, who gave his all for his son."

"And who gave his life for your mama," Glenn added.

It was a sober toast but a fitting tribute. Aida dropped the key back into the envelope and handed Emmit one of his new toy cars in exchange for the keys to the Ferrari.

CHAPTER 36
LUNCH WITH MOM

The next day, Aida scheduled two appointments, one with her mother and another with Malcolm. She was eager to speak to one of them and loathe to speak to the other. She met her mother at the spa for lunch in the dining room. Her hope was that the public setting would encourage Gloria to keep herself under control. The conversation was lopsided, with Gloria asking questions and demanding answers and then talking right over Aida without listening. Aida was unsure whether her mother got the information about Fraz right.

Gloria was more interested in Emmit and demanded to see him again. Aida reluctantly agreed. Gloria immediately started texting her friends about the baby, but Tony was standing nearby and intervened, informing her that her phone would be confiscated, and a tracker put on it if she revealed information about Aida or the baby.

Gloria was enraged by his interference. "How dare you," she started. Then she thought better of it, remembering her ride in the back of the black Suburban yesterday. She glared at him, but Tony was immovable. Gloria stood up, threw her napkin on the table, and stormed out, ending the meeting abruptly. Aida shook her head as she remembered making the same kind of dramatic gesture in one of her meetings with Bea. Tony got a kick out of it. In any case, Aida was glad that the meal had ended early. Gloria had not touched her food, so Aida invited Tony to sit with her and eat.

He gladly obliged. "Don't mind if I do. It's been quite a while since I've had a seventy-five-dollar filet mignon that I didn't hafta to pay for." He picked up Gloria's napkin and laid it delicately across his lap. "It has been quite a week down here with the Adams family," he continued. "Now this here is the high life. I could get used to this. Look at that blue sky." He turned to gaze out of the large picture windows at the manicured grounds. Picking up his knife and fork, he sliced into the juicy, tender meat.

"You deserve it and much more, really. Tony, thank you so much for all that you have done for me and Karen and Emmit. You are absolutely the best." She reached across the table and laid her small soft hand on top of his.

Their eyes met, and he held her gaze. He saw her beautiful hazel eyes swimming with tears again. She blinked rapidly but continued to look at him, unable to break away. He looked puzzled and uncharacteristically nervous but didn't drop his gaze, either. He swallowed the bite of steak almost without tasting it and held his gaze steadily upon Aida.

Aida loved Tony's face. She thought of all the times that she had watched him grinning at her in the rearview mirror of the limo. She had never really thought about whether he was handsome, usually being preoccupied with his reaction to whatever she was saying. She loved the way that he would try to keep a straight face when he delivered a comeback. Aida was not used to evaluating a face for beauty. If she had been pressed to describe Tony, she would have said that he was "average-looking"—not ugly, not handsome, just regular. As she continued looking into his blue eyes, she felt a flutter of attraction in her belly, and not for the first time. Usually she forced herself to think of something else, but she no longer had to. Their professional relationship was coming to an end and he looked so good to her.

"You're so beautiful," she whispered.

Tony's eyes opened wide, and he sat back a little as he said, "What did you say?"

Aida had shocked herself. She had no idea why she said that, but she wasn't going to take it back. She was uncertain how to continue the

226

conversation, but she was not going to stop. She kept her hand where it was and said, "What is your reaction to my giving up my House seat?"

Tony had been asking himself the same question. "Well, it has caused a political hullabaloo, but I think you're doing the right thing for you and Emmit. That city sucks the life out of people, and it was no good, you being separated from the baby."

"No, it wasn't," she agreed. "I feel like such a fool. I got myself trapped in a crazy scheme and just didn't know how to get out. I'm so sorry I was deceitful to you. You deserved better. You have been so loyal to me."

Tony wasn't sure where the conversation was headed, but he liked the feeling of her hand on his. He always loved being with her. She was the first woman he had ever really wanted to be with.

"Tony, the worst, the very worst thing about quitting D.C. is that you won't be my driver anymore. I hate that. I'll miss you. You have been my rock. You and Karen are family to me. I don't know what I'll do without you." She was tearing up again. It frustrated her. "I never cry," she said.

"Oh really? You coulda fooled me." Tony's tone was soft. They were still holding hands, and he was afraid to move.

"Well, I never cried until I got pregnant anyway," she said.

"I guess I wasn't around for that."

"No, no you weren't. Now, the thought of you not being—what will you do, Tony? Will you take on someone else to protect in D.C.?"

"Absolutely not! I'm done with that place, too. No more museums to explore, and I'm sick of the cold cloudy weather."

Aida felt suddenly hopeful.

"I know it's selfish of me, but I'd hate to think of you driving someone else around."

"I'm thinking of moving to Florida."

"Are you really?" Aida squealed. "Where?" She lit up like a thousand-watt bulb. Tony had not, in fact, been thinking about moving to Florida. He decided to be honest with her.

"Aida, I gotta tell you the truth. I really haven't had a clue what I was going to do, and I have been pretty miserable about losing you and your little family. It wasn't until just a few minutes ago when I got an impression—and please tell me if I'm wrong—but I got the impression that I might mean more to you than just a driver and bodyguard. I know you mean much more to me than any woman I ever knew. Do you think there's a chance this relationship could take a romantic turn?"

Aida jumped up out of her chair, and it fell over backward as she lunged across the table at Tony. She wrapped her arms around his neck and planted a long, satisfying kiss right on his mouth. The guests at the other table started clapping, and a waiter glided over and righted Aida's chair.

"I take it the lady said 'yes'?" he quipped.

"Umm, whatever she said seemed pretty nice," Tony responded. "I think I need to ask her to tell me again!"

The other patrons started hooting and clinking their spoons on their glasses. Aida was beaming and bright red. She didn't sit back down but grabbed Tony's hand and pulled him after her as she started through the restaurant.

"Let's get out of here."

"You made my day, lady," one of the patrons called after them. He turned to his wife and said, "How come you never do that to me, huh, Ethel?"

"Things are looking up," Tony laughed. "This is the first time she ran away and took me with her!" The laughter followed them all the way out into the lobby. Tony and Aida were tickled and started laughing, too. Then Tony remembered that the check had not been paid and started to reach into his pocket for his wallet.

The manager came power-walking up to them holding two carryout bags.

"Hey, you two, don't forget your food now. You can't live on love alone. Go find yourself a nice spot and have a picnic."

"Oh, wow. Thanks, man! How much do I owe you?" Tony asked.

"Ah, forgetaboutit," the man beamed. "It's on me and my pleasure, too! Have a good one!"

It was a perfect Florida day, with low humidity, clear blue skies, no rain, and refreshing breezes. Aida directed Tony to a lake that she loved where she knew there were picnic tables. They were both on an emotional high.

Aida was giddy. She kept giggling. Tony kept asking what was so funny, and, when she stopped giggling long enough to tell him, all that she could say was, "I'm happy! I am so happy! I never feel like this! I am so stinking happy!"

"Well, if I deserve a seventy-five-dollar filet mignon and more, you deserve a lifetime of happiness, and I'm gonna do my level best to make that happen for you."

"You already have!"

Aida's phone started beeping. She grabbed it and proudly announced to him, "I don't care who it is, they are not invited to this picnic. I'll just make sure it's not Grammy about the baby!" She giggled again. "Karen is Grammy, that's so hilarious." She scanned her phone. "Don't move, Tony, I'm not...Oh no! I forgot my appointment with Malcolm! I'm sorry, Tony; I just have to send him a quick apology." She paused to read the text from him. She scanned the message and read it out loud under her breath. "So sorry for bothering you but I have to leave for the airport shortly..." She looked up at Tony. "He's sending me an email that summarizes what he wanted me to know."

"He seems like such a good and gentle man," Tony observed. "I'm glad he's related to you. I like my Muslims to be of the mellow persuasion, don't you know, like your dad."

"I know," Aida answered. "Just look at the difference between my dad and Farah's father! My father has forgiven me for having a baby when not married. He's forgiven me for not letting him know his grandson. Farah's father paid a hit squad to come after her and murder her just for exploring a different religion!"

"Glenn took it all in stride, that's for sure." Tony offered. "Have you heard any more about Farah?"

"No, all I know is that she was quickly granted asylum. There was no further need to prove that her life was in danger."

"That's for sure. So, what does the email say? I'm curious about this distant relative of yours. A man likes to know what he's mixing himself up with."

"Give me a sec to open the email."

Tony sat back and turned toward the water. Aida's attention was riveted on her phone. She was curious, too. Aida gasped. "Tony!

Malcolm says that the ancient ancestor that we have in common is named Eleazar! Tony, Eleazar was in my dreams! I dreamed about him several times." She continued reading the email this time out loud to Tony. "'Our common ancestor, Eleazar, was a first-century Jewish priest who encountered the LORD Jesus Christ when He was still on the earth.' What in the world? A Jewish priest?"

"I didn't think any of the priests believed in Jesus."

"He's not seriously telling me that I have Jewish blood? Wait a second. He says that I should read John 12:42 for confirmation that some of the priests became followers of the Christ. She continued reading, "'Eleazar became a follower of Christ and was ejected from the Jewish priesthood." She stopped and looked at Tony again, "I have Christian blood, too? This is too much! Can it possibly be true?"

"Heck if I know," Tony answered. "What else does he say?"

"'Eleazar left Jerusalem during the first Diaspora and settled in Ethiopia, where he married, had many children, and led a network of churches that he helped establish. After he died, these Messianic Christian communities gradually stopped meeting, but they never forgot their Jewish heritage. In 2007, one of these family members, also named Eleazar, immigrated to Israel. I, Malcolm, am the son of this Eleazar, and your mother and I found each other through Ancestry.com.'"

Aida dropped her phone into her lap. She was speechless. She turned to Tony with concern on her face. "Tony, are you sure you want to get mixed up with such a woman?"

"Ha! Yes, I'm sure. Anyway, it's too late. I've been mixed up with you for quite a while already." This got him another kiss and then Aida pulled away abruptly. She leaned back and scrutinized his face.

"Tony, I never asked. What faith are you? You seem to be such a good man."

Tony actually blushed at that, but he didn't hesitate to answer. "I'm Catholic."

"That's Christian, isn't it?"

"It is, but I haven't been a good Catholic. To tell you the truth I've been thinking about that quite a bit lately."

"You have? So have I! Not about Catholicism, but about how much

I need something or someone spiritual in my life. I was really challenged by that conversation with Sandra Moore."

Tony was looking intently at Aida, slowly nodding his head. "Aida, I'm glad to hear you say that. I really am. Let's do this together, ok?"

"I'd like that," she grinned.

ACKNOWLEDGMENTS

I am so grateful to all who have helped me make this book a reality. My greatest supporter has been my husband, Rick Mathew. He provided a listening ear and sound advice as I made decisions. What an encouragement he has been.

When I started this project, I asked several friends to pray for me. I tried to keep them updated as I went along. They were all very excited about the concept and sure the book would be a best seller! Special thanks to each of them: Ramona Turner, Bing and Karen Henderson, Judy Rugh, Sandra Tyre, Ruth Krueger, Norma Pullen, Kathy Dolan, Vicky Rizzo, Rhonda Dillon, Sally Irwin, Terri Erler, Denyse Achinson, Millie Scaglione, Ruth Evinson, my sister, Rebecca Caufield, and my wonderful husband, Rick Mathew.

I have heard that an author's first book teaches them to write. I agree heartily with that maxim. Not that I claim to have learned to write. I have, however, started learning to write and *The Great Exposure* was my teacher. I also owe a huge debt of gratitude to Brad Pauquette and the School of Kingdom Writers (now called The Company) located in Zanesville, Ohio. In the fall of 2019, I signed up for a free one-year webinar this school was offering. Participants were led through the steps to writing, publishing and promoting a novel. I really had not thought of writing a novel, but that's what was being taught, so I accepted the challenge. It took me longer than a year, but thankfully the goal was met. Thank you, Brad for the many resources and for your support.

I would also like to thank Matthew Trinetti and Parul Bavishi, founders of The London Writers Salon. I wrote many hours in their company along with writers from all over the world. Their camaraderie and encouragement really helped.

After the manuscript was written I needed a publisher. My prayer team and I thought about this and prayed about it during the whole process of writing. The LORD clearly led me to Hallard Press, a private, independent publishing house. I found co-owner, Nancy Hellekson, on Facebook when I was looking for resources for writers. I was impressed with Nancy from the first phone call. She was very responsive to my inquiries and generous with her time. She kept in contact and promptly answered all my questions before I had even committed to Hallard Press. She invited me to a meeting of the Writers' League of The Villages and included me in a luncheon with a visiting successful published author. Thank you again, Nancy!

Once we had agreed to work together Nancy skillfully led me through the steps of preparing *The Great Exposure* for publication. She assigned me two editors, James Marks and Victoria Harding-Wakeen and I am grateful for their professionalism and extensive help. I had no idea that editing was a job as big as or bigger than writing.

Above all others, however, I thank the LORD Jesus Christ, who guided and inspired me. He called me a scribe before I even dreamed of being a writer. He enabled me and kept me going until this dream became a reality. I pray that this work of fiction stirs your heart to seek Him, the only one who is worthy of it all.

Made in the USA
Columbia, SC
29 June 2023

19722402R00145